Heart
of a
Kingdom

LISA BAIN

Heart of a Kingdom By Lisa Bain
Published 2019 by Your Book Angel
Copyright © Lisa Bain

Printed in the United States
Edited by Keidi Keating
Layout by Rochelle Mensidor

ISBN: 978-1-7330436-1-8

For all the women who have learned to create their own magic no matter what life throws their way, this story is for you.

I dedicate this novel to:

The Widows and Widowers in my life who never cease
to support, encourage, and inspire me daily.

And to the one and only Dan Bain; my soul mate,
best friend, co-conspirator, and guardian angel.
He never let me forget I was his queen.

Acknowledgments

I've always wondered if anyone, besides me, actually takes the time to read acknowledgments. They're kind of like an Oscar acceptance speech. I find them fascinating. So before the music starts playing and I get yanked off stage, there are few people I must acknowledge for their role in this story.

This book, and my survival through the fires of grief, wouldn't have happened without the cheerleading and encouragement of my inner circle, my real life Knights and Ladies-In-Waiting. Every character, place, and event in this story was inspired by real people I've met along my journey, and places I've been fortunate to visit. Jump to any conclusions you find entertaining, but remind yourself it's a work of fiction. Think you see yourself in a character? Then sure, it's you. Be sure to buy an extra copy of the book for everyone you know.

Mom, I love you. Thanks for always believing in me.

Jeremy, Will, Tommy, Gerald, RC, Maddi, Becky, and Kristin thank you for not allowing me to give up or walk away from this idea, even when I wanted to throw in the towel.

Amy, Mandy, and Ginger thanks for being there and keeping my kingdom in check as I went out on my adventure to figure out who this new me was supposed to be without him.

Maddi, Michelle, and Gerald thank you for having the guts to redline my drafts. You are fierce friends, and I'm so grateful for you.

My nieces and nephews, by blood and by choice, continue to give me the reasons to keep fighting the good fight. I will always work to make you proud of the life I squeeze out of every minute I have left. Your unconditional love is the true magic in my universe.

The musicians and poets who provided the ultimate playlist for my grief recovery and Libby's adventures, thank you for gifting the world your beautiful music.

My editor, Keidi Keating is my book angel. Sometimes the universe brings people together. I don't know what I would have done without your guidance, patience, diligence, and overall good sense. Thank you for taking a chance on a new author with a weird concept for a book about the grief journey.

Prologue

The figure at the bedroom door paused, listening. When she didn't hear any evidence that the door squeaking open had awoken her husband, the dark-haired woman quietly closed the door and in an exaggerated tiptoe headed to her closet to drop her high heels and change into her pajamas.

"Whew," she thought to herself. *"I think I may actually have achieved ninja status this time."*

She got changed and crawled into bed beside him. He rolled over and threw his arm around her.

"You could wake the dead," he declared, voice booming in the dark.

She jumped and started laughing.

"That was almost a quiet return. Did you and Dee have a fun night?"

Still laughing, she snuggled into his embrace. "I'm sorry I woke you. And yes, it was an epic Friday night in Belfast."

She was careful to never spend too long away from her responsibilities at home. Even on the nights like tonight, when she went carousing with her friends in Belfast, she almost always managed to make it home to her husband so they could wake up together. She'd sneak in to the palace in the wee hours of the morning and crawl into bed beside him, trying not to wake him. He often joked that the quieter she tried to be, the louder she was. He'd never confess that it wouldn't matter how quiet she was since he couldn't sleep without her and was always awake when she got home.

But that's not where this story begins. And all love stories should start at the beginning, even the ones that start with the happy ending and then get totally fucked up.

Chapter 1

Ships That Pass In the Night

Once upon a time, in a magical land a lot closer than you'd think, lived a king and queen. The McGregors governed the Kingdom of the Talking Trees with wisdom and humor. Under their leadership, the land prospered and the people were happy. They had the kind of love that burned deep into the bone marrow. It inspired poets to write and made young girls sigh to dream about. That kind of fire can both warm and burn. The flip side of their passion and romance was blazing anger when they butted heads. They were always friends first, so even when their knock-down, drag-out fights had them ready to battle to the death, they found a way to make peace. The King and Queen made a strong partnership, beyond what was expected with the traditional royal marriage contract. They were evenly matched in life, leadership, and strength. Yin and Yang. Two halves of a whole. Soul mates. Together, they were unstoppable.

The Kingdom was a magical place. It existed both within, and outside, of the living world, like an invisible snow globe that allowed the two worlds to overlap without the Normals, or non-magic beings, knowing. For the most part they were kept separate by a force field. Quantum physicists used string theory to try to describe how it worked. They weren't wrong, but it was easier to explain as magic.

The force field was powered by the King and Queen's combined life force. That barrier kept the kingdom both hidden and safe.

Residents of the Kingdom could cross back and forth if they knew the locations of the portals. Normals could technically do the same, but since the portals were magically hidden, they could rarely stumble upon them. And since the Kingdom could be relocated, it sometimes moved, making it almost impossible to locate a second time.

At the center of the Kingdom was the palace, although "palace" was a bit of a misnomer. It was the Kingdom of the Talking Trees, a land full of forests and glens and beautiful beaches. The palace wouldn't have been out of place in Colorado or Idaho as a resort lodge. It was large and defensible, constructed of strong stone and timbers. But it was also simple, and elegant—perfect for the kind of people the King and Queen were. Full of fireplaces and heavy tapestries, and huge windows to make the most of the views. It was a home to all who entered. Cozy, despite its size, and full of the treasures the Queen had collected from her travels.

The Queen, who'd been born in the kingdom, loved to travel and regularly crossed through the force field. She'd been all over the world. But, if she had to pick a favorite place to visit, it would have been Ireland. That's where she traced half of her ancestry and her given name, Aisling, although she usually went by Libby. So that's where the Kingdom was currently parked, anchored just outside of Belfast. It allowed her convenient access to her favorite town and all the fun it had to offer. Under her father's reign, it had usually been parked somewhere in the United States, which is why Libby and her sisters had a decidedly American accent.

King Dale was born in the Kingdom but raised in the Normal world. He didn't care where it was since he rarely traveled beyond the force field. He had everything he needed there and never quite understood his wife's fascination with traveling. But, like most things related to his wife, found it adorable. In general, he let Libby have or do whatever she wanted, and not just because she'd have done it anyway. If he hadn't wanted her to go, she would have stayed within and made the best of it.

Besides all the fun to be had there, the Queen knew that because Ireland was a source of ancient magic, anchoring the kingdom close to a ley line meant that she could have an exceptionally good time while she was there and not have to worry about the strength of the force field while she was out with her friends. It was a win-win for her. The Belfast pub owners loved it when she showed up in town. She drank fine whiskey, bought rounds, was always friendly with the staff, and tipped well. Plus, the nights she was there tended to be just a bit more crowded, and happier, although they couldn't explain why. They joked that she was magic for the night's profits.

They weren't entirely wrong; she was magic.

Drowning in an endless stream of tears
It's relentless and I'm defenseless
~Dolly Parton, "Endless Stream of Tears"

Libby bolted up from a dead sleep, fighting with the sheets as she gasped for air. Her flailing and choking woke Dale.

"Another bad dream?" he asked, startled.

He reached out an arm and pulled her close as she mumbled her apologies for waking him. Her heart was racing, and while she felt safer against his chest, she also had a sense of foreboding. This didn't feel like just a dream. It felt like a warning. And it was so real. She closed her eyes and tried to regulate her breathing, but the sensations of drowning were hard to dismiss. Her brain flashed through the images of darkness and looking up at the light getting farther and farther away as she sank deeper into the cold water. She felt the air being forced from her lungs, the panic as her lungs filled with water, frantically clawing to reach the surface but not knowing which way was up. She was so cold she was shivering, even with Dale's arm around her to warm her. She continued to count her breath. In for seven, hold for seven, out for seven, hold for seven. It felt like an eternity, but eventually she fell back into a troubled sleep.

Always a light sleeper, Dale lay there awake. He hated his wife's nightmares. He felt her fear deep in his chest and couldn't do anything to fix it. He'd do anything to protect her. Her nightmares were the one thing that made him feel inadequate. He listened to her breathing normalize and knew she must be counting. He was glad she'd finally learned that technique. It helped quiet the anxiety he himself felt. Sharing a heart had its drawbacks. At some point she stopped shivering and finally fell asleep. That's when he relaxed a bit. He buried his face in the back of her neck, took a deep breath of her lilac perfume, and drifted back to sleep himself.

Because they were both such strong warriors, Dale and Libby would take turns doing battle with the rare threats that would pop up. One day rumors surfaced of an evil witch in a far corner of the kingdom. Dale won a fierce game of rock-paper-scissors, so kissed Libby good-bye and prepared to ride out with his Senior Knight, Geoffrey Fitzgerald, to banish the witch from their lands.

"Don't forget your new armor," she called after him.

On one of the Queen's recent excursions outside the kingdom, she'd bought him a birthday present—Kevlar body armor that she'd had the Royal Wizards enchant to protect against magical attack. She'd bought herself a set, too, but he didn't need to know that. She liked it so much that she'd ordered a set for each of their knights and Ladies-in-Waiting, their royal protectors—although only their Security Chief knew about it since she'd run it by him first to confirm sizing. She planned to surprise them with it at their next all-hands training session at the palace in a few months.

"Thanks, Babe," he bellowed as he rushed back into the closet to grab it before heading to the stables. He came running back out, grabbed her by the waist and spun her around, kissing her.

"I love it. And you."

She laughed and kissed him back. He loved her laugh. He lived to make her laugh. It was when she was laughing that she was as far away from the bad dreams and ghosts that haunted her in the night as she could get. He couldn't get enough of it. She often had disturbing dreams. He knew she had visions and could see spirits. When she was awake, she could guard herself against unwanted communication, but when she was asleep, she was vulnerable. He shook his head, once again wishing she'd just learn how to manage it but respected her decision not to learn magic. He knew that the situation with her mother had pushed her into that decision, and once she'd made up her mind about something it was next to impossible to get her to change it. He sighed. Of all the women to fall in love with, it had to be the one who was as stubborn as he was. Maybe more so.

He knew she could damned well take care of herself. She was a natural with a sword and a bow, even on horseback. And she was a better shot with any firearm she got her hands on than he'd ever be. Hell, she could take care of herself, him, and everyone else better than he could. She didn't need anyone to take care of her, but he knew she loved that he wanted to. She would never ask for help, although she'd be the first to give it. He smiled.

"I love you, too," she laughed. "Are you okay if I head out to Belfast for a bit? Dee and I were hoping to get together, but I can stay here if you'd prefer I wait 'til you're back."

"No dear, give your Belfast Bestie a hug from me. I'll see you when I get back. Don't get into too much trouble."

She grabbed his face in her hands and kissed him hard. She looked into his hazel eyes and smirked. "Dalen Martin McGregor, there's no such thing as too much trouble."

He rolled his eyes, picked up his armor and sauntered out to the stables to meet Geoffrey. He paused when he reached the doorway. Turning halfway around, he said, "Ash, I do love you."

"I know." She smiled. "I love you, too."

Other than her sisters, he was the only one to ever call her Ash. Everyone else in the Kingdom called her Aisling or Libby. In the world outside the force field she was simply Libby McGregor, the quirky American art buyer who blew in and out of town like a hurricane.

He turned around, smiling, and continued out to get his horse, wiping her lipstick off his face. The Queen headed to her closet, softly humming the Old 97s song, "Thank God for Irish Whiskey, Thank the Devil for Pretty Girls," as she pulled her shoulder length black hair out of her face to figure out what to wear for a night out in Belfast.

Neither of them could possibly know those "I love yous" would be the last conversation they'd ever have.

Heav'n has no rage like love to hatred turn'd
Nor Hell a fury, like a woman scorn'd.
~William Congreve, "The Mourning Bride"

Dale saddled up his trusty horse, Hoss, a beautiful red stallion with soulful golden eyes and a sense of humor better suited to a human.

"Hey, Hossy Bossy, are you ready to go fight a bad guy?"

Hoss stomped his feet and snorted in Dale's direction, eager to get out of his stall to go riding.

"Yeah? Me too! Let's go get that evil witch and make her go away. Who's a good boy? Who's my little monkey face?"

Hoss rolled his eyes. "Monkey face?" He looked nothing like a monkey. Sometimes Dale was just ridiculous. "Monkey face." Bah!

Hoss was one of the smartest horses the King had ever ridden, and he'd grown up with horses. Hoss was so smart the Queen sometimes wondered if he had magical lineage. She knew shapeshifters existed but couldn't imagine one choosing to remain Dale's horse for so long. Libby swore that sometimes she saw Hoss laughing at Dale, and that he'd occasionally make eye contact with her and smile. Libby would also ride Hoss if she was out alone in an official capacity but wasn't as particular as Dale was when it came to her steeds.

Geoffrey cleared his throat to let Dale know he was there and could hear this goofy baby talk that Dale used on Hoss when he thought they were alone.

"Oh! Didn't see you there, Geoffrey. Ready to go?"

"As ready as I'll ever be," he replied.

Geoffrey Fitzgerald didn't love horses the way the King did, but he'd managed to saddle up his favorite horse from the royal stables. Dude was a shiny white stallion, with an annoying habit of taking a shit anywhere he wanted, even if it was in the middle of a formal military procession. Dude's lack of respect for protocol was secretly what Geoffrey liked best about him. The Senior Knight always fulfilled his responsibilities appropriately but hated the ridiculous nature of life at the palace. Protocol made him want to vomit on good days and kill people on bad days. As down to earth as Dale and Libby were, the trappings of court life were sometimes beyond their control. And they were down to earth. How many rulers would allow themselves to be called by their nicknames? King Dalen Martin went by Dale whenever possible, and Queen Aisling Elisabeth went by Libby.

The Queen's name came from the old Irish word for "dreamer." Since few people could get the Gaelic pronunciation Ash-ling correct, she usually went by Libby. Although she did adopt an Ash Tree as part of her crest in nod to the name. In her youth she went by Elisabeth for a time, but one day decided that there was only room for one Queen Elizabeth in the world, and the one who was there first was a badass. From that point forward, it was just Libby.

After a brisk ride, Dale and Geoffrey reached the witch's encampment the next morning. As they got closer, they could see her standing there in the clearing, waiting for them. Her short brown hair made her appear taller than she was. You could tell she had been pretty in her youth, before bitterness had taken its toll and sharpened the softness that used to be in her face. The look of recognition in her pale blue eyes as they got closer was mutual, and heart-breaking on both sides.

"Oh fuck," Dale muttered under his breath as he looked at Geoffrey.

In that moment, Dale embraced the universal truth that hell hath no fury like a woman scorned. He knew this wasn't going to be easy, but couldn't imagine how badly it would go. The evil witch was none other than Skarra Svensden, a princess that once vied for Dale's heart. She knew that if he married Libby he would become King, but was convinced she would win in spite of that. When he chose Libby instead, Skarra threw an epic tantrum and promised she'd make him pay. She wasn't a bad person initially, just a spoiled brat whose confidence was shattered when she wasn't the first choice. Her parents had convinced her she was perfect, and failure was a lesson in humility she'd been protected from her whole life. That is, until the moment Dale chose Libby.

Libby outperformed Skarra in every area of life, except one. Despite an innate ability, Libby refused to pursue any training in magic. So Skarra was determined to be the unquestionable best at it, including the dark magic. When she saw Dale ride up, she was crushed. She'd hoped it would be Queen Libby and that she'd have a second chance with Dale. Now one of them was going to have to kill the other. She steeled herself for the fight ahead. *That fucker made his choice, now he'll have to die with the consequences.*

Dale tried to take the high road and reason with her.

"Skarra, what are you doing?" Dale wasted no time on formalities.

"Hello Dalen, it's been a long time. I'm fine. Thank you for asking." She replied coldly. "Where is your lovely wife?"

"Why are you doing this, Skarra? It doesn't have to be this way."

"Oh, I think it does. You brought this on yourself, you know. You chose wrong. Admit it. You know I would have made the better wife." Skarra spat out the words as her anger came bubbling to the surface.

"Skarra, enough already. It's been almost fifteen years. Have some self-respect."

"Self-respect?" she screamed at him. "How dare you speak to me of respect. You humiliated me. You're the one that will learn respect. You and that whore you married."

Dale clenched his jaw in anger and determination. He glared at her, as he realized that talking was futile. He was furious that she was going to force him to fight her. He'd heard rumors that she had run off to study black magic and had moved beyond petty, selfish and manipulative to cruel and evil. He had his enchanted armor and a magical sword but wouldn't leave anything to chance. The time for talking was over.

He raised his sword and without another word Hoss charged at a full gallop. He caught Skarra by surprise, who didn't really believe he'd do it. His first run was successful; he pierced her heart. The look of shock on her face quickly turned into maniacal laughter as she used her dying breath to cast a curse on him.

"Say goodbye to your happy ending. Your love story is over." Skarra sputtered her last words as blood trickled from her mouth.

When a wizard infuses a spell with their life force, it takes on a special power and is next to impossible to break. Without the enchanted armor he'd have been killed instantly. Instead, it slowly took hold and he slumped over in the saddle and started to fall off. Hoss knew something was wrong with his rider and had already started slowing up when Geoffrey flew into action. Dale was fighting against unconsciousness. The pain was indescribable.

"What did that bitch do?"

"I don't know Dale, but we've got to get you home. Now."

Geoffrey grabbed his king and heaved him onto the back of Dude before Dale passed out and became deadweight. He grabbed Dale's sword and quickly chopped off Skarra's head to make sure she wouldn't come back as a zombie, and then he raced home, leaving Hoss to follow along behind. Nothing like standard military training to keep one prepared in these situations, and they didn't have time for a zombie outbreak. He pulled out his new phone, a gift from Libby, and voice dialed Sean Perry, the Security Chief, with the details so he could apprise the palace doctors of the situation. Geoffrey was the Senior Knight, but as Security Chief, Sean took care of all the logistics. They'd both been friends with Dale long before he became King. He trusted them completely.

Ships that pass in the night, and speak each other in passing,
only a signal shown, and a distant voice in the darkness;
So, on the ocean of life, we pass and speak one another, only
a look and a voice, then darkness again and a silence.
~Henry Wadsworth Longfellow, "Tales of a Wayside Inn"

Belfast had always been good to Libby. So had her friend Dee. She was one of the few Normals who knew the Queen's secret, although she'd never visited the kingdom herself. A typical Friday night would have found the two women at McHugh's Pub to watch Dee's husband Mark and his best friend Gary perform. But tonight, they were gigging at the Duke of York. And that's where they were when Libby felt Dale's injury.

Following protocol, Sean called Libby, but she already knew something was wrong. The moment the King was struck she'd felt it. She'd stopped mid-joke, turning pale and nearly dropping her drink, clutching her chest. Dee was alarmed, wondering if her friend was having a heart attack. When the phone rang, she could see the look of pain on Libby's face as she received Sean's report. Dale had been badly injured and was unconscious. Geoffrey was rushing him back to the palace, but it was bad. Libby needed to return immediately.

Dee helped Libby get outside the pub without much of a scene and get into the small alley behind the Duke of York so she could discreetly use the emergency portal. Despite being a clear summer night, a storm had opened up over Belfast. The alley was dimly lit and anyone who might have seen them would have seen two women walking in the rain, one helping her drunk friend who was leaning against the wall for support.

Libby quickly ran her hands over the Longfellow poem painted on the bricks and opened the portal back to the palace stables. She studied the poem. As many times as she'd read it, this time the words felt ominous. *Then darkness again and a silence.* Like her dream. She fought the sensation of drowning, the panic and edge of unconsciousness that threatened her. She felt sick and knew Dale must be in bad shape.

She looked up at her friend before she stepped through. "Thank you, Dee," she wheezed.

"Don't be silly," she replied. "Just message me later and let me know you're okay."

Libby nodded and stepped through as a peal of thunder echoed through the narrow alleyways of Belfast's Cathedral Quarter. A slight quiver in the brick wall was the only evidence that she'd been there. Dee took a deep breath and walked back into the pub through the side door instead of going around to the front, a perk of being a musician's wife. Fortunately, the band was on break or she'd have been walking right in front of the stage. She'd never get used to the idea that magic was real or that her friend was part of a whole other world. When Paul gave her a questioning look from behind the bar, she told him that she'd put Libby in a cab and sent her home. The handsome bartender shrugged and tossed her a clean bar towel to dry off.

"Bit unusual to see Libby get that pissed, isn't it, Dee? Ah well, nothing a good fry up in the morning won't fix," he chuckled.

Dee laughed in agreement, and slumped back into her seat at their stage side table to finish her drink. She was worried about her friend and gratefully accepted a kiss from Mark as he made his way back to the stage to finish that evening's set.

When the call ended, Sean put the phone down. He stood there for a moment thinking about his friend. They'd worked alongside each other for years. He recalled the day Dale asked him to join the knighthood. It was a no-brainer. He was angry. Angry at himself for not going with them, but at the time the threat assessment didn't indicate that level of response was necessary.

His face was getting redder by the minute. He needed to calm down. His wife was always on him to watch his stress levels and blood pressure. He took a deep breath and set to work preparing for a full roster recall. But first, he had to meet the Queen with a situation report. She should be back any minute. The emergency portal opened right into the palace stables instead of in the palace itself. In the unlikely event it was breached, they'd have additional time to prepare. In the event of a surprise attack, every minute mattered. Sean met Libby and gave her a briefing as they walked back to the palace.

"What the hell happened, Sean?"

Libby had gratefully taken the arm he'd offered when she stumbled. A solid 5'6", she was a good head shorter than he was. From a distance it looked like she was leaning into his embrace. Instead, she was leaning on him for support as they walked. She was breathing shallow and struggling to maintain focus.

"Short version? It was Skarra Svensden. Geoffrey says Dale charged at her and pierced her heart, but she cast some kind of dying spell. He's in and out of consciousness, but it looks bad. Libby, I've summoned the Royal Wizards and physicians. They don't seem hopeful. We need to prepare for the worst."

"The worst?"

"Yes. I'm sorry Libby, but my job requires I think in worst-case scenarios. You know the risk to the force field and the kingdom. I can see the toll his injuries are taking on you just looking at you. You look like shit, by the way. I want to believe in hope, but I wouldn't be a very good Security Chief if I put all my eggs in that basket."

Sean rarely cursed. Libby knew how worried he must be. She pulled back and raised her dark eyes up to meet his concerned gaze. "Right. Well, my job requires I think positive. But do what you need to do. I'll support any decisions you make. My sole focus right now is Dale."

Libby sat in silence, alone in her office, spinning her wedding rings around and around her finger like she often did when she was thinking. She was sweating and nauseated, and her heart hurt, so she knew Dale was still alive but that his condition was worsening.

She'd managed to get a look at herself in a mirror, and Sean was right. She did look like shit. She was pale and clammy, and the rainstorm that had opened up over Belfast as she was leaving had caused her mascara to run all over her face. Her hair was a stringy mess and her sassy night out attire was wrinkled and looked ridiculous under the circumstances.

She felt the sinking, cold foreboding and returned to the dream warning where she was drowning. She'd released Sean to make preparations to recall the knights and the Senior Lady-In-Waiting, the head of the elite all-female security team that protected the royal family, back to the palace. The logistics of housing an additional twenty soldiers and horses fell to him since he oversaw the training barracks and armory. She paused, dreading the phone call she had to make, but Dale's sister Kendra deserved to hear from her directly. Brushing her dark hair out of her face, she picked up the phone to deliver the news.

Kendra was remarkably calm as Libby explained the little she knew, but she and her son, Kurtis, immediately set out for the palace. They lived on a horse ranch half a day's ride away and would arrive shortly after Dale. It would be months before they'd return to stay at the ranch again.

Libby buried her fear deep and immediately burst into action. She knew that Geoffrey would be arriving with Dale shortly and was determined to have as much ready as possible. Her father had often jokingly referred to her as his Hurricane—which became HurriQueen after she'd assumed the throne—when she got into one of these bursts of action. Today she was a category five, and the staff did their best to stay out of her way. It wasn't personal and they knew it. Word traveled fast and they were all worried about King Dale. She'd left everyone abuzz and went to clean up and change clothes, so she'd be ready for Dale's return.

Libby was pacing nervously in front of the palace when she felt the familiar pressure on the top of her head, and the lights zigzag across her field of vision.

"Oh no. Not now, I can't right now," she pleaded.

A lifetime of unwelcome spirit visits had taught her it was going to happen whether she wanted it to or not. She just didn't have the energy to fight it this time. She squinted and looked around, trying to see through the lights, looking for an anchor to keep her steady. The pain in her head was getting worse. But then she saw him, standing at the edge of the group waiting for Dale. Her father. He was talking to her. She could feel her nose start to bleed as the vise around her head tightened further.

"Aisling Elisabeth, you must listen to me. There is a storm coming. A bad one. But you aren't alone. You must stop fighting us. Let us help you."

She felt clammy and fought back the waves of nausea. She closed her eyes and took deep breaths, counting. In for seven. Hold for seven. Out for seven. Hold for seven. After a few repetitions, she felt the nausea back off and the zigzags fade away. The pressure in her head would last a few more hours, but when she opened her eyes again her dad was gone.

Larra, who was always nearby, discreetly handed her a handkerchief and she wiped the blood off her face just in time to see Geoffrey and Dale come flying up the drive, Hoss just a few paces behind. They'd bypassed the stables and come right to the main entry. Dale was still in and out of consciousness and Libby's heart skipped a beat when she saw him. She shook off the uneasy feeling and the image of her late father, and got Dale ushered in and set up in their bedroom, with a full entourage of doctors and wizards.

"Ash?" Dale groaned as they got him settled in bed.

"I'm here, Dale. You're home and safe."

He mumbled something unintelligible as he faded back to unconsciousness. Libby took an unwilling step back to allow the medical team a chance to examine him.

Sean had been waiting with Libby, but he and Geoffrey retreated to the Knight's Tower as soon as they were assured the King was in good hands. Libby would be well protected by Larra and they had work to do.

It had been a hot dirty gallop back to the palace with Dale. So, while Geoffrey was in the shower getting cleaned up for the frenzy of activity that was coming, Sean did his job. With the exception of Sean and Geoffrey, all the knights had other jobs and lived with their families around the kingdom. They came in for regular trainings but having them strategically located around the kingdom helped to provide a sense of security to the citizens without the need to maintain a full army.

One by one he made the calls that put them on standby to come to the palace. He sighed when he got to the last name on the roster, Morgan. John Morgan was the one knight Sean hadn't had any input on, and the only one who lived outside the force field. Both the King and Queen had added knights to the Royal Corps over the years.

There were always ten, and Sean kept his eyes open for future recruits as other knights retired or left the service. The Queen had found John on one of her trips to the outside world. As if he were one of her art treasures, she'd brought back a Normal man with no connection to her or anyone else in the Kingdom and made him her Queen's Knight Grand Champion. Sean knew she had a reason for everything she did, but this was one he just couldn't agree with. John lacked discipline and respect. The man was a direct descendant of the pirate Captain Morgan, and proud of it! It was an insult to the Corps.

He gritted his teeth as he dialed, running his hand through his short blonde hair. The Queen's Champion was flying down a mountain on two wheels when the call came through. It was a miracle he'd heard it at all but knew that it must be important, so he stopped to answer it. Few people ever called his private phone, especially not Sean. Usually it was Libby seeing if he wanted to pop in to Belfast for a night on the town, or his wife with an emergency at home.

"John Morgan, this is Sean. There has been an incident. All knights are on standby. You need to be ready to return to the palace on short notice."

"You're breaking up, Sean. I'm out in the hills right now. Did you say I need to be at the palace?"

"You're on standby. You need to be ready to return." Sean felt his face getting red with irritation at having to repeat himself.

He heard John start to explain he was out mountain biking and cut him off.

"The King has been seriously wounded. He may not survive. The situation is urgent. This is your duty as a Royal Knight and the Queen's Knight Grand Champion."

"For fuck's sake, next time lead with that! I'll be there for Libby. I'm heading down now."

John rolled his eyes; he knew Sean didn't like him, he just couldn't figure out what his deal was and why he was so uptight. *What a control freak*, he thought to himself, as he flipped the face shield on his helmet back down and went barreling down the mountain on his bike. He had to get down the mountain anyway, he may as well have fun doing it. Like the rest of the knights he always had a go bag ready, so was already packed. *Stand-by? Descendants of the one and only Captain Morgan don't wait on stand-by. Nah, I'm going in to see what the heck is going on.*" He'd say goodbye to his wife and son and then head to the palace.

Chapter 2

The Spirit Council
Is Called to Order

Eye of a hurricane, listen to yourself churn.
World serves its own needs, don't misserve your own needs.
Speed it up a notch, speed, grunt, no strength.
The ladder starts to clatter with fear of fight, down height.
Wire in a fire, represent the seven games
In a government for hire and a combat site.
Left her, wasn't coming in a hurry
With the furies breathing down your neck.
It's the end of the world as we know it, and I feel fine.
~R.E.M., "It's the End of the World As We Know It"

The elderly Japanese woman was sitting in her kitchen sipping her tea when the alarm on the wall started beeping. Teruyo put down her crossword puzzle and pulled up a high-tech monitor to discover that the King had been critically injured in battle. He was alive, but not for long. She frowned and pushed the peacock-colored vinyl chair away from the chrome-edged table and shuffled across the black and white checked linoleum floor to the old enamel stove to put on the kettle, smoothing the silver hair in her neat bun out of habit. She knew she'd be joined by other members of the Council shortly. Their realm bordered that of the living, and they were intertwined. If the living world was destroyed, they would be too. They would soon be fighting for their own ghostly survival, ironic as that was.

The Spirit Council served as the advisors to the King and Queen in times of crisis, and could appear to them, and any other humans deemed necessary, while they were awake. Spirits usually preferred conversations in dream state, although they were less efficient. There were only five seats on the Council, but members came and went like players in an ice hockey game. It all depended on who had the skills needed for that particular play, and who the monarch was. Any spiritual being could be called upon to serve on the Council, and various incarnations included angels, ghosts, and other magical beings who had crossed over into their phase of the universe. King Dale wasn't going to survive in the living realm much longer. As head of the Council, Teruyo knew that her granddaughter, Libby, would need as much help as she could get, but that she'd resist. She drafted those from Libby's past, in the hopes the Queen would trust them more easily.

The first to arrive was the Queen's father, Kokichi.

"Hello, Son," she greeted him with a warm hug.

Kokichi was the newest member of the Council. He'd been dead less than a year but had taken his spirit training seriously. He'd already been communicating with the Queen via dream messages and other spiritual signs. Today was the first time he'd attempted to contact her while she was awake. Most new spirits took a lot longer to adapt and master skills like communicating with the living, but he had a willpower and determination in life that stayed with him in the spirit realm. This was, after all, the man who quit smoking cold turkey the day Libby was born. And even though the Council was only activated in times of crisis, Libby had seen and even interacted with members of the spirit realm for years. Mostly in her dreams, since she refused to acknowledge this particular talent. Libby had inherited both Kokichi's willpower and the stubbornness that went with it. She'd inherited her other gifts from her mother's side of the family.

"Hi, Mom. I saw Dalen. He looks bad. So does Aisling Elisabeth. I think she saw and heard me there, but you can never tell with her. How bad is it?" he asked. Her father and grandmother were the only two in her life who'd ever referred to her using both names, a habit they continued in death.

"Bad," she confirmed. "But we will do our best."

The other three members she'd summoned to the Council walked into the small kitchen together: a Japanese warrior woman in her twenties, a ginger-haired Irish grandmother, and a sandy blonde green-eyed toddler. Kokichi was the tallest at 5'7", and the women barely made it to 5'. Even though they were energy and had no physical bodies, they looked more or less like they did when they were alive, retaining their physical appearances so that they'd be familiar to those left behind in the living realm. The toddler was an exception and was one of the few allowed to choose his own form.

As the five took their seats, the simple kitchen transformed into a high-tech military situation room. There were video screens surrounding the round table and monitors at each seat. It was an exact duplicate of the council room in the palace.

Teruyo stood and called the meeting to order. "Thank you for coming on short notice," she began.

"As if we had a choice," barked the boy. The deep smoky voice didn't match the angelic baby face it came out of. Michael had been there a long time, almost as long as Teruyo. Maggie and Michie had been there centuries longer, but since Libby had never met them, Teruyo took the lead on the council.

Teruyo gave him a silencing glance and he stopped with a long-suffering sigh.

"Here is what we know," she began.

She stood up and began gesturing at the largest monitor. "At 8:24 this morning King Dalen Martin was hit with a fatal curse. Skarra Svensden was killed and beheaded so we don't have to worry about the threat of zombies, but this is a potential world-killer. The King will not survive. How long he has left is in question, but our Aisling Elisabeth is already shouldering the bulk of the force field. The Royal Wizards and doctors are monitoring both of their conditions. She is putting herself in a meditative trance a few times a day to help conserve energy. This will hold for a while, but when the King dies, we know that she will lose half her heart and all of his. Her survival, which is key to the survival of both the kingdom and our realm since there are no suitable heirs, is in question. It may be too much for her."

Kokichi sat there frowning. It was hard for spirits to feel much sadness about death, since they knew that life continued, albeit differently. But he was still new, having died just eight months prior, and held on to many of his old emotions and feelings. He was worried about his daughter. Unlike when she was seven and crashed her bicycle, breaking her leg and losing teeth in the process, there was no way to make this better for her. Even then, she'd refused to cry in front of him and wouldn't ask for help. There wasn't much he could do to protect her now, even if she was open to assistance. She was going to have to weather the storm and figure out how to save herself and the Kingdom. By herself.

Maggie cleared her throat and ran her fingers through her short red hair before turning her bright blue eyes on their leader. She was a direct ancestor of Libby's but was chosen for her magical knowledge and abilities over any tie to the Queen. "Fortunately, she doesn't have to rely solely on willpower. What do you propose we do, Teruyo?"

Teruyo shook her head. "We will do all we can. Aisling Elisabeth is strong, but she will need all of us if she is to hold the Kingdom together.

"We have another matter to address," she sighed. "Aisling Elisabeth is a stubborn mule of a girl. A woman," she corrected herself. "Almost as stubborn as Dalen. We've all tried communicating with her over the years, both in dream state and in waking, and she continues to resist our guidance. He is the only one she will listen to. I propose we get him trained as quickly as possible and add him to the Council."

They sat in stunned silence as they pondered this. There were only five seats on the Council. It's just how it was. One of them would be out once he was ready. Dalen was a hothead in life, and those personalities were the hardest to train. They all agreed he was probably the only one Queen Libby would listen to, but the likelihood of success was low, further diminished by their impossibly short timeline.

"I've been here a long time," piped up Michael, "and have never heard of a spirit learning to communicate that quickly. Not even Kokichi. But I agree, she will best respond to someone she knows, especially Dale. I will give up my seat on the council once he's ready. Besides, Libby doesn't even know I'm here."

"Don't be so sure about that." Maggie looked at him. "She has the gift of sight when she chooses to use it. She knows your face. She saw you the day you died, in this form." Maggie gestured at him. "You spoke to her and she heard you. I know. I saw it all."

Michael looked up at the ceiling without responding and blew his shaggy blonde hair out of his face.

Teruyo looked at Maggie and sighed. "If we survive the death of the King, you must find someone to teach Libby to use her gift. I have a feeling she's going to need it to survive. And you'd probably better do it as quickly as possible. She's too weak to take much more of the headaches and nosebleeds every time she resists us. Teach her that first. You of all people should have some ideas on how to help her."

Maggie smiled like a contented cat but said nothing. In life Maggie had also possessed the gift, and when her great-great-great-great-great-granddaughter was born she recognized it immediately. For those who can see energy, magic has a unique color for each person. In Libby's case it was the coppery pink glow of a rose quartz crystal. Maggie's was the sparkling blue of her eyes, but she recognized that Libby's magic came from the heart and was based in pure love. Libby's was strong, but she rarely acknowledged it existed and had refused to learn how to use it.

The situation with her mother caused her to fear magic. The Queen Mother had been strong and embraced her power and gifts. But, as sometimes happens, her brain was overpowered. While she was still a child, Libby's mother began to have difficulty separating her waking reality with the spirit realm she could see so clearly. As such, Libby grew up mothering her younger sisters, making sure they were dressed properly and did their homework. She loved her sisters but developed a strong resentment to this adult responsibility, and blamed magic.

There were times in her life where Libby couldn't hold it back, usually at times of great distress and loss. The day she'd fought to save a child she loved, she'd instinctively tapped into it, at great personal cost. And the day Kokichi died it flared and she could see him and all of the rest of them, but she'd forced it back down. It scared her. The only time she didn't fight it, was with music. She loved being able to see the color of music.

Maggie finally had the chance to send a teacher her way. With instruction, Libby could be the strongest of her line. Now that the Council had been formally convened, she could reach out to the one person easily available and talented enough to teach Libby. When Libby was receptive, Maggie could reach out to her directly.

"I do not agree," Michie spoke softly, yet always managed to be heard.

All four heads turned to look at her.

"There is too much at stake, and too much that can go wrong. Attempting to put Dalen on the Council is a distraction for all of us."

Teruyo's face expressed her displeasure, but she wouldn't disrespect her ancestor by interrupting.

Michie continued. "Still, you are correct, Libby will be most receptive to Dalen. We should expedite his training but keep him under close supervision. The risk of untrained communication could be catastrophic."

Michael barked, "Which one of us is going to get stuck with the nightmare job of training him?"

"Kokichi is the only logical choice. In life they'd had a good relationship so that will hopefully make the process easier. Dalen respected him, which was rare for him." Michie looked over at Kokichi with a tinge of pride.

There were no other suggestions, so Kokichi bowed his head in acceptance of this new responsibility. He had reservations. The King's impatience and stubbornness were well known. They were counting on the fact that his love for Queen Libby would outweigh his pig-headedness. He hoped they weren't making a mistake.

Teruyo addressed the group once again. "Are we in agreement then? We will train Dalen, but he will not be added to the Council?"

They all nodded. They knew Dale would try to take shortcuts. It was imperative that he wait until he completed his training to try to communicate with her or he may push her into madness. What many of the living considered hauntings were really just spirits who hadn't mastered communication yet. But even with experience communication was tricky and left far too much room for interpretation. Maggie liked to say, "Clarity is a rarity," and it was true. Clarity was never guaranteed.

Teruyo spoke once more before adjourning the Council. "While Aisling Elisabeth is in a meditative state, or asleep, I will contact her and assure her she is not alone. She is susceptible to attack in her weakened condition. I propose we take turns protecting her from any spiritual threats. The moment the King dies we are all at risk. We must help her as best we can. I will reach out to the Senior Knight and Senior Lady-in-Waiting to apprise them of our plan. I hope they remember their training and live up to their roles. Appearing to the living can go wrong in so many ways, even after the Council has been activated," she said, shaking her head.

Dale and Libby kept two full-time Royal Wizards on staff, and a third who was semi-retired. It quickly became clear there was neither a known medical nor magical way to save the King. The toll on the Queen was obvious so, with a little dream state suggestion from Maggie, a call went out throughout the Kingdom summoning all additional wizards and musicians to the palace.

The wizards and engineers could work their magic on the force field, but musicians had the power to boost one's life force itself. Out in the Normal world people loved music for how it made them feel. Music could change your mood, help you relive memories, or get a crowd going. There was latent power in all music, even outside the force field. But in the Kingdom, there was real magical power in every note. The Queen, at the King's bedside, received musician after musician, absorbing as much music magic as possible. Even that wasn't enough to keep her strong, but it kept both her and the force field from dying out under the strain.

One of those musicians was the Queen's dear friend, Fintan O'Toole. He'd been a world-famous musician and poet before he'd retired. He was a Normal, but when she'd convinced him to move to the Kingdom a few years earlier, she'd named him Poet Laureate. She was surprised and grateful to see him when he'd walked into their bedroom one afternoon with his mandolin, a small sprig of fresh lilac tucked into the button hole of his lapel. She'd hugged him, but neither had any words, so he'd just started playing.

The curse was fatal, and it was only a matter of time before Dale died. When he pierced Skarra's heart, the curse she cast started in his. It would slowly consume his internal organs before spreading to his brain and killing him. Eventually he wouldn't regain consciousness at all, which would be a blessing. It was a gruesome and painful way to die. In the end, he wouldn't be able to walk or talk. He wouldn't know what was happening, and wouldn't even know who Libby, the love of his life, was anymore. He'd be helpless, unable to do anything for himself but die. Not the death befitting a warrior or a king.

At the same time Geoffrey was racing back to the palace with Dale, and the Spirit Council was debating how to proceed, one of the Royal Wizards was about to get the shock of her life. In her home, at the far edge of the Kingdom, Krystal felt the giant malachite crack a split second before she heard it. She rushed to her altar and saw the beautiful green stone lying in pieces.

"Oh, Sweet Goddess," she cried as her hands reached up to tug at her long silver braid. She knew that when a malachite—a powerful protection crystal—cracked it meant danger was near. She quickly dropped her braid in favor of her amethyst amulet and reached for her favorite black tourmaline wand as she set new wards around her home. As she was making her way around to each corner, she stopped dead in her tracks when she saw Maggie appear. Krystal was a Royal Wizard, although she was semi-retired these days. Unlike her counterparts, she could easily communicate with spirits, and she recognized Maggie as such so she wasn't afraid, although the malachite had her on edge.

"Krystal Johns, you must return to the palace immediately. The King has been injured. The Spirit Council has been convened. I am Maggie O'Brien, and I will fill you in on the way. You must make haste."

"Wait, is that what caused my malachite to shatter?"

"Yes. And that's not all that's at risk. You must hurry."

Krystal was already loading crystals and white sage into her bag and hollering for her grandchildren to go home. She lived several days journey from the palace. She wouldn't take her crystals through a portal since that could potentially change their molecular structure, so she had to travel by horse. She knew that if the Spirit Council had been convened things were bad. As much as she'd studied crystal lore, she'd never before seen a malachite shatter like that. *At least I have practical evidence that the legends are true*, she thought. *I just hope it's not as bad as I think it is.* There was no time to clean up the altar, so she finished blessing the room and closed the door behind her.

She got her wagon packed with the necessary provisions and set out at a brisk pace for the palace. The wagon had everything she'd need, her mini-house on wheels. Not having to make and break camp would shave at least half a day off the three-day journey. As she departed, she dialed the Palace to inform her colleagues she was en route.

Chapter 3

Death Comes Knocking

L ibby knew she was dreaming but couldn't force herself to wake up. She was cold. She was at home in the palace, but it was too quiet to be real. Everything she looked at had sharp edges and was washed out. She recognized their bedroom and walked towards the bed where Dale was lying. Her footsteps echoed loudly on the stone floors and it seemed to take forever. With each step the temperature dropped. By the time she reached the edge of the bed, she could see her breath on the air. She looked down at Dale. He was alive, but just barely.

His body was shriveled, and he looked more skeleton than human. His breathing was labored and rattled. He was looking at her, but his beautiful hazel eyes were a solid yellow. She could feel a scream start in her belly at the same time blood came pouring out of his mouth, yellow eyes just staring at her in accusation, blaming her for his death. She was still cold, but felt a warm wetness spreading across her chest. She looked down to see blood pouring out of her mouth and running down her body. The screaming that started in her belly was lost in a gurgle as she drowned in her own blood.

She woke up to the sound of her screams still hanging in the air and weapons being drawn as her Ladies-in-Waiting sprang into action to defend their Queen.

Since their official title was Ladies-in-Waiting, or LIW for short, those not from their kingdom might assume the LIWs were tea-drinking frilly dress-wearing ladies. That couldn't be further from the truth. The Ladies-in-Waiting were an ancient order of female knights, and a group of elite warriors. On more than one occasion a Royal Knight got his rear handed to him by a LIW, including John Morgan. When he'd first arrived in the Kingdom, he thought it was funny to refer to them as Lulu Belles, playing off the sound of the acronym LIW. They'd quickly expressed their discontent with the nickname, and he now only referred to them as *The Ladies*.

Unlike the knights, the LIWs stayed at the palace in shifts. They were the immediate bodyguards of the royal family, as well as the Queen's advisors and trusted friends. Since the universe likes balance in all things, there were ten LIWs, to mirror the knights, with one junior LIW, Dyanna Chaney, Libby's niece. Like the knights, each LIW was appointed, but in this case the Queen had the final decision. Sean did background checks on all of them, but even the King didn't have an official say in the matter.

The day of the attack the Queen had moved to the neighboring bedroom to accommodate all the wizards and doctors tending to the King, so at least there wasn't a large audience. When the LIWs on duty realized it was another nightmare, there was awkward silence. They were the Kingdom's fiercest warriors and her best friends, but they didn't know what to say. Nothing in their training had prepared them for this scenario.

Larra wordlessly handed the Queen a flask of uisce beatha, the faery whiskey that literally translated as water of life. Mortals knew it better as whiskey, although the magical version was a hell of a lot more powerful. After a hearty swig the Queen collapsed, sobbing into her pillows. She'd seen the future in her dream. She'd felt the truth of it, although it would be some time before she'd accept it. As the uisce beatha coursed through her veins she fell into a troubled sleep, shivering from the cold that she'd dreamed about. Larra sat quietly at the foot of the bed and motioned for her counterpart, Harley Gallagher, to go back to guarding the door from the hallway.

Harley looked at Libby with concern and compassion. She fought back the tears welling in her big dark eyes as she returned to her post. "Larra, what do we do? This is almost too much to endure just to watch." As much as she loved Dale, her heart was breaking for Libby.

"We do our jobs," the tiny girl replied. "Go back to your post. I'll stay with Libby."

She looked over at Libby, who had returned to a fitful sleep. Over the years she'd grown to care for, and respect, her human liege. An unlikely friendship had developed between the two women, despite the enormous difference in their ages. Libby was in her mid-forties. Larra was a good 200 years older.

Larra would outlive almost every human she'd ever know and care for but, since she was part human herself, she'd also eventually age and die. She was unlikely those of pure fey lineage who were immortal unless killed. Larra had never been accepted in the faery world, despite having been born to the royal family. She was tiny for a human, but larger than most of the fey. They were pale and fair, and she had dark hair, dark almond eyes and an eternal tan. Everything about her screamed that she didn't belong there. Her existence was an embarrassment to her family, so she rarely spent time in the faery realm.

She'd met Libby on one of her adventures before she'd become Queen. Larra may have been hundreds of years old, but she looked like a beautiful human teenager. She'd been in a pub one night when some men were giving her a hard time. Larra was a deadly warrior, but she kept a low profile whenever possible. Libby had been carousing at the bar and noticed the young girl being hassled by a bunch of drunk goons.

She sauntered over to Larra's table and said, "Hey Sis, there you are. I've been looking for you. It's time to go home."

Larra looked up at her, and before she could say anything one of the men started in with, "Why don't you just leave us alone with her, or better yet, join us." As he grabbed Libby's ass, she brought her heel down hard on his foot, then her elbow up into his throat. Libby looked at Larra and said, "Let's go," with such authority that Larra followed her, amused and intrigued to see where this would all go. She'd never have imagined it would have brought her here.

Libby needed to be surrounded by music twenty-four hours a day just to survive. With additional wizards and musicians to support the Queen's energy field, Sophia and Awen, the Royal Wizards, attacked the archives in a desperate attempt to find something they could use. Krystal, their colleague, was already on her way when the call for help went out. They hadn't even questioned how she knew before most everyone else, but it was still going to take another day for her to arrive. Libby was tougher than most people, but that was due more to sheer willpower than physical strength. With her suppressed magical abilities, maybe there was something that could be done to save the Kingdom, if not the King.

They spent days with dusty old scrolls and leather-bound books. The old stuff hadn't been digitized yet, but they had search algorithms running for everything else, including anything that may have been lost outside the force field in a Normal library. They were exhausted, dusty, and desperate. Sophia was massaging her temples with her eyes closed, when she heard Awen yell, "Yes!" from across the library.

"Oh please, Goddess, let this be it," Sophia prayed.

Awen came running from around the stacks with an old dusty scroll under her arm, her knees bouncing up and down like she was running hurdles. Her active lifestyle made her forgo the traditional robes in favor of athletic attire, which came in handy today as she leaped over stacks of books and dodged reading tables.

"Sophia! I found it! I think I've found it! Oh, please let this be it!" she yelled.

They made quite the pair. Sophia Sabino was the blonde and blue-eyed earth mother, the Healer, who took care of her kids and grandkids and everyone else. Her hugs were famous, as was her cooking. Taco night at Sophia's could cure pretty much anything that ailed you.

Awen Aymara was a tall leggy brunette. Drop dead gorgeous, athletic and sarcastic as hell. A good twenty years younger than Sophia, Awen was a stronger wizard when it came to raw power, but not as confident or experienced. Sophia came from a long line of wizards, and Awen was new to all of it. They made a good team.

They poured over the scroll and Awen explained what she'd found. "There isn't much in the way of specifics, but it's been done before. This text is ancient and I couldn't even find a year on it. It was hidden within another scroll, which is probably the only reason it survived. There was a warrior queen whose husband died slowly from wounds received in battle. I think her name is Michie, but it's hard to make out. It's a dialect of ancient Japanese. But it *is* possible for the Queen to survive the loss of the King."

"Wait, are you seeing this, too? If I'm reading this right, if the Queen survives, she'll become the King?" Awen asked incredulously.

"Whoa, that's how I read it. I guess it's never needed to be written down because historically the throne has passed to the heir before the elder king or queen can die. Or maybe none of the other scrolls have survived? This is one of the oldest looking texts I've ever seen. I wonder, if a queen dies does the King become the Queen?" Sophia mused out loud.

"Don't be ridiculous," Awen snorted. "There is no way a king could survive the loss of a queen. Have you heard of man flu?"

Sophia laughed, "If I didn't know the universe demanded balance, I'd say you're probably right about that. But if a queen can survive, that means a king can, too. Even if it seems improbable." She thought about Dale and knew that in his case he'd never survive the loss of Libby. He could barely function when she was away for more than a week. As bad as this was, at least they had a fighting chance. Since Dale and Libby had no children of their own it complicated things. They'd identified two potential heirs, but both were far too young to be married, and still untrained, to even be considered an option. Saving Libby was their only choice to saving the kingdom.

Awen was about to roll the ancient scroll back up when Sophia stopped her. "Wait, what's that?" She'd noticed some markings on the innermost portion of the scroll.

Careful not to tear the scroll from the inner dowel, Awen unrolled it completely. The two women could see a drawing of a dragon, and additional text in the margin.

"A curse." Sophia sighed. "Of course, there is a curse. Why is there always a curse?"

"It says that Queen Michie is doomed to an afterlife without her king, until a queen tames the Black Dragon." Awen squinted as she made out the tiny calligraphy. "Huh. What the heck do you think that means?"

"No idea, but since it's about this Queen Michie I'm not going to worry about it. Right now, we need to focus on Libby."

The two wizards spent the rest of the night reviewing the text and coming up with a plan. After three all-nighters in the archive, they both fell into bed with a faint glimmer of hope.

Three months had passed since Dale incurred his injuries. The knights continued to come in to the palace for monthly training but spent the remainder of their time at home with their families around the Kingdom. While Geoffrey and Sean both had quarters at the palace, they also maintained their own homes close by. The two took turns so that one of them was always on site, but both went home as often as possible. It was Geoffrey's turn, and he was sitting under the moonlight in an outdoor bubble bath smoking a joint when Teruyo appeared beside the tub. "What the fuck?" he exclaimed as he dropped his joint into the water and reached instinctively for his sword, that was leaning up against the edge of the tub, more out of habit than any threat. Years of military training had ingrained a certain amount of hyper-vigilance that would never go away.

"Calm yourself, Geoffrey Fitzgerald," Teuryo laughed. "I mean you no harm. Do you know who I am?"

Still gripping his sword, Geoffrey looked at her closely. He realized that the tiny Asian woman who had just materialized wasn't quite solid and he could see through her a little. *Oh hell, how stoned am I?* he wondered.

He stared at her as recognition finally made its way through his still fuzzy brain. "You're the Queen's grandmother," he answered. He'd seen photos of her at Dale and Libby's, but also knew that she'd died years before they'd married. His mind was racing. He knew from his studies that the Spirit Council was said to communicate to the living only in times of great crisis. This definitely qualified. This was bad. This was so bad. He'd hoped for the best for his friend and King but knew in that moment that Dale was going to die.

"Well done, Senior Knight. That's correct. I head the Spirit Council. We convened the moment the King was hit by that curse. We are here to help the Queen save the Kingdom. Call your knights back to the palace. I need to meet with you and Scarlett first thing tomorrow morning."

She started to shimmer and phase out, and then added, "Oh, and stop with the happy weed. I need you sharp."

Geoffrey sighed, took a wistful look at his now soggy joint and looked up at the night sky. "Dale, my brother, I'm so damned sorry it's come to this. I'll do everything in my power to protect Libby and the Kingdom. Godspeed, little buddy." He didn't have any kids of his own, but there was a woman in his life. He wished she was with him now. He knew Awen had her hands full at the moment and he'd see her soon enough back at the palace. Still, the knowledge that they may not have much time left made him regret not marrying her before all this happened.

That's the big lie of life, he thought to himself. *You always think you have more time.*

Scarlett was baking cookies with her granddaughters when Teruyo appeared in her great room. She'd announced her retirement plans earlier in the year, and training her successor had allowed her to spend more time with her grandchildren. Until now. Now everything was uncertain, but she still spent as much time with them as she could.

"Hey girls, keep decorating these cookies, Grandma Chezel will be right back," she instructed as she headed into the living room to chat with Teruyo.

"You are aware of the King's situation?" Teruyo asked.

"Yes. I've been with Libby since Dale returned to the palace but came home to spend some time with my girls." Scarlett had known Libby long before she became the Queen. The Queen's best friend, she was there when Libby and Dalen met, and even stood up with her at the wedding. Aisling Elisabeth McGregor and Scarlett Chezel had been friends for a very long time.

"Do you know what is likely to happen when the King dies?" Teruyo pressed.

"Yes. I do. It's one of the reasons I took time off to spend with my granddaughters. While I still could."

Teruyo looked over at the girls and smiled. "Good call. Enjoy your evening with them. We'll need you at the palace tomorrow. Geoffrey and the wizards will be there as well. Please put the other LIWs on notice. Their service will be needed. All of them."

Scarlett's eyes filled with tears as she nodded. She took a moment to regain her composure and then went back to baking with her granddaughters. The girls were having a good time and didn't even notice all the extra squeezy hugs and kisses they were getting from their grandma. It was a good while later before she responded to Geoffrey's text message confirming what time he'd pick her up in the morning. She also sent out the recall order for her team. By tomorrow afternoon they'd all be at the palace.

The next morning Geoffrey met Scarlett so they could talk as they headed out early for their appointment with the Council. To anyone paying attention, they were a study in contrasts. Geoffrey was tall and thin, with long dark wavy hair. Scarlett was petite with glossy black hair and sparkling blue eyes. She was the oldest of the LIWs. She rode a black stallion whose mane was almost as shiny as her hair. Both would have preferred to travel by car, but horses were always used for official transportation. Science and technology were just as welcome as magic, but some things were tradition, like a knight on a white horse.

Their presence and sense of purpose were unmistakable. Even without their armor and weaponry, they weren't a pair to be trifled with. They compared notes on their surprise visitor, and what it could mean. They already knew the situation was dire but were eager to get an update on the plan ahead. It was now their job to get the rest of the knights and LIWs ready. The shit was about to hit the proverbial fan.

The three wizards rounded the corner, arms full of scrolls, and slowed to meet Geoffrey and Scarlett, who had paused at the heavy wooden doors leading to the council chambers. After a nervous exchange of good mornings and a "Let's do this," Geoffrey opened the door and ushered the women in.

Even after their late-night visits with Teruyo, when they walked into the council chambers the two Seniors had to struggle to keep their composure. Knowing ghosts exist and seeing one was one thing. Walking into a room and seeing five of them, including one you knew in life, was disconcerting.

Scarlett recovered first, "Hi, Mr. Aodamo. It's good to see you." She forced a smile and looked around at the rest of the group.

"Good morning, Sir." Geoffrey hadn't realized that the Queen's father was on the Council. It took him a second to process that information. It had been less than a year since he'd led the processional at his funeral. This was surreal. The Queen's father was beloved. Even Dude was on his best behavior that day.

Kokichi nodded and boomed a hearty, "Good morning." He looked just as he had in life. Regal. His thick hair and beard were pure white and trimmed neatly. Instead of the formal attire they were used to when he was King, he was wearing the simple black gi he'd favored in his retirement. He looked equally ready to take down an opponent or drink tea.

Teruyo thanked them for arriving on time. "Since we'll be working together it's important you know who we are. We, of course, already know you. You've already met me."

The five humans nodded.

"Same for me," said Kokichi.

Maggie stood up. "I'm Margaret Aisling O'Brien, the Queen's great-great-great-great-great-grandmother. You can call me Maggie. I'm the reason Libby was born with red hair, no matter what color it may be now. I'm also the reason she has magic and other special gifts, something she will need to acknowledge and learn to master if we are to survive." Maggie was looking pointedly at Krystal, who was tugging on her silver braid.

Scarlett nodded, slowly. She and Libby had talked about it before so she knew about the Queen's prophetic dreams and that she could sometimes see spirits. Geoffrey kept a straight face but was still freaking out a little about what he was seeing and hearing. He knew the Queen was into the metaphysical new age hippie stuff, but they'd never really talked about it. Now he was hearing ghosts talk about her having special powers. Like a wizard. Ghosts! It was hard to process it all. He wished he were still stoned. *It might be funnier that way. Or less terrifying.*

The beautiful young Japanese woman stood up, without making a sound. Geoffrey guessed she was about 4'6" and not older than 25. She was tiny but exuded a strength he wouldn't have messed with on a good day. Her stature and "don't mess with me vibe" reminded him a little of Larra. She'd have easily gone unnoticed, but for her exceptional beauty and a confidence that was a lot larger than her petite frame. She was wearing blue-lacquered samurai armor, carried a bow on her back and a katana and tanto on her hips, the traditional swords of the samurai.

Awen gasped when she began speaking. "I am Mori Michie. I've given up trying to count how many greats separate us." She smirked at Maggie. "But I am the Queen's grandmother many times over. Libby is my direct descendant. Although she has never heard of me by name, she has had dreams of me from the time she was a child, and that's why she is a natural swordswoman and archer. She has wielded my blade and my bow in her dreams her whole life. Maggie O'Brien is correct about her gifts. They will be an asset and she must accept and master them for the good of the kingdom. You will need to encourage her when she finally agrees. Push her if necessary."

Maggie's eyes grew wide at this confirmation. Michie rarely spoke much, so this volunteered information was unusual. It was even more gratifying than the rare times her husband admitted that he was wrong, and she was right.

Awen and Sophia were staring intently at each other. Sophia raised her hand to interrupt. "Excuse me. By chance are you the

Queen Michie that survived the death of her king? The one from the ancient texts?"

Michie nodded, "Yes," but offered no additional information.

Awen's jaw was hanging open in shock. All three wizards were deep in thought, minds racing as they tried to process what this meant for their current predicament. As such, they missed Michael's introduction.

Scarlett and Geoffrey noticed the sweet boy standing up on his chair so he could be seen by the others around the conference table. He was wearing tiny sandals and a green tropical shirt and shorts, as if he was on his way to the beach in Hawaii. Scarlett figured he was about five years old. Geoffrey didn't even hazard a guess. Kids were out of his area of expertise. "I'm Michael." They were taken aback by the man's voice that came out of the sweet toddler's face, "Queen Libby is my mother."

Geoffrey lost all attempts at composure at this announcement and a "What the fuck?" echoed around the council chambers, recapturing the attention of the wizards.

Scarlett's eyes filled with tears and a smile took over her face. She was the only one outside of Libby's private physician, who knew the Queen had lost a child. She'd been there as Libby dealt with the devastation in private. It was made worse when accompanied by the news that the damage ensured she'd never be able to have children. Scarlett wasn't sure if Dale had even known, since Libby had sworn the two to silence and forbade them to ever bring it up again. "Oh, sweet Goddess," she whispered.

"Yes, Aunt Scarlett. I'm here on the Council but have been watching over my mother for years."

Teruyo gave the group a moment to digest that information and then began the briefing.

Geoffrey paused to look around at the Council. *Interesting*, he thought. Despite the Queen's Irish heritage and love of Ireland, only one member of the Council was Irish. The rest were Japanese. Geoffrey knew that Libby was quite in touch with her Japanese heritage and had lived in Japan for years. It was only in the last ten years or so that she'd focused on learning more about her Irish ancestors. Yet, her name was Irish. She was even born a ginger, before her Japanese DNA asserted itself and her red hair started growing in black.

His eyes came to rest on Maggie and he guessed she'd had something to do with Libby's sudden interest in her Irish past. The Irish were famous for spreading out everywhere on the planet. Libby often joked that you could find an Irish pub no matter where you went in the world, and that the Irish were taking over the world one pour at a time. It seemed that slow Irish takeover also held true when it came to Libby's DNA. Well, at least parts of it. *That girl sure does love her whiskey, music, and fun,* he mused.

He felt Scarlett kick him under the table and snapped back to paying attention, with the realization they were all looking at him. Awen was unrolling the scroll in front of her and looking at him with irritation.

"Sorry. Pulling it together," he said with a small salute.

Teruyo continued. "We believe that Libby's survival is possible but will be difficult. It's been done before, but Libby will need all of us."

"How did you do it?" Awen demanded. "The scroll doesn't give any details, just that you did it."

"The details aren't important right now," Michie replied. "Libby will need your support, and we will need your cooperation. Nothing we discuss is to be mentioned to anyone outside the Queen's Council. There are too many delicate pieces that we can't risk being messed up by the well-meaning but uninformed. That includes your knights and LIWs, and the rest of the family. Do you understand?"

Geoffrey and Scarlett both nodded. The wizards rarely discussed their work with anyone but the King and Queen, so this wasn't a big change for them, but the two Seniors rarely held information back from their teams.

"We'll do anything to help Libby," Scarlett assured them.

"Very well." Teruyo interjected. "The Queen is weak. We will work to protect her from any spiritual attack, but she is vulnerable to a physical one. That is your primary responsibility now, ensure her physical safety at all costs. We will give you additional instructions as needed. We will meet here as a group daily, but it takes a lot of energy for us to appear to you this way, so we will communicate with you in dream state as much as possible. Be prepared."

With a slight bow, Teruyo silently dismissed them. The group stood up to leave, when Maggie addressed the wizards, "Not you three. We have more to discuss." Geoffrey and Scarlett looked at each other and walked out of the council chambers before the spirits could change their minds. They paused outside the door. Scarlett looked up at Geoffrey and gave him a small smile and wrapped her arms around him. No words were exchanged, but they nodded and went in separate directions to fulfill their duties to the Queen and the Kingdom. They had a lot of work to do. They knew that they—and everyone they knew and loved—could die at any minute.

When the three wizards were finally released, they headed off to get to work on their new assignments. Sophia went to make preparations for Dale's impending death, and Awen went to find Libby.

Krystal headed to the vault to get her supplies. Maggie had given her an impossible task, but she was going to die trying if she had to. She snorted; she'd really die if she didn't try, so at least this was a way to feel useful. She was going to need all the help she could get, in both realms. Somehow, she needed to convince Libby, who had suppressed her magic her whole life, that it was not only a good idea, but critical to the survival of the Kingdom. *Where do you even start? Lessons were one thing if you had a willing pupil. How do you drag someone kicking and screaming and get them to learn in spite of themselves?*

"The mute button," Krystal said too loudly for someone talking to herself. "I'll teach her how to use the mute button first. Yes, that's the way in, to solve her problem of unwelcome visitation. Once she learns how to mute a spirit or change the channel on her spirit radio, she'll be able to avoid the headaches and nosebleeds. From there I can teach her other things. That's my way in with her."

Krystal passed the palace steward on her way to the vault, which was conveniently located next to the wine cellar. He watched the wizard walking down the hallway, nodding and talking to herself. He looked around to see if he could see any spirits, then shook his head at the attempt and continued towards the kitchen.

Awen found Libby at the King's side, holding his pale waxy hand in hers. Beads of perspiration dotted her tired face. The inhuman effort the Queen expended to compensate for the King's declining energy was taking its toll. She stayed at his side, but at great cost to her own health. She didn't even look like herself. Her skin had taken on a gray pallor, not too different from that of the King's, and the dark circles under her eyes made her look ghoulish. And wow, she looked a lot older than forty-four. The amount of energy the force field required had an unexpected effect in that the Queen's rich black hair had faded to a brilliant white, as if all the color and life had been sucked dry—an outward visual indicator of what was happening within her body and soul.

She didn't look up as Awen entered the room.

"I need to speak with you in private," she informed the Queen.

"I can't leave him." Libby waved her off.

Awen looked at the doctors in attendance, and the King's sister. "Can you handle things for a few minutes? This is urgent."

"Of course," said Kendra, mildly offended. Why wouldn't she be able to care for her brother? She'd known him longer than anyone, including Libby.

Awen took Libby by the hand and, since the Queen was too physically weak to resist, pulled her to the other side of the room. "Libby, we think we have found a plan to save you, the force field and the Kingdom, but we must take immediate action."

Libby's eyes welled up with tears when she noticed that Awen didn't mention saving the King. To be honest, she knew he wasn't going to make it. A lesser man would have already died. He was a fighter, and he was a protector. Dale would do whatever it took to protect both her and the Kingdom. She'd held out hope for a long time, but even that had waned in recent days. When you share a heart, it's hard to deny what's happening no matter how much you'd like to. Then, of course, there was the dream. The horrible blood-soaked nightmare and accusing yellow eyes that haunted her each time she dozed off.

She wanted to curl up and bawl her eyes out, but her responsibilities to her people outweighed her personal crisis. "Let's hear it," she wheezed, leaning against the dresser for support.

"Sophia and I have found an ancient text that describes how a queen was able to survive the death of her husband. Just like King Dale, it wasn't sudden so there was some time to prepare." Awen stopped here. Michie deserved to tell Libby about their connection herself. Awen was still dumbstruck by the whole thing anyway. What were the odds that the Queen referenced in the text was Libby's ancestor? And that she was a sitting member of the Spirit Council?

Awen picked up her explanation again. "I'm sorry, I haven't had much sleep either, so here is the short version: You go into a meditative trance and focus on the force field. You can stay with the King; the location doesn't matter. Every energy worker we have, me included, will be with you to help shore up your energy."

The Queen looked at her blankly and Awen had a sinking feeling. *Oh shit, I wish Sophia were here*, she thought. *She's better at the hard stuff.*

"I don't mean to be insensitive or crass, but do you understand what will happen when the King dies?"

The Queen looked up as her eyes filled with tears, "Yes. I do. The moment he dies, the part of my heart that is grafted to his will die with him. In addition, the part of his heart that is grafted to mine will die as well. I will have only half a heart. No one has ever survived with half a heart, let alone maintained the force field which requires the strength of two full hearts."

Awen breathed an inward sigh of relief. "Actually, the queen I mentioned earlier did, at least until she could regrow a full heart."

Libby's eyes snapped open wide. "What? Is that even possible?"

"I won't lie to you, it won't be easy. It would be painful on a good day, and in your weakened condition there is a lot that can go wrong. But we want to try."

Libby sat and pondered this a minute. She knew she had to try for her people. She knew Dale would want her to fight and not let it all end with him. She wished he'd wake up so she could talk to him, but she knew that he'd never wake again. She knew it was close. Probably less than a day. She'd never felt so afraid or alone in her life.

The Queen nodded weakly and Awen laid out the rest of the plan they'd developed with the Spirit Council. It was fairly cut and dry. They'd keep Libby alive until she could learn to regrow her heart. She'd have to learn some magic and talk to ghosts, but if it worked the Kingdom and her people would survive. *Seems easy enough,* she thought sarcastically. There was only one thing left for her to do.

As Awen departed, Libby asked everyone to leave the room. She didn't want anyone else around when she spoke her final words to him. He'd been in a coma for several days now, but she wanted to say the words out loud. Somehow, she knew he'd hear them. As she walked to the bed where he was lying, she was instantly transported to the dream. When she reached the bedside, she saw the skeletal face and yellow eyes. Although she could feel the scream starting in the pit of her stomach, she knew they weren't looking at her in accusation like in the dream. This was just the face of death. She couldn't bear to see him like this. She knew it was time. She choked back the panic, took his hand in hers, and dug deep to find the words she needed to say.

"Dalen. My sweet brave Dale, I know you can hear me. I need you to know that it's okay for you to let go. I know you've been fighting to stay. You've been fighting to protect me and everyone else." Her voice cracked as she started sobbing. "I know you've been in so much pain, and that breaks my heart. What's left of it." She laughed dryly. "I will be okay. We will all be okay. We have a plan, and we are going to fight. We are going to be successful. It's okay for you to let go. I won't say good-bye because I know we'll be together again someday, just like we found each other in this life and in many past lifetimes. I love you. I will always love you. I thank you so much for the life we've shared." The words were barely intelligible as the wracking sobs tore through her body. "Let go, Baby. It's time to let go. Have faith in me. Trust me to do this. Please let go."

She looked up as she sensed him relax a bit. As she gazed at her best friend and soulmate, she suddenly saw her dad standing beside him, hand on his shoulder. He was looking at her with a gentle smile, something he did often when he was alive and knew she needed his support. She knew that he'd be waiting for Dale. She didn't like to acknowledge the spirit world much, but at this moment seeing him there was comforting. The love of her life wouldn't be alone. Being alone would be her burden to bear. "Thank you, Daddy," was all she could get out before she collapsed into tears again.

She ran her fingers through his short silver hair. Despite knowing his body was shutting down, she was startled to see his hair fall out in her now shaking hands. She gently shook it out of her fingers, then she laid her head on Dale's chest and sobbed until she had nothing left. When her breathing finally regulated she began to prepare for her meditative trance. If she focused on the plan, she wouldn't have to focus on losing her husband. If she focused on the plan, it would give her something to fight for.

She summoned the head physician and sent word to family, the knights, and Ladies-in-Waiting that it was time to say their good-byes if they were so inclined. She spent the next 24 hours sitting at his side, his hand in hers, but was in a deep trance. She didn't notice people coming and going, nor did she hear their final words to Dalen. During this time she did see faces of those who'd gone before...her grandmother, her parents, and others she couldn't quite place. She knew she wasn't alone, even though it was the loneliest feeling she'd ever endured.

Chapter 4

The Knight's Rally

Geoffrey issued the recall order as soon as he and Scarlett left
the council chambers. It was a formality. All eight knights
had already convened at the palace within the last twenty-
four hours. They'd started preparing as soon as Sean contacted them
after the initial attack on King Dalen. As word got out that the King
probably wouldn't survive the night, they'd made haste. After saying
good-bye to their families for what may have been the last time, they
left home. They would all be onsite at the palace when he died. The
knights would now serve the Queen for the good of the Kingdom. It
was likely they wouldn't survive the next 24-hours, but they would try.

Nine men and one woman made up the Royal Knights. They
were joined by one junior knight who was also a potential heir to the
throne. They'd gathered in the great room of the Knights' Tower. It
wasn't actually a tower, but throughout history that's what it had been
called. John watched Sean pace and make continuous notes on his
tablet. He'd occasionally talk to someone through his communications
gear, but it was otherwise a somber room.

Under normal circumstances the room would be full of lively
banter. Knights would be trying to one-up each other with whatever
crazy adventure or financial success they'd just had. Instead, weapons
and gear were being cleaned and checked for readiness, and soft
conversation was the only noise. It was too warm out for a fire, but
food and drink were laid out on the counter. Only Will O'Malley, the
Weapons Master, was true to form. He was sitting quietly, sketching

the scene and writing a few words to capture the moment for his future use, occasionally breaking to twirl the ends of his silver handlebar mustache.

John couldn't stand it anymore and finally broke the silence. "I don't mean to sound like an ass. I know it's awful that the King is dying. But why is everyone acting like we're going off to war never to return?"

His voice trailed off as ten heads turned to stare up at him in shock. He had no military bearing, and wore his wavy blonde hair long and shaggy, looking more like a lanky California surfer than the Queen's Knight Grand Champion. At 6'7" he was the tallest of the bunch, but that's not what made him stand out. The fact that the Queen had personally recruited him from the outside world was what made him the odd man. He didn't have any shared history with the rest of them and clearly this part had been glossed over in his studies.

Sean flat out stared at him in contempt. *This is why you don't bring in an outsider,* he thought to himself, shaking his head.

"What is wrong with you?" screamed Leia, her dark curls bouncing around as she gestured wildly. The only woman in the history of the Royal Knights, she was barely five feet tall, and a fierce warrior who had been friends with Libby since they were teenagers. It didn't take much for her to get fired up, and since most men didn't expect the cute tiny woman to be a berserker on the battlefield, she always won. Geoffrey routinely warned new knights to underestimate her at their peril. She should have been a member of the LIWs, but had a Scrappy Doo complex that forced her to compete with men on a level playing field. If she were forced to be truthful about it, she loved it. It was fun.

Geoffrey motioned for her to stop before she got started and ran through several responses in his head before speaking. She sat back down muttering under her breath, daggers shooting from her eyes.

"John, we sometimes forget that you're still new. I appreciate your loyalty to the Queen in spite of the fact you don't fully understand the seriousness of the situation."

Geoffrey raised his hand to cut off John's defensive rebuttal.

"By all rights, if the Queen fails, we will probably all die soon."

John looked bewildered. *The Queen? What was it that she might fail at?* His mind was racing. He was regretting not paying more attention to the Knighthood 101 studying that had been thrown at him when he'd accepted her offer.

Geoffrey continued. "Out in the Normal world, have you heard marriage described as two hearts become one?"

John nodded, still confused.

"Well, that's based on fact. When a royal marriage occurs, it's not just a contract or love oath. The King and Queen are bound by a magical covenant both to each other and to the Kingdom as a whole. It's complicated, painful, and permanent. The Royal Wizards complete a heart graft. They each have a part of the other's heart permanently grafted to their own. They make each other whole. This process makes them even stronger when it comes to protecting the Kingdom. This is what enables the force field to surround the Kingdom like a snow globe. The barrier is quite literally tethered to, and powered by, their combined life force."

By now all the knights were listening intently. Outside of the wizards, the Senior Knight and LIW, and the King and Queen themselves, no one really knew any details about how the force field worked. Not even heirs to the throne were trusted with this information until shortly before they assumed the throne.

"Can you imagine feeling the same pain you cause your spouse? It only happens once, and you spend the rest of your life avoiding doing anything to hurt them. To hurt the other is to hurt yourself. This magical bond is why Libby and Dale stayed together even after their monster fights. They were better, stronger, and more powerful together than they could have ever been apart. The marriage contract solidified that magically. Separation meant death.

"The risk to the Kingdom if one dies is too high and it's why the King and Queen are always protected at all costs. It's also why the details of the heart graft are a closely guarded secret. People know that there is a magical component to the marriage contract, and a link to the force field, but not the particulars. That is too high of a risk. You are the first outside of that list to hear how it works. Our situation is unique. And your loyalty is not in question or I wouldn't be sharing it with you now. Even Skarra didn't know that, which is why she thought she could just replace Libby."

Geoffrey paused to take a breath. "Normally, the link to the force field is transferred to the heir before the King and Queen get too old to put their dying of natural causes at risk. That's what happened when Libby's father retired. The marriage of the heir is always tied to the retirement of the reigning king and queen. That's when the transfer happens. It's why the forcefield survived the death of the elder King. As you know the elder Queen passed not long after her husband. That's because surviving with half a heart is next to impossible. Since Dale and Libby never had children of their own, and since their niece and nephew were born much later, the traditional training of the potential heirs never happened. Both are far too young to even think about marriage and, as you well know, Dale and Libby never got around to identifying the heir at all."

He paused and looked pointedly at Kurtis. The young man, and one of the potential heirs, flushed as he felt the surreptitious glances of the rest of the knights.

"Wait, you mean that... We all die when the King dies?" John demanded incredulously.

"Yes," Geoffrey continued. "And not just die. Our entire Kingdom implodes, taking the entire living world and spirit realm with it. By all rights, the Queen should be killed when he dies, taking all of us with her. If it had been the reverse, our demise would be a certainty. Dale is my best friend and a strong stubborn man, but he would never survive her loss. Queen Aisling Elisabeth has more abilities than most people realize, and her sense of duty was second only to her father's, but this burden is too much for any one person, especially in her weakened state."

"There is only one other Queen in the historical records who has ever survived in this situation, so we know it's possible, albeit unlikely. All we can do is everything in our power to give our Queen every opportunity to do the same. It's why the wizards, the LIWs and the knights are here. But even with our help and support, only Libby can save us. As powerful as she is, it may be too much for her."

"What?" exclaimed Leia. Even Sean's head had snapped up at Geoffrey's bombshell. No one had really believed it was possible, and now they learned there was precedent for their success. Geoffrey knew he shouldn't be sharing this much information without the Council's blessing, but at the moment he didn't care about the repercussions.

"Yes, there is a Queen who survived. The wizards have a plan. Oh, and the Spirit Council has been convened. This is end-game serious. We all have assigned roles to play. It is unlikely we will succeed, but we have a plan, and that's something."

John and the other knights sat in silence and sorrow. But, for the first time since they'd acknowledged that the King would die, the knights had hope. It had been done before. Just once, but that was precedent. If any Queen could do it, it would be their Libby. Geoffrey gave them the rest of the briefing and they dispersed to their quarters and began implementing shifts to protect the palace from any physical threats during their rulers' weakened states.

Only Sean kept up his quiet conversations. He'd go down fighting and would do whatever it took to protect Libby. Assuming she did the impossible and survived, both the Queen and the Kingdom would be vulnerable to attack. It was up to the knights and LIWs to protect them from any physical harm. The wizards had the burden of protecting their borders from magical threats. And the Spirit Council had to help the Queen survive.

As soft chatter resumed in the Tower, John left the knights' headquarters and went outside for some air. When Libby had asked him to be her Knight Grand Champion, she'd explained that once he left his home in the Normal world it would be difficult for him to return often. He was always up for an adventure, and there was something about the Queen that made him want to protect her. He couldn't explain it. He loved his wife and was faithful to her. His relationship with the Queen was purely platonic, but there was something there that was more than friendship. Libby called it Destiny, but he hated that mystical bullshit. He laughed at himself. "So says the guy living in a magical kingdom being given instructions by ghosts. For fuck's sake Morgan, what kind of mess did you get yourself into this time?"

He'd signed on and taken the oath without regret. He paced around the quad and tried to decide what he thought about all this. It had been easier to accept that Libby was a queen than to accept magic was real. Did he regret his decision to accept her offer? He thought about it. No. Being Libby's Champion had brought excitement and adventure back to his life, the kind worthy of a descendant of Captain Morgan. He was where he needed to be, in the middle of all the action. He felt horrible for her. He'd had no idea how much she shouldered. He wished he could hug her and make it better, but propriety wouldn't allow for that here at the palace, and he didn't want to intrude right now. Anyway, he hated the emotions, so it worked in his favor. He liked making her laugh but didn't think he could bear to see her cry.

He thought back to how they'd met. A mutual friend had introduced them at Harp Bar in Belfast, and they'd hit it off, surrounded by good music, good craic[1], and that god-awful red velvet. They shared a love of travel, adventure, and learning other people's stories. And drinking. They both enjoyed drinking a lot. They were two sides of a coin. Tall and short. From two different worlds, literally. They had different cultures and sometimes spoke different languages. She cursed like a pirate despite having been raised to be a proper lady. He was descended from pirates, but was loyal and honorable, in his own rogue way. He loved being in the middle of everything, and she preferred to stay on the fringe. When they'd go carousing in the non-magic world, she'd often tell people they were twins separated at birth. Maybe on a metaphysical level they were. Champion. Twin brother. Whatever it was, their connection was instant and real. John could get away with saying things to Libby no one else could, and she took his counsel seriously.

"Maybe that's why Sean doesn't like me. He thinks I'm a threat. Oh, my God! I bet that's it." John laughed out loud and started back towards the Tower in a slightly better mood. He respected Sean but found this idea entertaining. Poking the bear would be a good diversion from the disaster looming ahead.

"I don't want to die, but this is still one hell of an adventure. I guess we all gotta go sometime." He thought about his family back

---

[1]   Craic is the Irish word for fun or having a good time.

home. He now understood that if Libby failed, their world would also disappear. He wished he could hug his wife and son but being here was the best way he could protect them.

Geoffrey watched in silence from his fourth-floor office window. He'd always said he had faith in John, despite Sean's doubts, because he had faith in Libby. He didn't realize he'd been holding his breath until he watched John head back to the Tower and he finally exhaled. He could tell John had decided to stay by his body language. That was good. The Queen couldn't handle any more loss right now. Something about John made the Queen laugh. Since John didn't have any background info or preconceived notions, the Queen could trust that he liked her for who she was, not her title. "John Morgan," he said under his breath, "I hope you can be the Champion she needs. The one we all need."

Geoffrey turned back to his desk and picked up the phone to call Awen. Now that they were both back at the palace, he hoped they might steal some time for each other. While they still had time.

Chapter 5

The King Dies

Less than 24-hours after Libby told him he could let go, the King died. Libby was deep in her trance, Dale's hand still clenched in hers. As much as the waxy yellow eyes had haunted her nightmares, she was spared witnessing the final gruesome end. Those in attendance weren't so lucky. In the final hours of his life, Dale began to aspirate. As his organs shut down, he could no longer clear fluid from his lungs. As the fluid accumulated, it sprayed out of his mouth, covering his face and chest, and sometimes Libby, with a layer of foam spittle. The nurses continued to clean him up every few minutes. It felt disruptive, but they couldn't bear to see him like that.

It would get worse. So much worse. At the moment his heart stopped beating, Libby collapsed, falling unconscious over her dead husband's body. The wizards, doctors, knights, and LIWs had been ready for this. Because she was in a deep meditative state, she didn't even know they were there. The LIWs immediately took up defensive positions around the Queen and all entrances to the rooms they were in, weapons close by.

Scarlett, Awen, and Sophia rushed to the Queen's side and carried her to the neighboring bedroom, while the knights locked down the palace. They quickly got her set up on oxygen while making preparations for magical surgery. She didn't have to be awake to witness the blood pouring from the King's open mouth, or the gasps of the medical team tending to him. She'd seen it in her nightmares for months. But for the rest of those present it was horrifying and felt like an omen of things to come. The knights and LIWs couldn't get out of there soon enough. They needed an enemy they could fight. They couldn't fight death or the grief and terror that accompanied it.

At the moment of Dale's death, a wave of energy rippled through both the living and spirit realms. No announcement was needed, the entire Kingdom knew their King had died. So did the kingdom's enemies. Deep in a cave in Northern China, far from the force field border, the shock wave was enough to awaken the great black dragon, Jasper, from a deep sleep.

He gave a big stretch and a sleepy smile and started chuckling to himself. "Finally, Queen Aisling is mine for the taking." The dragon was a serial collector of strong women, and Libby definitely fit the profile. He'd been wanting to add her to his collection for years, but that damned force field was too strong. Oh yeah, she was going down. He dozed off again with an evil grin on his face and purred like a 747 engine.

Chapter 6

Long Live the Queen

From the spirit realm, the Council watched in silence in the Queen's bedchamber. The Queen couldn't see them, but they had linked arms. Well, not really linked arms, since they didn't technically have any, but had joined together to share as much of their spirit energy with her as possible to protect the force field while they stabilized her. It was working but couldn't last forever. Kokichi, the newest spirit on the Council, was already starting to flicker.

Confident she was still alive, Teruyo looked at the Council and with a quiet, "Now," they directed all their energy in a single beam at the dying piece of Dalen's heart in the Queen's chest. It slowly burned away, cauterizing the wound and leaving an angry pink scar that could only be felt and not seen. Once they were confident it had been removed, they severed their connection, spent. It had to be removed in order to make space for the Queen to regrow her heart the way a lizard regrows its tail. Being unconscious was a blessing. They couldn't risk drugging her right now.

The Council faded out, except for Michie, who lingered. She alone knew what the Queen would be up against and the pain she'd have to survive. "Fight, Granddaughter," she whispered. "You must fight with everything you have. Even when you don't want to. You must fight even when you want to lie down and die. Fight. Remember everything you have been taught. Remember your duty and honor. I will not leave you, but you must fight." Then she too faded out back to the spirit realm to rest and regroup.

Sophia, Awen, and Scarlett continued to work on the Queen. They didn't hear a word of what Michie said. That's the thing about the spirit realm. They had to let you see them, and you had to be willing to see them. At this moment the Queen had 100% of the wizards' attention.

Libby survived the night, but the pain was indescribable. She faded in and out of consciousness. In her waking moments she was aware of the LIWs, the wizards, her sisters, Geoffrey, and even her friend Fintan. She could hear them talking but couldn't latch on to any of the conversation. She saw her sisters quietly talking at the foot of her bed but couldn't make out what they were saying.

She dreamt of the samurai woman. Libby knew she was talking to her, but her words were blurry. It felt important and she strained to hear her, but the warrior woman disappeared before she could say anything.

Libby was also pretty sure she saw Dale.

Am I dead? she wondered. Reality was phasing in and out, like looking through a wall of water. She saw Dale, flying around above her, with the sun behind him. He was so shiny, she had to squint to see him. He was laughing hysterically. Happy. The relief was what led her to believe it was real. *Oh good, he made it to the good place*, she thought as she drifted back to the quiet relief of unconsciousness.

On the third day after Dale's death the Queen was finally able to remain awake for a few hours at a time. Sophia had her full of acupuncture needles to help with her energy flow and pain, Krystal surrounded her bed with a grid of protective and healing crystals, including placing them on Libby's body. And there was a steady stream of musicians rotating through, even when she was asleep. With instruction from both Maggie and Michie, they were doing everything they could to keep the Queen alive. As uncomfortable as she was, they needed her as alert as possible.

Adding insult to injury, Libby now suffered from fainting spells. Even without the searing pain and overwhelming grief, without a full heart to pump oxygenated blood to her brain, she was prone to fainting and the doctors had her on full-time oxygen therapy. Since she was a fall risk, she was restricted to her bed. The warrior Queen who hated being told "No" was now too weak to care that she's wasn't allowed to leave her bed without help.

Geoffrey and Scarlett arrived at the Queen's bedroom while the wizards were there. The five of them looked at each other, and then at Libby.

The whir-pump-whir-pump of the oxygen machine was the only sound as they stood there trying to figure out how to begin.

"What?" she wheezed. "What is it?"

Scarlett cleared her throat and spoke for the group. "Sweetie, we can't imagine the pain you're in right now, but there are some important things we need to do."

Teruyo chose that moment to appear.

"Grandma?" Libby whispered. "Grandma, I've missed you." Libby assumed she'd fallen back asleep and that she was dreaming.

"I've been here the whole time. And I'm not alone." The rest of the Council shimmered into view. All royals knew of its existence, but they almost never encountered the Council. Since Libby had been able to see ghosts since she was a child, she didn't realize it was the Council at first. Of course, she already knew how bad it was. She could barely breathe, could barely stand the pain, and the force field was collapsing.

Libby looked at them and forced her eyes to focus.

"Daddy?" Tears started streaming down her face when she saw her father. "Daddy, I don't think I can do this."

"You can do it, Aisling Elisabeth. We will help you."

She looked at the rest of the group. She recognized the Japanese woman from her childhood dreams. The warrior queen who rode horseback and fought with both arrow and sword. This was the woman she'd dreamt was talking to her. Michie nodded in recognition.

She looked at Maggie. She didn't know her but recognized her somehow. Maggie smiled, knowing it was her energy that was familiar.

She gasped when she got to Michael.

"Michael," she whispered as tears overcame her again.

"Hi, Mom. I'm impressed you remember me," he said.

Libby looked at Scarlett. "Are you seeing this, or have I had a mental breakdown? Am I dead? Are we dead? Did we fail?"

"We are very much alive, Sweetie. We see them too. The Spirit Council is here to help you, just like we are." Scarlett took Libby's hand in hers, patting it reassuringly.

For a brief moment Libby realized that she didn't have a headache or nosebleed, and there were no zigzags flashing across her field of vision. Scarlett must be right. This must be the Council. They alone would be able to speak to her without any of the usual side effects. They could also speak to her without her consent. Although at this point, she was too weak to put up much of a fight, and Libby was so sad she no longer cared about trying to fight. For the first time in her life she longed for them. For the first time she had a reason to. She hadn't processed the thought yet but wanted to speak to Dale.

Teruyo spoke first, snapping her fingers to get the Queen's fading attention. "Aisling Elisabeth McGregor. I know you're in pain, but I need you to focus a little while longer before you rest again. While you were unconscious, we removed the part of Dalen's heart grafted to yours. In an ideal world you'd have months to recuperate. We don't have that luxury. Threats to the kingdom are already on their way. Do you understand the plan that Awen explained to you?"

Libby felt like she was under water. Cold. Dark. Sinking. It was so hard to concentrate. The pain was excruciating, and it was hard to breathe. "Yes," she slurred. "I understand. Step 1: Don't die. Step 2: Regrow my heart." She giggled at the ridiculousness of it all.

"Good. Rest now. We'll begin tomorrow."

The Queen drifted off to sleep mumbling something about "my baby boy" before Teruyo's words faded.

Libby was fast asleep when she had her first visit with Michie. This time Michie wasn't in samurai armor but appeared in the tactical gear Libby herself wore.

"Hello, Mago-chan. I'm Michie and I am here to guide you. I will help you as you sleep and meditate. I will visit you in dreams to use as little of your energy as possible. My presence here will also prevent your night terrors since your mind can't process both at the same time."

"Mago? Granddaughter? You're my ancestor?"

"Yes."

"All those dreams."

"Yes, those were dream memories. My memories."

"I always thought they were mine from a past life."

Michie laughed, "No, Mago-chan, those were mine. But you and I are linked for some reason. Usually when one dreams of an ancestor it's like watching a movie, not like living it. You and I have much in common. That story is too long for one night's dream, but I am here to guide you. Will you follow my instructions and let me teach you?"

"Yes, I suppose."

"Listen up grasshopper, there is no I suppose. Will you follow my instructions to the letter?"

"Yes, Grandmother, I will. I will do anything to protect my people."

"Good. That's the correct answer, by the way. The answer of a queen. Sleep now, Granddaughter. Our lessons will begin soon. One last thing, for the time being you mustn't speak of our visits to anyone outside your Royal Council. Promise me."

"I promise," Libby mumbled as she drifted back into a dreamless sleep.

The Queen woke to a soft knock on her bedroom door. The pain assured her she was awake and that it wasn't another dream lesson.

"Come in," she groaned.

"Aunt Libby?" came a soft voice, as her nephew came into view.

"Hey, Kurtis. How are you?" she asked. As close as they were, this was the first time he'd ever visited her bedroom, and it made him uncomfortable. Of course, nothing like this had ever happened before.

She motioned for him to come over and sit on the edge of the bed. He swapped out the lilacs in the vase next to the bed with the fresh bunch he had in his hand and took a seat. Bringing her favorite flowers was the only thing his almost fifteen-year old mind could come up with to try and make her feel better.

"I'm okay. How are you?"

She looked up at the young man. He looked uncomfortable. And sad. She could tell he'd been crying. His hazel eyes, just like his Uncle Dale's, were red and swollen. He wore his hair short but kept running his hands over it nervously.

She'd never held back or treated the young ones like kids, so she was honest. "Miserable. Everything hurts and I miss Dale."

"I miss him too. And I'm not the only one. That's why I'm here," he started. "Um, Aunt Libby, I need a favor."

"What do you need?"

"It's Hoss." He paused. Kurtis found all the emotions and tension too much to take, so would regularly retreat to the stables and take care of the horses. Most of the horses in the royal stables had come from his family's ranch, so he knew them. He'd been there at their births, and even named most of them. He'd been in a stall brushing his horse when Dale died. The energy wave had been scary enough, but Hoss started screaming at that exact moment. He was distraught and had been throwing himself against the stall door. Kurtis had finally managed to get him calmed down so he wouldn't hurt himself, but Hoss was a mess.

"Aunt Libby, Hoss is a wreck. He hasn't eaten anything since Uncle Dale died. I'm scared for him. I know you're hurting too, but if you could visit him a little, I think that would help. If he doesn't start eating, I'm afraid he'll..." His voice trailed off and his eyes welled up with tears. He couldn't bring himself to say that he was afraid Hoss would die of a broken heart. It was true but seemed the wrong thing to say to his aunt.

Libby thought about it. It broke her heart to see him hurting so much, and she'd do anything for him. She didn't know how, but she'd find a way to make it work. She reached for him and he leaned in for a hug. "I'll find a way. I love you, Kurtis. Thanks for taking care of Hossy for me. And thank you for the flowers."

The teenager wiped his eyes on the back of his sleeve and mumbled an "I love you, too" before heading back out to the stables.

Chapter 7

Waking the Dead

T he moment Libby was moved to the neighboring room, after
Dale died, a different ritual began in their bedroom. While
Awen, Sophia, and Scarlett tended to Libby, Krystal took care
of Dalen. She cleared the room of the negative energy still lingering
from the King's tormented passing, and any residue of Skarra's curse
before bathing Dale's body in sage and lavender infused water and
drying him with clean linen towels. When she was done blessing
his body and soul, she wove a small spell to keep his body fresh until
the funeral. Then, Libby's sister Corrine and her daughter Dyanna,
in place of Libby, joined Kendra and Kurtis as his closest family
members, to dress him in his formal robes. By that evening he'd be
lying in state in the palace ballroom.

It was in the palace ballroom that Dale came to. He didn't know
where he was at first and couldn't understand why he was swimming.
How did he get into the lake? The last thing he remembered was
charging Skarra. Then he remembered the pain and seeing his wife
sobbing over him. "No, not swimming," he realized, "but I'm floating.
Or weightless. Oh shit, I'm dead. Where is Ash? Ash! Aisling!" He
screamed out her name, desperate to find her.

"That's enough of that," Michael scolded him. "Time to come
with me."

He looked down and saw a beautiful boy looking up at him in
amusement. Dale was confused; who was this boy who could speak so
disrespectfully to him? And why did he sound like a chain-smoking

truck driver? Something about him seemed familiar. "Who are you? You can't tell me what to do." But Dale was new and had no control over his incorporeal self, so Michael just grabbed him by the leg and dragged him along like a helium balloon.

He looked down and saw himself lying in formal robes. There were flowers everywhere, and people coming and going.

"What the fuck is happening?" he demanded. "Am I dead? I'm dead, aren't I? What happened?"

"You'll see Dad, you'll see. Just calm yourself. We'll explain everything. Just try to be calm. Breathe through your nose."

"Dad? What the fuck is happening here? Why are you calling me Dad? Are you mental? Where is my wife? Why can't I move? What is happening?"

"Dalen-san," Kokichi greeted him as Michael tied Dale to a chair in the council chambers to keep him from floating away.

"Pops? What is happening here? Where is Ash? Is she okay? Why am I tied to a chair? Why can't I walk? Why'd that boy call me Dad?"

"Dalen, calm yourself. We will explain everything. In time you will gain control over this form. Are you willing to stop fighting and listen to what I have to tell you?"

Dale kept fighting to move, but no matter how much he flailed about, he was going nowhere. With an exasperated sigh he nodded at Kokichi and tried to focus.

"Good. I know this is all very confusing. You probably feel like you're underwater and that you can't see or hear clearly."

Dale stopped fighting and looked right at Kokichi.

"I know, I went through it only eight months ago," Kokichi reminded him.

"Fuck. I'm really dead?" he asked.

"Yes. You are really dead." Kokichi raised his hand to stop him from interrupting. "Before you ask, Aisling Elisabeth is still alive, and so is the Kingdom, although the force field is collapsing, which could end us all.

"Dying is simply moving from one plane of the universe to the next. Since our souls are energy, we must shed our physical forms to reach this plane. The living and spirit realms are connected. If one is destroyed, both are, not just the one that took the blow."

Dale looked frustrated.

"With me so far?"

"Yes, I think so."

"Good. Our realm is immediately next to the living world you just came from. I don't know what's next for us but theorize that there are an infinite number of planes to pass to. For now, we are focused only on two. We are connected. We who are now energy can pass between the realm we are in and the one we came from. Those with physical bodies cannot."

"So that's why we sometimes see ghosts?" Dale asked.

"Yes, that's why the living sometimes see ghosts." Kokichi was careful to use the correct language to help the King process the fact that he'd died. It was going to take a while. Time they didn't have.

"I know it's a lot to process, but we don't have a lot of time. From the spirit world we try to guide and support our loved ones in the physical world."

"Wait, can I go see Ash now? As a ghost?"

"No! You may not. You need training first or you will do irreparable damage to the woman you loved most in the world. I promise you will be able to communicate with her when the time is right, but you risk pushing her into madness in her weakened condition. Do you understand? I'm serious, Dale. What the living often perceive as hauntings are really just impatient spirits who haven't learned how to master communication. They cause irreversible damage to the living. It's dangerous and you must not attempt it. I will teach you, but you must be patient."

Dale looked disappointed, but as he couldn't control his own energy body, there wasn't much he could do but pout.

"Where was I? Oh, yes. As you know the Council appears to kings and queens in times of great crisis, as a way to formally assist. It's not discreet like dream messages, but in a crisis situation it works."

At that moment the other members of the Council appeared. Dale was frantically trying to untie himself from the chair, but the most he got was a slight breeze. He was getting pissed off.

"Hey, I know you. You're my wife's grandmother," he said far too loudly. "Why am I yelling? Apparently, I can't control my volume either," he cursed to himself.

"Yes," Teruyo confirmed, "I am the Queen's grandmother. I also head the Council. You know Kokichi, who also sits on the Council. He will be your instructor in how to navigate the spirit realm. I will let the rest of the Council introduce themselves."

It was much like when they'd introduced themselves to Geoffrey, Scarlett and the wizards, until they got to Michael.

Michael floated up on the table so he could look the King in the eye.

"I'm Michael. Allen Michael McGregor, if you want to get particular about it. You asked me earlier why I called you Dad. It's because I'm your son."

Dale squinted at him. "There is no way you're my son. We never had any kids."

"You are partially correct; you never had any children born, but I am your son. Do you remember when you were out on a hunting party with the knights shortly after you and Mother married? You felt through your heart graft that something was wrong. You felt her pain and her sadness, but when you called her, she said she just wasn't feeling well and to enjoy your trip. Do you remember this?"

If he'd still had a body he'd have been shaking by now. Dalen suddenly remembered the moment vividly. He'd known something was wrong but when she told him to stay, he did because he was enjoying himself. He'd written it off as adjusting to the new graft. Now he knew what an asshole he was and that he should have returned home immediately.

Michael continued. "That was when I died."

Dale floated there in silence, tears streaming down his shimmering face. "Oh my God Ash, why didn't you tell me? Why did you go through it alone?" Although he already knew the answer. She was protecting them both from the grief. She was one of those people who kept her true pain to herself, while the rest of the world got a smile. He was one of the only people alive who knew how much pain that was, and that was only because of the graft.

"Don't feel guilty about it. She didn't want you to know. She'd only just found out about me and was going to tell you when you got home from that trip. Because I wasn't actually born, I entered this realm without needing the type of re-training the rest of you get. But because Mother had named me, I have full spirit rights and responsibilities on the Council."

Dale was now furious. He'd had a right to know. Later she did tell him she'd never be able to have children but had omitted this part of the story. "Damn it Ash!" Dale shouted to no one in particular. "We weren't supposed to have any secrets from each other! I know you were trying to protect me, but you didn't even give me a chance to screw it up, let alone get it right."

"I need to see her immediately," Dale demanded.

"Not going to happen," Kokichi interjected. "Not until you finish your training. How quickly you complete your training is up to you, although I'd encourage you to make haste. She will need you."

We were born before the wind
Also younger than the sun
Ere the bonnie boat was won as we sailed into the mystic
Hark, now hear the sailors cry
Smell the sea and feel the sky
Let your soul and spirit fly into the mystic

Just like way back in the days of old
And magnificently we will flow into the mystic

When that fog horn blows you know I will be coming home
And when that fog horn whistle blows I got to hear it
I don't have to fear it

Too late to stop now...
~Van Morrison, "Into the Mystic"

In the midst of all this, Dale's funeral had to happen. When she'd assumed the Queenship, Libby's sisters automatically took on court duties. It was possible to refuse, but refusal was never an option they would have considered. Each of them lived close to the palace with their families to help their sister.

The sisters were close but had grown even closer in the months since Dale's injury. Libby was the oldest of the three and had grown up taking care of her two baby sisters. Those roles quickly reversed when the King was cursed.

While Scarlett, Geoffrey, and the rest of the royal staff took care of security, logistics, and everything else she'd need as Queen, Libby's sisters took care of her as a regular person and the grieving widow. Ava, the youngest, had already been taking care of the Kingdom's books as Royal Accountant. Corrine, the middle sister, didn't have an official appointment but took care of their family and was well-known in the kingdom for her generosity and ministering to the broken. While she continued to sleep most of the day away to hide from the pain, Libby's sisters took charge of planning Dale's funeral.

Despite having almost nothing to do with planning it, Libby still had to attend in an official capacity, even though she wanted to curl up in a ball and die. She knew her people needed to see her. It wasn't a secret that parts of the force field had become very weak. Even though she was still so weak she shouldn't be standing unattended, the Queen did her duty.

Corrine Chaney was famous for the parties and events she put together. No detail, no matter how small, was ever overlooked. This was no exception. It was a beautiful funeral, befitting a well-loved king. The Queen observed from the main palace balcony. That way the oxygen machine was discreetly out of sight, and the fact that staff kept her from falling was hidden from the general population. Harley's artful make-up application covered up the Queen's gray pallor. She looked sad, but not dying. The knights and Ladies-in-Waiting lined the palace steps as the King's body was carried down into the courtyard where the funeral pyre waited.

Bright colored bunting draped most surfaces, and everyone wore similar vivid colors to celebrate the King's life. Even the Queen wore bright colors instead of her normal dark blue, although she'd dyed her hair dark blue for the occasion. She'd hated the glaring white reminder that Dale, and life as she knew it, was gone every time she looked in the mirror. After all the formal words were said, the Queen shakily stood up to speak. Corrine felt the pangs of nervousness. She wasn't sure Libby would be able to get through it.

Corrine handed her sister the speech Libby had written earlier, and the Queen addressed her people.

"Citizens of the Kingdom of the Talking Trees. On behalf of our family I thank you for being here today to honor the life and legacy of our King, Dalen Martin McGregor. In life, he possessed a strong will, a loving heart, and fierce drive to protect those he loved. And he loved all of us. All of you.

"It is true that we face a great challenge in the days that lie ahead. I will not lie; the odds are against us. But I vow to you, as I stand here before the body of my King, that I will fight to the very end, just like he did. I challenge you to make the most of every minute of the life we've been given, the life that has been stolen from our King. Live now. Live every minute of every day. Do it for Dale. I know I will."

The population was afraid but put all their hope in their Queen. It wasn't like they had any other choice. The Queen's knees buckled, but Sophia and Awen kept her from falling, so few people noticed.

Corrine signaled the orchestra to play one of the King's favorite songs, "Into the Mystic." Then John, as Queen's Knight Grand Champion, fired a burning arrow and set the pyre alight. Sophia gave the flame a little magical boost, and the pyre was instantly engulfed. As all eyes were on the rainbow flames, Ava and Corrine quickly got the Queen back inside where she collapsed, sobbing, in her bed while her beloved was returned to ash.

The banquet that followed the funeral was exactly what Dale would have wanted. It was a party for the ages. There was feasting, music, and the Queen's dear friend and Poet Laureate, Fintan O'Toole, read the epic tale he'd composed about King Dalen's great deeds. It was a party Dale would have loved. It was only missing two people— Dale and Libby.

Love of mine
Someday you will die
But I'll be close behind
I'll follow you into the dark
No blinding light
Or tunnels to gates of white
Just our hands clasped so tight
Waiting for the hint of a spark
If heaven and hell decide that they both are satisfied
illuminate the no's on their vacancy signs
If there's no one beside you when your soul embarks
Then I'll follow you into the dark
I'll follow you into the dark
~Death Cab For Cutie, "I Will Follow You Into The Dark"

Libby woke up screaming. Again. It had become a nightly occurrence. As soon as her dream lessons ended, she was once again susceptible to the night terrors, but they couldn't do lessons all night. Her brain waves needed a break. The LIWs were used to it by now, but it was still unsettling. They knew she desperately needed sleep. She couldn't remember anything, couldn't focus for long, and struggled to complete a thought. She was drifting inwards. She was no longer a person they recognized. They'd never seen anything like it, and the Wizards couldn't find any reference in the library, so relied on Michie and Maggie for guidance. The LIWs didn't know how to help.

Libby dozed most of the time or sat with her eyes closed. People left her alone because they were worried about the force field, and no one really knew what to say or do anyway. Even Fintan, one of her best friends, stopped coming by to see her. She didn't talk to anyone about what she saw in the night terrors. The LIWs only knew about them because they were her personal protectors.

She was desperate. Libby knew she needed to get some sleep but couldn't bring herself to ask for help. Instead, she took to self-medicating. When she couldn't get her hands on the uisce beatha, she'd dig into her whiskey or bourbon stores. A small part of her sleep-deprived brain knew that mixing alcohol and the sleeping potion

Sophia had cooked up for her was a bad idea, but it numbed the pain and helped her fall asleep, however briefly, so she kept doing it.

Most nights she would wake up just after falling asleep. The dream lessons were a lot shorter than they felt. This night, it wasn't even an hour. She was groggy and frustrated and exhausted. Not thinking clearly, she helped herself to more sleeping potion, washing it down with the last of the uisce beatha. She smiled when she saw Dale standing at the foot of her bed. He was nodding and smiling with approval.

Finally, she thought. "I've missed you. Please visit me in my dreams," she pleaded as she drifted back to sleep.

Dale stood there, feeling useless and afraid. "Ash!" he screamed, "What are you doing? I told you not to do that! Why did you do that?"

Dale watched, helpless to do anything. He saw her breathing slow, then stop as the deadly mix of drugs and alcohol took effect.

"No!" he screamed. "No! It's not your time! Wake up! Ash! Wake the fuck up! No! Aisling! Libby!"

Libby was dreaming. It's a miracle how the brain's synapses continued to fire even after the heart stopped beating. In her dream she could see Dale outside the window. She was happy that he'd come to visit her like she'd asked. But he was so angry. He was pounding on the glass, screaming her name. She was confused and afraid. At the moment the glass shattered she awoke choking, gasping for air. She could still hear the sound of the glass breaking and shards hitting the floor.

Dale. She could still hear his voice screaming her name.

She started crying as she realized that she'd been dying, and Dale had brought her back.

"Why, Dale? Why wouldn't you just let me join you? I didn't do that on purpose, but if it meant us being together you should have just let it happen."

But Libby's sense of obligation to her people was strong, and as soon as the words left her lips, she regretted them. Her selfish desire to be with Dale would cost everyone their lives. As much as she wanted to be with him, she knew he'd done the right thing. That didn't make it hurt any less.

Now that she was awake, she couldn't hear him anymore. She couldn't hear the alarms blaring in the spirit world as they felt their realm start to fade. She didn't know that the Council had jumped into action to grab Dale and that he was getting an ass-chewing like no other. She heard the alarms blaring in the palace as the force field was fading, but her sudden start awake stabilized it.

Kokichi was livid when he found Dale. "I warned you!" he yelled. Kokichi never lost his temper, so Dale was a bit surprised. "I warned you to leave her alone, that you weren't ready and would screw it up! But no, you had to do it your way. I can't believe you are such a selfish fool! Baka!"

Dale knew Kokichi had to be furious for him to yell out the worst insult the Japanese can give. Baka meant fool and was serious. In all the years he'd known Kokichi he'd never heard him utter the word.

"Selfish? For wanting to tell her I'm okay and that I'm still with her? She's so sad and I'm trying to comfort her!" Dale yelled back. "And I saved her!"

"You almost killed her! I warned you that when spirits try to communicate with the living, before they've learned how to do it properly, it's haunting. When you visit her in dreams, she doesn't see the healthy you or hear the words you are trying to say. She sees the visions she had of you at your death. The ugly, gory, bloody images of you. She thinks you blame her for your death. She's not sleeping because that's when you visit her. Don't you remember how much you hated her nightmares when you were alive to protect her? She has no one there at night now. This is your fault! Tonight, she thought you were encouraging her. You idiot!"

Dale visibly paled. "I miss her! She misses me! She's been asking for me. She has to know I love her still."

Kokichi sighed and said bluntly, "She doesn't. Out of everything she questions, which is almost everything, whether you loved her is one of them. I know you mean well, but you're going to kill her, and everyone in your kingdom and our realm if you don't stop. I promise you that the day will come when you can communicate with her clearly, but until that day comes you must leave her alone. You can observe, but no communication attempts or you *will* kill her. Promise me."

"I promise." Dale hung his head in shame and guilt. He missed her. He hated seeing her so miserable and was just trying to comfort her. But Kokichi was right. She was all alone now. He wasn't there to protect her from the bad dreams. Now he was one of them. He shook his head in disbelief. How had this happened?

"Babe," he whispered, "I'm so sorry. I'm sorry I've failed you. I'm sorry I left you all alone. Please forgive me. I have to leave you alone a while longer, but it's because I love you. Please don't doubt me. Have faith."

Maggie had come to Krystal and given her specific instructions on what to do after Libby's failed accidental suicide so she waited until Libby was in the council chambers for a meeting and, with the help of two of the LIWs, entered the queen's bedroom. While the LIWs cleared the room of liquid spirits, the wizard cleared the room of the other kind. She was sweating and wobbly by the time she'd finished.

No wonder Libby's been a mess, she thought to herself. *The energy in here is awful.* She made a note to have the room cleansed daily and to place a huge order for white sage. *Ironic. It's Libby who's creating the bad energy without knowing it. It's time to get that girl to finally face her gifts and learn to use them.* She'd resisted her whole life, but now it was time for her to do it for the greater good. Krystal was going to teach Libby everything she knew whether she wanted to learn it or not. With Maggie O'Brien's spirit constantly hounding Krystal, there was no way she was getting out of it.

Chapter 8

The Dragon

ichael looked at one of the monitors, "Well, word is obviously out. Has anyone else seen the dragon off Donegal?" All eyes turned to look at the map. Sure enough, there was Jasper. He'd been waiting. He'd had his eye on Queen Libby for decades and sensed his chance. The force field continued to weaken, with significant damage caused during the few minutes Libby's healing heart had stopped beating. It was just a matter of time before it went down completely.

Jasper had left Shenyang and was camped out on the edge of the Kingdom, on a small uninhabited island just off the coast where it overlapped with Donegal. Every now and again he'd tap the force field with his tail just to watch it quiver like a Jell-o mold and laugh, clapping his tiny hands. He hated strong women who refused to be intimidated by him, and Libby had laughed at him one too many times. Oh yeah, she was going down. He'd have her begging him to save the kingdom before he was done with her.

The Queen's Council, which included Geoffrey, Sean, Scarlett, Catherine, Awen, Sophia and the Spirit Council convened in the council chambers to discuss options. Libby was still on oxygen.

Libby began with, "We all know why we're here. I don't have the energy for formalities so let's just get to it. Geoffrey, the assessment?" Her words were barely audible over the sound of the oxygen machine keeping her alive.

"The knights and engineers are doing regular border inspections of the force field, and Fynnigan Van der Linden is working with the engineers so that any possible repairs are as strategic as possible. I can see why you like him so much. young Fynnigan is brilliant. We anticipate we have a matter of weeks, if not less, before Jasper and any other threats breach the border. We've given the local residents the option to relocate to the palace or return to the Normal world. We don't have any known way to fight or defeat a dragon of his age. By his size alone, he must be ancient."

Awen jumped in, "There is no way Libby will be able to fight a dragon in just a few weeks. It's too soon; she's not ready."

Teruyo chimed in, "That is correct. But the confrontation will happen. What we must do is find a way to buy more time."

"How do we do that, Grandma?"

Michie cleared her throat and all eyes turned to look at her. "Dragons are cunning and proud. They are also sticklers for tradition and rules. I propose you challenge him to a duel."

Whir-pump-whir-pump went the Queen's oxygen machine, the only sound in the room as they all processed Michie's suggestion.

"Libby will agree to fight him alone, beginning with a battle of wit and skill, ending with an actual physical fight. By calling the duel, she will get to choose the time and place."

Geoffrey's eyes narrowed as he started to grasp what she was proposing. "How far out can we push it?"

"One year would be the maximum that tradition would allow."

"Okay. Do it," wheezed Libby.

"Libby, perhaps we should explore other options," started Scarlett. "You're talking about a physical fight with a dragon! Even a year from now that is insane."

"No. There are no other suggestions, and it has to be done. This gives me time. It gives the entire kingdom a fighting chance." She looked at Michie.

"Grandmother, can we trust Jasper not to attack until the duel?"

"Yes. As far as one can trust a dragon. At the moment, it's the only option we have."

"No. Absolutely not!" Interrupted Sean. "Have you all forgotten we're fighting to keep Libby alive? If she is killed by a dragon it means death to everyone. The heirs are too young, even a year from now, to be bound to the force field. There is no way she can duel a dragon. It has to be someone else."

"There is no one else," snapped Michie. "It must be a Queen. The Queen," she corrected herself. "The duel has specific rules that must be adhered to. And you know that Jasper will accept no one else. There are precautions we can take, including magical ones. And Libby has a year to study and train. Libby must be the one to face the dragon."

That last was said with a vehemence that surprised even Libby. She looked at Michie with a question in her eyes before turning to face Sean. "We don't have any other options and are running out of time. Sean, by issuing the duel we give ourselves a year to figure something out. Maybe even how to separate me from the forcefield without destroying it. I don't like it any more than you do. Trust me."

Sean glowered at the rest of the Council members but remained silent. If the Spirit Council had reservations, they didn't show it. Those that were alive couldn't have hidden their opposition to this plan even if they'd tried.

Libby nodded at Geoffrey and the rest of the Council took over planning the duel terms while Libby sat back and closed her eyes.

And just like that a third item was added to Libby's To-do List: Step 1: Don't die. Step 2: Regrow her heart. Step 3: Defeat a dragon.

She sighed and reached her thoughts out to Dale. *I don't know if you can hear me. I'm not sure I can do this. I'm going to try my best, but I'm pretty sure I'm going to die. If it weren't for our people, I'd have already given up just so I could be with you again. Where are you? Why can't I see you? I can see the others, just not you. I just want you to be happy and at peace, but damn I miss you. It was always you and me against the world. Together we were unstoppable. Alone... I don't know what I am anymore. I don't know who I am anymore.*

"Libby? Earth to Libby?" She opened her eyes when she realized someone was speaking to her. Her Council was looking at her with concern.

"I'm alright, just resting my eyes." She winked at her dad. That was always his favorite response when he'd get caught napping. He gave her a big toothy grin in reply. "What's the plan?"

She couldn't know that Dale was standing right behind her, tears running down his face. It pained him to let her believe he was gone and not to respond, but he'd promised Kokichi, and he wouldn't risk her safety further.

Two days later the Queen's envoy set out for Donegal to deliver the challenge. Larra as the Queen's personal bodyguard and John as Queen's Knight Grand Champion, departed after hours of protocol review with Michie. It was critical to follow it to the letter. Any mistakes could give the dragon the upper hand. They rode out to the border to meet with Jasper.

Neither of them spoke much until they reached the edge of the Kingdom that currently overlapped the coast of Donegal. That was when they got their first glimpse of Jasper, sunning himself on a secluded beach.

"Holy fuck!" John exclaimed. "It's an honest to goodness fucking dragon. Libby is going to have to fight that thing. Oh my God. This is a terrible idea." He was speaking way too fast.

"Be silent. They have excellent hearing. Do you remember the protocol Michie explained?" Larra spoke softly to get him to calm down.

"Yes. Sweet Jaysus, it's a fucking dragon. I can't believe dragons are real."

"Get ahold of yourself, man."

"Fuck me. Okay. Let's do this." He reached up to pull his shoulder-length blonde curls back into a band and out of his face. He wanted to make sure he could see everything.

They dismounted and left their nervous horses behind to continue through the force field on foot.

As they got closer to the beach, they could see him clearly. He was bigger than a two-story house. Black scales glittered in the sun. The end of his tail was a tip that one could only guess was as sharp and lethal as that of an arrow. He had pale silver fur scattered haphazardly on his head. Dwarfed beneath his huge leathery wings, he had tiny arms and claws, like a T-rex, surprisingly disproportionate to his massive size. They wouldn't want to get close enough to them to find out how much damage they could do, but both were assessing any potential weaknesses they could bring back to Libby.

His eyes stood out—a brilliant blue. John had been expecting green or yellow. The blue was scarier. *When they describe the reptilian brain fear response, this is what they're talking about*, thought John. He was terrified and had to fight the urge to flee.

John halted, not taking his eyes off the dragon. "Jasper of Shenyang. You are in lands which are protected by Aisling Elisabeth McGregor, Queen of the Kingdom of the Talking Trees."

"Can't a dragon of Shenyang visit his sister city Belfast? No?" Jasper's laugh rumbled through the clearing. "Libby is exactly why I'm here. Did she send you as an offering? I am rather hungry."

John couldn't help himself, his hand was already on his holster and he slowly eased the latch open.

"Jasper of Shenyang. Since you refuse to depart willingly, as her champions we speak on behalf of our Queen. Queen McGregor hereby challenges you to a duel."

Jasper raised his furry brows and roared with laughter. This was a surprise. He'd expected bravado but figured it would be empty. It was a miracle the Queen was even still alive. This was getting more entertaining by the minute.

"What are the terms you propose, Queen's Champions?"

"One year from today you will battle on wit, skill and physical strength. The location of the duel will be neither Shenyang nor the Kingdom of Talking Trees, but the uninhabited island off Donegal. You will depart immediately and remain outside these protected lands until the date and time of the duel."

Jasper paused. This was interesting. If he defeated Libby so publicly, it would make his victory all the sweeter. But he wasn't about to let her dictate terms.

A slow smile crept across his face. It made John's fight or flight response go into overdrive, and he had to force himself not to move. "I accept the challenge, but it will be one year from the death of King Dalen, eleven months from now, and in a location of my choosing. I choose the clearing where King Dalen took his fatal blow."

John was livid, this was a deliberate attempt to mess with Libby's head, as if the dragon didn't already have a huge advantage. He was about to retort when Larra quietly answered. "On behalf of our Queen, the duel is accepted."

Jasper had seen John's reaction and felt smug. He knew they were afraid. The Queen's defeat was certain. If she wanted to drag it out and make it public so be it. It would give him more time to savor every moment. He roared with excitement, then spread his wings and took flight, heading back to Shenyang.

Chapter 9

The Color of Magic

With Jasper's acceptance of the duel, Libby now had eleven months to prepare. It was hard to imagine surviving that long, but if she could keep the force field up, they'd at least bought a reprieve from Jasper. The engineering team continued to research ways to preserve and protect the force field.

Daily training became part of the schedule for the knights and the LIWs with their return to the palace. Libby was still too weak and on full-time oxygen for any physical training, so her focus was on meditation to strengthen her mind and control her fear. Fear would be a fatal weakness in a duel with a dragon. She'd always been fearless, but since Dale's death she was afraid of everything. Well, everything but death. She was afraid of being alone, of being lonely, of the dark, of failing her people, of what people might think, and that she'd never be whole again. Death seemed relatively easy next to all of that.

"Libby!" Krystal shouted to get her attention.

"I'm sorry." Libby had fallen asleep again. In her weakened state, even something as non-taxing as meditation was exhausting. She'd often fall asleep in the middle of it, until one of her wizards would gently wake her up to begin again. Libby would persist without complaint, but the tears would flow freely as soon as she was back in her bed and crying herself to sleep became the norm.

"You must focus," Krystal continued. "I know you are weak, but you will remain so until you're able to regrow your heart."

She was lying down with a grid of pink and green crystals fanning out around her. The wizard had given Libby a rose quartz crystal talisman on a leather cord to wear around her neck. The cord was long enough the crystal could easily be tucked out of sight in Libby's shirt. It rested right at heart center. She held the crystal in her left hand, and tried to follow Krystal's instructions to use it to focus her intention.

Libby sighed and turned her focus inwards, to her heart. She forced herself to see the scarred half heart, weakly pumping. She visualized the cells along the scar, willing them to divide and multiply. It was a slow process. It was painful. And she was lying down, so it was easy to fall asleep again, which she did. At least until Krystal woke her to begin again.

The LIWs knew how much Libby was suffering. The lone widow among them suggested a change of scenery might help with Libby's healing. After all, everything and everyone in the palace reminded her of Dale and his death. After some heated discussions, Scarlett and Geoffrey came up with the idea to spend time away from the palace while working on her training. It would also give them time to inspect the forcefield and border villages. It was more of an extended camping trip than a quest, but that's the format they came up with when they proposed it to Libby.

"A pseudo-quest?" She chuckled. "Well, I'm up to getting the hell out of Dodge for a bit. We have eleven months before I must face Jasper. When do you propose we start this little adventure?"

"As soon as you're off the oxygen," Scarlett answered.

"That also gives us time to coordinate logistics with the team," Geoffrey added. "We anticipate we'll be on the road for at least a few months. Since we can't take everyone, we figured we'd structure it like a quest, taking five knights and five LIWs. This group will also be the one to accompany you to the duel."

"Better bring a wizard while we're at it," Libby sighed. "Okay. Let's do it."

Duels have specific rules. So do quests, even pseudo ones. The Universe always demands balance. Since there were five on the Spirit Council, there were always five knights and five LIWs who would join a quest. The symbolism of repeating fives wasn't lost on Libby. She knew from her studies with Krystal that repeating fives were a spirit message of major changes and transformation, new freedoms, and living inner truth. Part of her wanted to scream, "No shit?" at the Universe, but she knew that was pointless. In the meantime, decisions needed to be made as to which five would travel and which would stay behind to protect the Kingdom. She'd tasked her two Seniors to prepare their formal recommendations.

The next morning, Geoffrey, Sean, Scarlett, and Catherine met with the Queen to make the final decision. Corrine joined them for the first time, unofficially joining the Queen's Council. They anticipated she would soon be named Regent during Libby's absence.

Libby's color was better, and she could converse without getting winded. Since Dale had been keeping his promise to leave her alone, she'd started sleeping again, if only for a few hours a night. Those few hours made a huge difference. "Let's hear it. Who will be questing with me?"

Since Sean was responsible for recruiting and logistics, he spoke on behalf of the knights. As much as he wanted to go, he had reluctantly agreed with Geoffrey that he was the strongest resource to stay behind and protect the kingdom. The Regent would need his knowledge and expertise in the event of any physical threats, especially with the gaps that remained in the barrier.

"Libby, every single one of your knights has volunteered for this. But since only five can go, we formally recommend the following: Geoffrey Fitzgerald, Senior Knight, will travel with you. John Morgan is your Queen's Knight Grand Champion. By tradition he must go since he delivered the duel challenge. And I don't think we'd be able to keep him away anyway."

Libby smiled because she knew he was right. John had the worst case of Fear of Missing Out she'd ever encountered. His only character flaw was his insane jealousy of anyone having more fun than him. He'd find a way to go even if he wasn't selected.

"Will O'Malley, Weapons Master, will go. He will continue to assist in your training and can also handle weapons acquisition and minor repairs on the road, should it be necessary. Leia Pineda would go even if she wasn't selected. Her talents on and off the battlefield will be invaluable. Wrapping up the group is Fynnigan Van der Linden. While young, he is both a fierce warrior, and brilliant strategist. His engineering background will be helpful and he'll work on inspecting the forcefield borders. He'll also run point on field security since I'm staying behind. Plus, he's your favorite and you enjoy his company."

Libby rolled her eyes and chuckled, but knew he was right. She did love Fynnigan's company.

"The rest of the knights and I will stay behind to aid the Regent and help manage any other threats against the Kingdom during your absence."

Sean took his seat while Libby sat in silence pondering the list. She loved all the knights. She knew them, their stories, their families, and it was difficult to choose one over the other.

"Thank you, Sean. I know it must be killing you to stay behind, but I agree that you will be a bigger asset here. I approve this roster with one addition."

The group was surprised at this. Quests only had five knights. What was she doing?

"I'm adding my nephew, Kurtis McGregor, Junior Knight. He's begged to go. And to be honest, I'd love his company, too."

Geoffrey interrupted, "Out of the question. Libby, he is one of your heirs and completely untested. He is too young. It is unwise to allow him to participate. Protecting him will be a distraction to the rest of the group."

"I considered that, Geoffrey," Libby agreed. "But he's tougher than you think and won't need protection. And this isn't a real quest, right? He loved his uncle Dale and I will not deny him this opportunity to learn about the Kingdom that may one day be his to rule."

Geoffrey could see she'd made up her mind. He could veto the young man's participation as a knight, but as an heir only Libby had that authority. Besides, she did have a point. As much as he didn't like it, he acquiesced. He glanced over at Sean who was already making adjustments to the training schedule and gear list to get the young man as prepared as their limited time would allow. *This is a really bad idea*, he thought, *but what about this entire thing isn't bad?*

The Queen then looked at Scarlett.

"What do you have for me, my friend?"

"I will, of course, be going. You wouldn't dare leave without your best friend and Senior Lady-in-Waiting at your side." Scarlett had announced her plans to retire, but this situation put her retirement on hold. "Harley Gallagher will be assisting with your physical strength training and has already been working with Awen to develop your program. Larra is your personal body guard, so she will of course be coming. Tradition demands her presence since she delivered the duel challenge. Cristina Sobreiro will also be joining us."

"Last but not least, Kendra McGregor." At this Libby's face expressed the surprise they all felt. Kendra was a late addition to the LIWs, very capable and what she lacked in brute force she made up for in motivation and love for her family. But as the late King's sister it seemed fitting. Dalen and Kendra's parents had raised prized horses, and Kendra had taken over the ranch when they'd died. Her skills would come in handy.

Scarlett looked over at Catherine before continuing. "Catherine O'Michael will run point with the remaining LIWs, and work directly with Sean and the Regent." Scarlett had been grooming Catherine for years to take over. She could handle it.

"I approve." Libby paused and looked at Corrine. Corrine's heart dropped. She knew what was coming. The quest demanded symmetry. With Kurtis questing as junior Knight, she knew her daughter would be going too as the only junior LIW. She held her breath. At least Ash'd had the decency to talk to her about it in advance.

"Dyanna Chaney, my niece and heir to the throne with Kurtis, will also be coming. Symmetry will be maintained. My two heirs will learn more on this quest than they could ever learn remaining behind.

This will make them better rulers, and better people. And, to no fault of their own, they are dangerously behind on their training. Effective immediately, they are to be included in all Council meetings. We will need to find some office space for them, although at this point I think they can probably share one. We're a bit squeezed in with all the extra people and the steward may kill me if I ask him to carve out more."

That's just fucking great, Geoffrey thought to himself. *This just keeps getting better and better.*

Sean was typing away to make the adjustments, but his red face indicated his disapproval. Scarlett was equally unhappy with this decision but knew better than to challenge Libby about it at this juncture.

All eyes turned to look at Corrine. She gave a slight nod, but it was clear she was holding back tears. As much as she didn't want to be alone, she'd hoped her husband would be one of the knights selected. He would have helped keep an eye on Dyanna. At least she knew that the LIWs would fight to protect her both as one of their own and as an heir. She knew her sister wouldn't have carelessly made the decision to bring the two heirs along. Still, Dy was her baby girl and Corrine hated the idea.

With the roster approved, the meeting adjourned so the Queen could get some rest. Geoffrey and Scarlett returned to their teams to make the roster official.

Libby was exhausted, and quickly fell into a deep sleep. She was dreaming in Irish. It was about the time she realized she didn't speak Irish that Maggie appeared.

"Hello, child." Maggie smiled at her. "I've been waiting for you."

"Hello, Maggie. I hope you weren't waiting long."

Maggie chuckled, "Longer than you can imagine, but that's not what I meant. You are finally strong enough for us to begin lessons."

"But I've been doing lessons for weeks!" Libby protested.

"Ach no, child. I mean you are finally strong enough for lessons with me. Lessons about magic."

"Oh." Libby said quietly. She could feel her stomach knotting up. She'd been dreading this.

"Relax. Your education in this area has been woefully lacking. In my time, your training would have begun with your first visions and dreams as a child. But you are smart, and I have full confidence in your abilities. Your wizards will help you practice when you are awake, but I will teach you while you are asleep. Time doesn't run the same in dream state, so we can make up some lost ground."

Libby sighed. "Okay. Where do we start?"

"Good attitude. Thanks. I know how you feel about magic, but this is important and will be necessary for the protection of the kingdom. I need your promise that you won't discuss this training with anyone outside your Council. You're going to duel a dragon, and he will underestimate you if he doesn't know you have magic. Do you understand?"

"Yes. I'll take any edge I can get."

"Good. There are three areas you will need to master: seeing and manipulating energy, balancing your chakras, and summoning and speaking to spirit."

"I can learn to summon spirits? I want to speak to Dale. Teach me that first."

Maggie rolled her eyes. "No. You're not ready for that yet. We'll get to that, but we must go in order. We need to build your spiritual and mental strength just like you're working on your physical strength and stamina. Do you understand?"

Libby was annoyed but wouldn't argue. "Fine. Where do we start?"

Maggie smiled. Libby's irritation was a good thing. It would motivate her to train even when she didn't want to. "We'll begin tonight. Go to bed early, we have a lot to cover."

After her nap, the Queen completed her daily training and healing sessions. This was a lot more taxing than it sounded.

Each day, she'd meet with the wizards. It wasn't as simple as lying back and letting them work on her energy or healing spells. She was an active participant. In addition to being difficult, it hurt the way scar tissue goes on hurting for years. And it itched! That was even worse than the pain. The itch was deep in her chest and she couldn't do anything about it.

Why does healing tissue have to be so uncomfortable? she wondered as she took a break, rubbing her chest in a futile attempt to ease the itch and the pain. She sweated more in this regrowth process than she'd ever done in the sparring ring. She was still so weak, and it required a crazy amount of effort. Plus, she still had to keep the force field intact while growing a new heart. In her last dream visit with her ancestor, Michie had given her some tips that the wizards didn't know about, so it wasn't as painful as when she first started, but it was still exhausting. In this process she had to visualize the healing tissue, down to a cellular level, and focus on reducing the inflammation. She'd mentally will the nerve receptors that relayed messages of pain and itching to her brain to slow down. She couldn't turn them off entirely, but it helped.

Libby took multiple naps a day to rest between her sessions. Harley showed up in her room after her latest break.

"How are you today?" she inquired.

"If I were any better, I'd be twins," Libby lied.

Harley smiled at her and got to work setting up for their yoga session. Few people recognized the value of yoga to stay in fighting shape. Core strength and flexibility were important to a warrior. But more than that, it helped to heal and clear the pathways between chakras, something Maggie had emphasized as being mission critical. Libby was going to battle a dragon and needed to be physically, mentally, emotionally, and spiritually clear if she was going to have a chance at defeating him.

She was glad when their yoga session ended. Now that she wasn't on full-time oxygen she could visit the stables on her own, although it was a slow walk there and back. After promising Kurtis she'd visit Hoss, she'd had to find help getting there. She'd sent John back to the Normal world to get her a wheelchair. Libby hated the idea but refused to allow anyone to carry her, or break her promise, so gave in to practicality no matter how much it hurt her ego to ask for help.

John wheeled her down to the stables the first time she went to visit Hoss. He was running full speed until he was sure he heard her laughing but slowed down after he almost dumped her out on a turn. There were limits to having fun, even for the descendant of a pirate. After he had her set up in the stables, she waved him off and asked for some privacy.

Libby managed to get herself out of the chair and into the stall next to Hoss, who was so weak he couldn't stand. He whimpered as she sank down and curled up next to him on the floor of the stall, wrapping her arms around his neck.

"Oh, Hoss Boss, I'm so sorry I haven't been to see you since you got back. I know you miss him, too. I promise not to wait so long next time, I just needed to get help to get here."

He lifted his head and turned towards the wheelchair she'd left blocking the open stall.

"Yeah, I can't walk either. It's why I need you to get strong. I need you to eat. I need you, Hossy. I can't lose you, too."

Libby collapsed into sobs, still draped over Hoss.

"Please, boy, please eat. I love you. And I know you did everything you could to help Dale. He wouldn't want you to just give up. He'd want us to stay together."

Hoss listened, too weak to do anything but blow in her face. Eventually they both cried themselves to sleep. That's where Kurtis found her a few hours later, tear-stained, and sleeping with Hoss, like a kitten in its mama's chest. He paused. Hoss opened his eyes to look at him, and then turned his head to look at Libby. The young man thought he saw Hoss nod his head. Kurtis bent over to wake Libby and help her into her wheelchair. The ride back to the palace was a quiet one. He didn't know what to say.

That evening Hoss ate and drank for the first time in over a week. Libby kept her promise, visiting Hoss almost every day. Once he'd built up enough strength, Kurtis would walk him up to the palace portico and Libby would visit with him there. Until today.

"Hey Hoss Boss," she greeted him, as she plopped down, winded, on the comfortable sitting chair that had magically appeared next to Hoss's stall. She'd guessed Kurtis had brought it down for her. *Such a thoughtful boy.* She smiled to herself. She unlatched the door. Hoss pushed it open with his head and stuck his face close to hers so she could bury her face in his mane and wrap her arms around his neck, a bit of a challenge while seated. She laughed at him as he nosed her pocket, looking for the apple he knew she'd brought for him.

"Yeah, yeah, you only want me for my apples." She burst into a fit of giggles which quickly turned into a coughing fit.

"I'll be okay," she assured him as he stopped moving to look her in the eyes. "Hossy, I'm going to go on a trip soon. I'd like you to come with me, but you don't have to. It's going to be long and will involve a lot of riding. And it may be dangerous. But I need to go."

Hoss started shaking his head and stamping his feet. There was no way he was going to let her go without him. He grabbed for her hair, and since she was still slow-moving he caught a mouth full.

"Sonofabitch that hurts!" Libby yelled. "But okay, I get it. You're coming with me. Although if you try to bite my hair again, I'm leaving you behind."

Hoss snorted at her, knowing full well she wouldn't leave him. Satisfied he'd made his point, he nuzzled her other pocket for the extra apple he knew she'd have. He backed into his stall and pulled the door closed, dropping the latch to catch the apple she'd tossed at him.

Libby laughed at him, "You really are the smartest horse I've ever met, Hoss Boss."

That night, after a lifetime of denying it, Libby McGregor had her first magic lesson. Maggie appeared shortly after she'd fallen asleep. She was wearing a bright green scarf, which made her red hair and blue eyes that much more vibrant. Libby had half expected her to show up with a magic wand a crystal ball. Instead, the two women sat cross-legged on cushions on the floor of an old cottage.

"Every living thing is made of energy." Maggie began. Your engineers use science to explain the energy of the force field. They draw pictures and diagrams so that they can see something that can't be seen. Some will say that magic is science we don't yet understand. It is more accurate to say that science is a way for those who can't see, to visualize what those of us with the sight can."

Libby had to will herself not to roll her eyes. She felt a sudden rush of empathy for her young heirs and hoped she didn't sound like this in their lessons.

"Those with magic are blessed with The Sight, the ability to see energy itself. Once you learn to see it, you will be able to manipulate it, to weave it into your intentions. Normals refer to it as weaving a spell. That's a crude description, but not wholly incorrect."

Libby felt herself tense up again. She rolled her neck and shoulders and focused on her breathing. This was for her people, she had to focus. "How do I prevent what happened to my mom from happening to me?"

Maggie blinked at the question. "Always direct. I appreciate that. What happened to your mother is rare. It's all about balance. You can't live in two worlds at once. Your mother was left to learn largely on her own. Her mother died in childbirth and would have been the one to have taught her. And her mother did teach her what she could from the other side. She was fine with that limited instruction until you were born and your magic manifested. When she realized you were having the dreams and visions, she was determined to help you in a way that she wasn't. She sought out advice and instruction, and ended up taking risks she shouldn't have, including spending too much time in our realm.

Libby sat in silence, thinking. She'd never heard this before. All this time she'd believed her mother had been selfish in her pursuit of magic, and it turned out that it was all for Libby's sake. For the first time she viewed her mother's situation with empathy. As frustrating as it was for her to grow up without her mother's guidance, she'd had her dad to teach her what she needed to be Queen. Her mother had no one to help her growing up.

Maggie continued. "You must learn to focus your vision so that you can see the energy. It may be difficult, since you've fought it for so long, but you're going to have to work on it both awake and asleep."

"How do I do that?" Libby demanded, impatient to get started.

"Close your eyes. Take three deep breaths. Quiet your thoughts. Focus your intention on your third eye chakra, that's the one between your eyebrows. When you open your eyes, look at me. Keep your intention and look at me through your third eye. Keep breathing."

Libby did as Maggie instructed and then opened her eyes. She looked at Maggie. Nothing. Nada. Zilch. She couldn't see any energy, just Maggie.

"What exactly am I looking for?" She asked, frustrated.

"Usually a color. Most energy has a color."

"Like music?"

"Yes. Like music. How do you see the colors of music?"

"I don't know, I just do. I feel it more than see it, but I can see the colors when I really let myself surrender to the music."

"Aha!" Exclaimed Maggie, throwing her hands up. "Surrender! Of course, a warrior would think in terms of surrender. Yes, that's it. Let's try that again. Send your intention to the third eye, and then surrender to the sight."

Shaking out her shoulders, Libby started again. She went through the steps, and when she opened her eyes, she still saw nothing.

"Why isn't this working?" Libby wailed.

Maggie frowned. This was going to be more complicated than she'd thought. Most people with magic could just see it, the same way you just open your eyes and see. She'd never heard of someone with selective sight. *Think, Maggie. How do we do this? She must be able to see something if she can see music magic. Perhaps a little music?*

"Let's try it again. Did you think it was going to be easy? Just relax. I have an idea. Do you know exactly how it feels when you surrender to the music?"

"Yes."

"Good. Think about that." Suddenly a soft mandolin began playing in the background of her dream.

Libby closed her eyes. She took three deep breaths. She willed her intentions to her third eye. And she thought about how it felt to surrender to the music. She slowly opened her eyes and smiled. Maggie was surrounded by a bright blue light, the color of her eyes. No, not a light. It was pulsing, or vibrating, but it was definitely emanating from Maggie. It was the color of her magic; her energy or aura. Libby could see the frequency of the color and started to analyze it. Suddenly it was gone.

She frowned in disappointment, but looked Maggie in the eye and said, "Blue."

Maggie laughed. "Excellent! That's enough for one day. But I need you to practice. Practice with me when you're asleep. Practice with your wizards when you're awake. When you're able to see the energy at will, we're ready to move to the next level. And if you have questions, you don't have to wait for our trainings. Just set the intention you want to talk to me and call me."

Libby nodded, gave her a soft smile, and went back to a dreamless sleep.

Chapter 10

The Heirs

As her strength and stamina continued to improve, the Queen added daily meetings with her two young heirs. She'd had years of training with her father and grandmother to prepare for the throne. These two may have less than a year to learn as much as she could teach them. They could deal with the informality of their lessons in her current situation.

Today they pulled up a chair near their aunt's bed. Between their physical training and endless meetings and studies, they were exhausted but thrilled to get these private lessons with her. It made the fifteen-year-olds feel so grown up. Today's lesson was a continuation on diplomacy, with a focus on etiquette.

"As a king or queen you must interact with all kinds of people, in all kinds of situations. No one should ever leave your presence without feeling like they had your full attention, and most definitely should never leave feeling inferior. There are basic rules to follow, especially in formal situations:

"You must always address others by their title and surname, until such time as they ask you to call them something less formal."

"You will always stand when your guest enters the room."

"You will always offer a hand to your guest."

It didn't take long for the two teenagers to begin shifting their weight in their chairs and fidgeting.

"Never agree to a formal proposal or contract without first consulting your Council."

"Do not allow your facial expressions to reveal your true feelings. Mastering your breathing will help with this, especially when you are struggling to master your emotions."

"You will learn the language of your guest whenever possible." Libby droned on until she saw Dyanna roll her eyes. "Dyanna Chandra Chaney, I saw that eye roll, which is definitely poor etiquette for a young lady who may one day be Queen."

"Aunt Libby, these etiquette rules are archaic." Dyanna moaned. Kurtis agreed wholeheartedly but wasn't about to voice that opinion.

"They are tried and true, Dy, and decorum is the first rule of diplomacy. You disrespect others, and yourself, when you fail to behave properly. A queen is born to this role and has a duty not only to her people, but to her ancestors. The antics and lack of decorum you see from elected leaders in today's world are beneath you. Never forget that. If I ever see either of you behaving like a president or prime minister you will be disowned in the blink of an eye."

Kurtis snickered when Dy got three-named, and Libby now turned her attention on him. "Laugh it up, Kurtis Travis McGregor, you have your share of etiquette rules."

Dy smirked at him. Being three-named was serious, but misery loves company.

"I expect both of you to demonstrate your mastery of etiquette at all times, including with each other. Once you have proven to me that you will not embarrass the Kingdom in an official capacity, I will allow you to relax your etiquette in private. Do you understand?"

"Wait, you want us to act this way all the time? Twenty-four-seven?" asked Kurtis

"What about when we're in battle practice?" demanded Dyanna.

"Yes. At all times. It must become habit. How you address individuals and groups, how you carry yourself, the words you choose and the expressions you wear on your faces are all part of it. Do you understand?"

"Yes," they answered, although they looked at each other with doubt. As they stood up to leave, Libby cleared her throat and looked pointedly at Kurtis.

He sighed and reached over to assist Dyanna with her chair and extend an arm for their exit. "Miss Chaney?" he asked.

"Thank you, Mister McGregor." Turning to look at her aunt, she said with a slight curtsy, "Good bye, Aunt Libby. Sleep well."

"Good bye, Aunt Libby. Thank you for meeting with us today," Kurtis forced himself to say, willing himself not to roll his eyes.

Libby smiled. "Good job you two. Now get the fuck out." She laughed at their shocked expressions. "What? I already know the rules so can say whatever I want and still be queenly. Now go so I can take a nap." She was still laughing as the door closed behind them and it turned into a coughing fit.

As time progressed, Libby's physical condition did as well. She was able to incorporate moderate physical training into her daily schedule. It consisted mostly of long walks and taking Hoss out for rides. She continued her yoga sessions with Harley but added in light strength training.

In addition to her physical and magical training, the Queen was working diligently to formally prepare the Kingdom for her extended absence. As such, she assigned her sisters Ava and Corrine as Co-Regents in her absence. Ava hated this responsibility, especially since she was pregnant with her first child, but her experience as the royal bookkeeper made her an ideal choice since she already had a good overview of how things were run. Ava would work directly with Sean for logistics support.

Since Ava already had an office in the palace, Libby gave Corrine her office and moved into Dale's. No one had dared, or cared, to step foot in his office since he'd died, and it was wasted space. This made the most sense. Libby assigned the job of overseeing the packing up of Dale's things to her heirs. It wasn't fair, but this didn't fall under the scope of anything she could ask her knights or LIW's to help with, and she couldn't bring herself to do it. It needed to be family, and they may as well learn early that responsibility sometimes sucked.

Since there was a real chance the Kingdom would implode if the Queen died, people were afraid. One of Corrine's responsibilities was to organize parties, meditations, and other activities to make the most of whatever time may be left. She redecorated the palace in calming peaceful colors and piped in meditative music. She wasn't thrilled her daughter would be going with the Queen, but also understood the responsibilities that come with being part of the royal family.

Her daughter had begged to go along. As Junior LIW, and an heir to the throne, it was impossible to deny her. If the Queen failed, Dyanna would die no matter where she was. But it was all Corrine could do not to lock her in her room and forbid it. Her baby girl going off on a quest—it just felt wrong. She wiped the tears from her face and got back to party-planning.

To Dyanna it felt so right. Once it was announced she'd be joining the group, the teenager started flexing her muscle, walking around with an unladylike swagger whenever Aunt Libby wasn't around. She wanted so badly to be a warrior and worshipped the ground Leia and the LIWs walked on. No one would treat her like the cute, helpless princess ever again. Shortly after the announcement, she'd cut her long blonde hair and dyed it blue like her aunt Libby's. She'd never be mistaken for a boy, but it was one of those spur of the moment rebellious decisions that made her mother shake her head.

Dyanna still couldn't believe her aunt Libby was letting her come at all, and that her mom and dad didn't fight it. As much as she was jumping ahead, she was no slouch. Always an overachiever, she doubled up her training, even asking Larra to spar with her. Her efforts didn't go unnoticed and Kurtis, not to be outdone, did the same. The two teenagers were out on the practice field before anyone else and stayed until they had to run to their lessons with Libby.

One afternoon found Dyanna and Kurtis sitting on the edge of the training ring, waiting for their lesson with the Weapon's Master. They were engaging in a verbal sparring match about which of them was better. What started out in friendly banter quickly turned into a challenge to pick up real weapons and prove it.

"You're not too bad of a fighter, for a girl," Kurtis remarked.

"For a girl?" Dyanna was outraged. "I'll take you or any other boy any day of the week."

"Oh, you think so," Kurtis snorted.

"Yeah. I'm the heir to the throne. I'll be just as badass as Aunt Libby when I'm grown up."

Kurtis burst into laughter. "You're only one of the heirs. Aunt Libby hasn't chosen yet. And I'll still kick your ass no matter how tough you think you're gonna be."

"You're not even in the royal bloodline," Dyanna retorted.

"You know that doesn't matter," he scowled, feeling his temper start to flare as she hit a sore spot. "How about you put your sword where your smart mouth is?" he challenged.

Like many battles of the sexes, this one drew an audience. Knights and LIWs routinely sparred with each other. But in this case, the two youngest and inexperienced of their number were going at it hard. There was no more talk, only grunts and the sounds of swords and shields making contact. There were no practice swords here, and the knights and LIWs observed with pride and a bit of concern, even if there were a few wagers made. They didn't need any severe injuries at this juncture. If they all survived, one of these two would end up running the Kingdom. Until that day, they would do their best to make Aunt Libby, their Queen, proud.

Will O'Malley stepped in with, "That's enough of that. Let's see what you can do without your swords and shields." He knew that they weren't ready to be done yet, but that hand-to-hand sparring would lessen the likelihood of severe injury. Dy, the first to put down her weapon, never took her eyes off Kurtis but exercised care. The Weapons Master wouldn't be forgiving of a lack of respect for their swords and shields.

Kurtis was a good head taller than Dyanna, but just as winded. There was no way he was going to let himself be beat by a girl, even though he'd seen his Aunt Libby best Uncle Dale in the ring on more than one occasion. Dy was just as determined and competitive as their aunt.

Connor Chaney shook his head. He was proud of his little girl. He was also worried. He knew how headstrong she was, a lot like her aunt, and he wouldn't be around to protect her from herself. He shook that feeling off and started shouting instructions to her and cheering her on. No way his girl was going to lose to a boy, not even a fellow knight like Kurtis.

Kendra was just as fired up as Connor, and they had a side wager going on which of their kids would come out on top.

Libby could see what was going on from her office window but chose not to participate. She smiled. They were definitely her heirs, and struggling with the etiquette requirement, but doing reasonably well given their age and the unique situation they were in. Kurtis and Dyanna were evenly matched in their integrity, fighting skills, and healthy ambition. She was relieved she didn't have to choose a successor yet. The forcefield was holding, and they were far too young for either to get married and assume the throne.

"You know you'll have to choose one, eventually," came the deep voice behind her.

Libby turned to see Michael sitting on the chair at her desk, swinging his little legs back and forth.

She smiled. "Hello, Michael."

"Hi, Mom," he replied. She'd never get used to hearing that. She'd desperately wanted to be a mother, and it had taken years to resign herself to the fact that would never happen. She'd made the best of it and doted on the young people in her life. But seeing Michael here made her healing heart swell.

"Mom, I've been watching over you for a long time. Since the day I died."

Libby didn't know what to say, so remained silent. Her heart hurt at the reminder.

"I know how hard it was for you. How you blamed yourself. I also know that you shut off that part of your heart to protect yourself from the pain."

"Michael, how could you know that?"

"I just do. And that's what I want to talk to you about, because I see you doing it again, only this time there is too much at risk and I can't let you."

"What are you talking about?" Libby knew he spoke the truth but didn't want to rip open the old wound. It was so much easier to deny it than to feel the emotional pain that came from confronting it. Still, she didn't want him to go.

Michael climbed on to the desk and motioned for her to sit down so he could look her in the eye.

"Mom, you have to know that my death wasn't your fault. Neither was Dad's. Back then, you still had a strong, healthy heart. And when you walled part of it off, the rest of your heart compensated. You don't have that luxury now. Compartmentalizing any part of your half heart will kill you. But I can help you, if you're willing to let me."

Michael stared into her eyes, searching for her answer. Libby knew she didn't have a choice. She couldn't bear the thought of him leaving her again.

"I don't suppose it can hurt worse than what I've already been dealing with," she replied.

"Well, it won't hurt worse. Just different. But it will get better, I promise. Mom, you're going to have to feel the feelings, even the ugly ones, and then let them go." Michael climbed off the desk and into her lap. She wrapped her arms around him and the tears started to flow. The anger and sadness she'd denied herself to feel after he died came pouring out. Losing him had been unfair.

"Good, Mom. Feel it all. And then you have to forgive."

"Forgive what?" she asked, sniffling.

"Everything. Everyone. Forgive yourself for something that was beyond your control. Forgive Dad for not being there. Forgive the universe for not letting you have children. Forgive everyone else for having healthy children. Forgive. You have to forgive."

"How do I do that?"

"Gratitude. Simplistic, I know, but effective. Find all the things you are grateful for about the experience. Say them aloud."

Libby stared at him, mouth agape. How could there be anything about losing him that she could be grateful for? She was horrified at the thought but was suddenly desperate for his company.

"I'm grateful for you," she began quietly. "I'm grateful I got to love you and know you existed. I'm grateful I got to see your spirit so that I could recognize you when the Spirit Council convened." She stumbled. "I'm grateful I get to have you now, even though it's only because Dale died."

She was openly sobbing now. "I'm grateful my sisters have healthy kids. I love them and I'm grateful to have Kurtis and Dyanna in my life. And Fynn, too. None of them were you, but I love them as if they were."

Michael let her cry it out. When her sobs quieted, he put his hands on her face and smiled. "You did good, Mom. Gotta go now. I love you. I need you to love yourself, too."

Libby closed her eyes and took a deep breath. When she opened them again, she was alone in her office.

Chapter 11

Memories

Michie arrived shortly after Libby fell asleep, like she often did. "Hello, Mago-chan," she greeted Libby with a slight bow. "Hello, Grandmother. What lesson do you have for me today?"

"One you already know well, and we're going to cheat. After all your hard work, we finally have a shortcut available to us. Do you remember all the dream memories you had as a child? Riding my horse into battle? Wielding my sword and my bow?"

"Yes, of course."

"Well, it's time to start your training again while you're awake. You're still weak, but I'm going to run you through the dream memories while you are asleep each night. While you are awake, it will simply be a matter of letting your body and brain remember it and building up your stamina."

"Finally," Libby laughed, "something easy."

"Not easy," corrected Michie, "but hopefully a way to make up lost time. Are you ready?"

"Yes."

"Good. Okay, just sleep and dream. I will be there but will not participate unless needed. Remember, these are my dream memories, not yours. This is just for your brain and body to remember battle skills. Nothing more."

"Thank you, Grandmother."

"Good luck, Aisling. Good luck, my dreamer."

The dreams were like they always were when she was a child. Libby dreamt her ancestor's memories like they were her own. She was fierce and fearless, and she was a master. She could feel the weight of the katana in her hand. She felt herself wield it in battle, on foot or on horseback, but without the pain her body felt during the waking hours. She fought and hunted with her bow. The dreams were a lot more detailed now that she was an adult and could process things differently. She could see and hear the pennant blowing in the wind in front of them, a white dragon on a black field. She remembered how to balance arrows, and dream-learned how to restring her bow and make her own arrows. She learned how to bear the weight of her armor, and the difference it made in battle. She fought battle after battle, trained hour after hour, all in her sleep, until the motions were ingrained in her. Her muscles would remember them without her having to consciously will them.

Michie left her alone but was always close by. When Libby saw her husband take an arrow, she felt the anguish and pain at the same time she heard Michie's voice next to her telling her it was just a dream. That it wasn't Dale, it was Ryunosuke, to keep going. Many times, this was enough for Libby to pull the panic back in. When it wasn't, Michie would yell for her to wake up. Those nights looked the same to the LIWs, who assumed she'd awoken sobbing from another nightmare. The grief was almost unbearable. To be forced to carry both hers and Michie's was cruel, but it was the only way.

Michie, like the other spirits, no longer held the emotions of that memory. She knew there was more than this physical life. It pained her to see her granddaughter suffer. She wished there was another way, but they had no other options. She thought back to when she was alive. Time didn't have the same power it did in the living world, especially without the added weight of emotions. She remembered the day clearly. She and Ryunosuke had fallen in love despite being in an arranged marriage. It was unusual and it was envied. They were stronger because of it.

In the ancient Japanese tradition, any king who didn't have sons would marry his daughter off to a respectable second or third son of a good family, and legally adopt him to carry on the family name and be the figurehead of the Kingdom. Michie had been groomed to run the Kingdom her whole life. Battle strategy, weapons, finance, law, and anything else her father deemed necessary. As a Japanese woman she was also trained in the feminine arts of flower arranging, diplomacy, household finance, kimono, art, and music. She could have run the Kingdom as both King and Queen if societal norms would have allowed it. She resented being forced to marry, and no one was more surprised than she was when she fell in love with Ryunosuke after the heart graft. He was a good man, a loving husband, and a fair king. He was her equal and respected her as such.

Unlike Dale and Libby who, with knights and LIWs, took turns facing threats to the Kingdom, Ryunosuke and Michie always rode into battle together with only a minimal escort. On this day, they'd set out for the border to deal with an oni, an ogre, who was threatening a small village. They didn't know that the oni had been allowed in by Tanaka, a samurai who'd been one of the many suitors for Michie's hand. When Michie's father had chosen Ryunosuke, Tanaka was furious. He was power hungry, and the only way to gain the throne was by marrying Michie. He didn't know about the heart graft. Nor was he aware that if Ryunosuke died, Michie would likely follow and the Kingdom would cease to exist. He'd plotted for years, and on this day, he succeeded in part of it. While Michie and Ryunosuke were battling the oni, Tanaka fired an arrow that pierced Ryunosuke's armor, lodging in his abdomen

Michie and her bodyguard had time to get Ryunosuke back on his horse and ride hard back to the palace. Through sheer will, Michie kept the force field alive while the wizards tried to figure out a solution to keep Ryunosuke alive as long as possible. She'd dispatched the knights to finish off Tanaka and the oni. She forced her feelings down. She was a queen. And she was Japanese. It was inappropriate to demonstrate emotions in front of others, but she was screaming on the inside.

Against the odds, her knights destroyed the oni, but not before he cast a dying curse. Michie and Ryunosuke would not be reunited in the spirit realm, until a queen managed to tame a black dragon. Michie had been too distracted with surviving the loss of Ryunosuke and regrowing her heart to pay much attention to the oni's curse. At least until she herself crossed over into the spirit realm and couldn't find him. Fortunately, her wizards had chronicled everything. Despite thousands of years of fires, floods, and wars, a single scroll survived to end up in the royal archives of the Kingdom of the Talking Trees. The scroll that Awen had found.

Michie looked over at her sleeping granddaughter. Maybe that's why she and Libby were linked, why Libby experienced Michie's memories as her own. Their lives were on a parallel path that somehow overlapped across the centuries. Maybe Libby would be the one to break the curse and reunite Michie with her beloved. All this time Michie had assumed Ryunosuke had moved on to another plane of existence. When Michie first saw Jasper she'd felt a glimmer of hope. Perhaps the oni spoke truth that day.

After weeks of Michie's dream memories, Libby finally began to incorporate archery and sword training into her waking routine. It was moderate since she still got winded easily, and she remained on oxygen at night and between trainings. The first day back in the ring was emotional. It was the first time she'd put on her armor and weapons since Dale had been injured. Each buckle and tie brought back a flood of memories of the morning he'd left to face Skarra. Libby paused when she got to her sword. It had been her father's. Kokichi had retained the katana after his retirement from the throne, but after his death Libby had replaced hers with his. She slowly unsheathed the sword to examine it more closely. The katana was flawless, lightweight and perfectly balanced. It still had his crest on the tsuba[2], and every time she held it in her hand, she remembered his lessons. Now, after training with Michie's dream memories, she wasn't quite sure who was wielding the blade.

She finished dressing and headed out to meet her friend Will in the training ring, hand on her hilt. Will O'Malley was responsible for the bulk of her weapons training, but as she regained her strength,

---

[2]   A tsuba is the hand-guard between the blade and the hilt of the katana.

she'd spar with each of the knights and LIWs to keep sharp. She'd always loved training with the wiry Weapons Master. He made her laugh, which made the ass-kicking she usually got a little more tolerable. This was the first time they'd entered the practice ring since Dale's death and the Queen struggled to keep going. A simple parry that she should have been able to do in her sleep, saw her lose her balance and end up on her hands and knees. Will didn't cut her any slack, and she loved him all the more for it. He was able to show her how to rebalance her sword and shield to accommodate her weakened physical condition.

He was also a history buff. Will's chatter about the history of weapon design and how they were used and implemented in different parts of the world reminded her of Dale. She smiled as she remembered the two of them talking for hours between dodges and parries. The smile quickly turned to tears as she felt the sting of his absence. If Will noticed he was too much of a gentleman to mention it, instead saying he needed a break.

Libby nodded gratefully and quickly turned away to the attention of her heirs. Will watched her walk off with concern. He knew the kind of pain she was suffering. Losing his wife to cancer almost broke him. Even now it still hurt, and he'd had years to get used to it. He wanted to hug her and tell her it was all going to be okay but knew that might be all it took for her to lose the composure she was fighting to keep in front of everyone. It was unfair for her to be saddled with this duel and responsible for the death of everyone on Earth. He admired her strength and resilience, but worried about her. They all did.

He stood, absentmindedly stroking his bright white goatee, as he looked around at the group they'd assembled. Each of them had a personal relationship with the King and Queen. They were friends before they were knights and LIWs. They were a family brought together by bonds of love and loyalty. As he scanned those assembled, he made eye contact with Geoffrey. He knew Geoffrey was thinking the same thing. Libby's sword work was impressive given the circumstances, but she was still weak and lacked stamina. They must continue, no matter how painful it was. After an almost imperceptible nod, Will picked up his sword and shield and shouted at Libby that he was done with his break if she was.

Libby grunted quietly as she forced herself out of the chair. *Oh my God, it still hurts to move.* She was exhausted, but there was no way she was going to embarrass herself by quitting.

"Bring it on, old man," she challenged.

Will laughed out loud and with his thick Belfast accent flipped back, "I intend to. Old man, eh? I hope those sassy pants you're wearing protect your ass from the whooping you're about to get."

Awen had an armful of scrolls when Maggie appeared behind her, tapping her on the shoulder. The scrolls flew out of her arms as Awen jumped, then scrambled to catch them before they fell to the ground.

"Are you trying to give me a heart attack?" the wizard screamed at Maggie. Communicating with spirit was Krystal's talent, and Awen was still easily startled when one of the Council made an appearance.

"Apologies, wizard. We have some things to discuss." Maggie motioned for Awen to close the door to her office.

Awen dumped the scrolls on her desk and complied with the request. "What's up, Maggie?"

"Since you are going on the road with Libby, the burden of this task will fall to you."

"Great, this sounds fun, what kind of burden exactly?" Awen asked with a nervous feeling in her gut.

"Libby is making progress physically, but she is still weak spiritually. In order for her to be ready to defeat a dragon, she will need to clear and balance her chakras."

"Okay? That seems reasonable enough and she's been working hard at yoga and meditation." Awen wasn't sure where this was going.

"All of her chakras. She will not object, except for one which will be an obstacle, because she doesn't believe she deserves it."

Awen felt her heart sink as she quickly figured out what Maggie was trying to say. "Sweet Goddess, you're telling me that I have to convince her to find the pleasures in life? Beyond what she's already been doing?"

Maggie nodded, "She has to remember what that joy is, and not shut it out or resent it. It's possible she'll reach it eventually, through good food and music, massage therapy, among other things. But that's not guaranteed, and the quickest way to do that is for her to connect with a man. I don't need to remind you that the clock is ticking."

Awen lost it. "Are you kidding me? Her husband just died! How the fuck am I supposed to even bring it up in a conversation? It's beyond insensitive, it's ridiculous! Why can't you do it?" She demanded, grateful the door was closed since she was yelling.

"I will set the stage, but you are the one that will find the opportunity to speak to her about it. And she doesn't need to fall in love, just to remember and appreciate the joys of physical pleasure."

Awen's head was spinning. She couldn't believe what she was hearing, and plopped down in her chair, hands on her face in disbelief. "No. You have no idea what you're asking. Again, her husband just died. And you don't know Libby. She's not that kind of woman. There is no way this is going to work."

"Well, we're just going to have to figure out a way to make it work. As for not being that kind of woman, there is nothing wrong with finding pleasure in life. Without it, one is incomplete." Maggie disappeared before Awen could retort.

"Sweet Goddess, what am I going to do?" Awen prayed.

Chapter 12

Breaks and Bards

After weeks of training, they could all see Libby needed a break. She was regaining her physical and mental strength, but that didn't stop the grief from taking its toll. It was Scarlett who demanded the day off. She knew Libby would never ask, but she needed it. She also knew Libby would deny needing one, so said she herself needed it, that this Grandma was out of practice and if they were going to head out in the next few weeks, a break would do them all good.

Using the unexpected day off from training and pre-departure logistics as an excuse, Libby quietly saddled up Hoss and headed out to the countryside. She welcomed the quiet and the solitude. She hadn't had a moment alone since Dale was injured. Hoss was eager to stretch his legs but kept a steady pace since he knew his rider wasn't up for it yet. Forty minutes into their ride they came around a bend into a valley. Next to a small thicket of birch trees was a hunting lodge. A stream ran nearby, and purple and yellow irises bloomed along the banks. It was idyllic, the kind of place a poet might retire. She smiled for the first time in days and with a "C'mon boy," urged Hoss to pick up the pace, although he needed no encouragement to open up to a quick trot. By the time she reached the front door, Fintan was waiting for her with a big bear hug.

"Hi, Finn, I've missed you," she breathed into his chest as she let his arms envelope her.

"Oh Girl, I'm so sorry. I've missed you, too."

He'd been at the royal funeral, but in her weakened condition he wasn't able to see her that night. Although he'd written and read the tale of King Dalen at the banquet following the funeral, the Queen had been noticeably absent. He'd visited her privately a few times, but eventually he pulled back from that too.

The unlikely pair had met years earlier in an Irish pub on one of her outside adventures in the south of Ireland. That chance meeting began a twenty-year friendship. She'd decided to visit today because she was feeling the pressure of the task ahead and fighting her grief, and really wanted to see her friend. Plus, she felt like she should say good-bye.

Fintan ushered her in and grabbed a bottle of her favorite whiskey and two glasses and sat down on the leather couch in front of the fireplace. He was always cold, so the fireplace burned almost year-round. Tall and lanky, she noticed his favorite red sweater was getting a bit loose. Since his wife had died a few years ago, his healthy eating had gone downhill. Now, he ate whatever was at hand, if at all. Libby sat down, although her feet didn't quite touch the floor. She wasn't cold but tucked her feet under her. Normally she wouldn't have presumed to be so rude as to put her feet on someone else's furniture, but Fintan was an old friend. She knew he didn't care.

"How are you?" he asked without making eye contact. He felt so bad for her, but the King dying had brought up a lot of old grief over losing his wife. It was one of the reasons he'd kept his distance. It was just too hard. It was so hard that at the time, he'd packed up and finally taken Libby up on her offer to move into the Kingdom. He'd needed a fresh start without all the reminders of his beloved. He still crossed the barrier regularly to see his grandchildren, thanks to a special portal the queen had located for him but that was it. He'd left his old life behind him.

"I'd be better if you looked me in the eye, Fintan O'Toole," she snapped.

He winced but looked down into her eyes. He was painfully shy, and it had been a running joke between them that he needed to look her in the eye or she'd think he was lying. She was one of the few people who understood how someone who had been a world-class performer and could sing in front of thousands or read his award-winning poetry to auditoriums, could still be so shy. It was something they had in common. With a lifetime of training she'd learned to cover it well, but hated being in the public eye. But that role came with her ascension to the throne. She'd learned to deal with it, just as he had when he was still performing.

"I'm sorry, that was bitchy. I feel like shit but that's no excuse for poor behavior."

"It's okay, Aisling. You've got a lot on your mind. But really, how are you?" He almost always used her given name. He felt it suited her better than Libby, and it made his old Irish poet's heart happy to hear it aloud. Queen Aisling, the Dreamer. And she was a dreamer. Unlike him. For a poet, he was unusually pessimistic. She had nicknamed him Cranky Bear years ago, and it suited him.

She sighed and took a big swallow from her whiskey glass. "How am I? Well, it hurts to breathe. It causes me physical pain. It hurts to be alive. I'm exhausted. I can't think straight. Trying to keep the force field up on my own is killing me. But if I don't, my people will die. I'm supposed to fight a dragon or my people will die. If I fail, two worlds will die. I love my people, but I want to die. I'm surrounded by people but have never felt lonelier in my life. I'm doing fucking fantastic."

"Do you think you can do it?" he asked softly. He was one of the few people who would ask the hard questions, and always seemed to be able to get her to answer.

"I have no choice." At this she started crying quietly into her whiskey.

He hated crying. It reminded him too much of a time in his life he wanted to forget, but he scooched over on the couch, put his arm around her, and let her cry it out. When she was done, he kissed her on the top of her head and told her, "I've known you for a long time, Aisling. If anyone can do it, you can."

She wiped her face on her sleeve and started laughing. "Oh Jaysus, now I know we're all going to die. You just said something positive."

"Fuck off, your highness, it does happen sometimes." But he started laughing too.

"Sing for me?"

"You know I don't sing anymore."

"Don't make me order you."

"You know I don't give a fuck if you try."

"Fine. I'm asking you. Please sing for me. It might be the last time. It always cheers me up. Plus, the wizards say the healing music is good for me. So, do it for your country?" She laughed until the laughter turned into a coughing fit. Just like Dale had aspirated at the very end, she was always under water. Drowning. For a split second she was reminded of the dream she'd had before Dale died, the one where she was drowning. She shook it off and smiled at Fintan.

He sighed but went behind the bar and took the mandolin off the wall. He came back and sat beside her, quietly strumming a tune. Then he started singing her favorite song. It was the first song he'd ever sung for her, in Irish, "The Irish Phoenix." She was always a sucker for the mandolin and those blue eyes. That song had new meaning for her now. She would either be burned up in the fire or become the phoenix rising.

She closed her eyes and listened, but her mind drifted back in time to when they first met.

> It was a sunny spring day in the south of Ireland, and she was a bit hungover from the night before. Oh my God, it's way too bright out here, she thought to herself as she meandered up and down the cobbled streets of Killarney. She needed a break and a drink, so she ducked into the first whiskey pub she could find. She wanted someplace quiet and managed to locate the back side of Murphy's Whiskey Bar. Perfect! It took a moment for her eyes to adjust to the dim lighting. She wasn't even sure it was open since there was no one there. Most patrons went to the front part of the bar during the day.
>
> She asked the bartender, "Are you open?"
>
> He snarked back, "They don't pay me to be here if we aren't."
>
> She laughed, took a seat at a corner booth, and ordered her favorite Irish whiskey. "Wow, what a cranky bastard. Maybe he's hungover too," she mused.
>
> "That's a fancy whiskey. Where are you visiting from?" came a voice from a few tables over.

She hadn't noticed the other customer when she'd come in. Damned hangover was putting her observation at risk. Pull it together, Libby! *she barked at herself.* "What makes you think I'm visiting?" *she asked as her eyes found the blue eyes hiding in the shadows.*

"No one around here pays that much for anything. Let me guess, American?"

She laughed, and confirmed, "Yes. And rule number one is life is short, so enjoy the good stuff while you can."

"Rules about life? How very American. And cliché," he snorted.

Rather than be offended, she laughed. It had been awhile since anyone had flipped her shit for no reason and this was entertaining.

That's how Libby McGregor and Fintan O'Toole struck up a conversation. He was a local, and well-known in the area for being a bit of a curmudgeon. His wife, on the other hand, was charming and well-liked. Proof that opposites attract, is how people wrote off the unlikely pairing. Most people left him alone, which was exactly how he liked it, and why he was hiding out in the back of Murphy's that day, He eventually moved to Libby's booth when other customers showed up. They didn't have much in common in the way of life experiences, but both loved music, poetry and art. She learned about his family and that he was a poet and musician before he retired. He learned that she had a lot of responsibilities at home, so when she traveled, she unleashed her inner wild child. They learned that sometimes the universe brings people together who need each other. They found that rare friendship that instantly sparks with recognition that you were meant to know each other. One day, in the future, he'd describe their friendship as two sides of a magnet, with Libby the positive and him the negative.

The bar staff were amazed since he rarely spoke to anyone. They kept coming as close to their booth as possible to try to assess what was going on. Here was grumpy Fintan O'Toole, chatting up the American. A woman! A much younger woman at that. And he was smiling and laughing. So was she. It was almost like he was being charming. They couldn't believe what they were witnessing. This was going to be hot news in their small town. When the first regular showed up, it became a full-fledged gossip fest until Libby and Fintan decided to part ways with promises to stay in touch.

"I hope your wife isn't the jealous type. I'm pretty sure you're going to be front page news tomorrow."

Fintan looked around the bar and everyone's eyes quickly turned elsewhere. "Who gives a fuck what these small-town losers think?" But he was secretly pleased. "No, Sheila's not jealous. In fact, she'd love you. You should come for dinner some time."

"I'd love that." Libby smiled and gave him a kiss on the cheek, laughing at the expression on their waiter's face.

At some point she'd dozed off. Now, she woke up covered with a light blanket and with the realization they'd missed lunch. Fintan had moved to the easy chair on the other side of the room and was reading when he realized she was awake and looking at him.

"Thanks. I needed that." She smiled. "I haven't slept that peacefully in a long time."

"I know. Although I must confess, I was a bit annoyed. I'm not used to putting people to sleep. Once upon a time, women found me interesting."

Libby laughed. "Trust me, it's not the first time, and you're not that interesting. Are you hungry? I'm hungry."

She dodged the pillow he threw at her and got up to make them some lunch.

He sang and played for her while she prepared a late afternoon meal.

The sun was on its descent when they said their good-byes, possibly for the last time. Libby and Hoss set out on the return path. She slowed at the edge of the thicket and announced to no one, "Thank you. Thank you for not stopping me. Thank you for coming with me."

"You're welcome," a tiny voice replied. The black horse silently left the shadows, its petite rider almost invisible to those who didn't know who they were looking for. Dark hair, dark eyes, and stealth made the faery woman almost impossible to track. Libby hadn't told her where she was going but knew that she would follow her. "Shall we? It's getting dark."

"Yes, Larra, let's go home."

Chapter 13

The "Quest" Begins

You can dance, you can jive, having the time of your life.
See that girl, watch that scene, digging the Dancing Queen.
~Abba, "Dancing Queen"

Since Corrine was in charge of morale, she'd made the decision that a traditional pre-quest banquet was in order. Libby groaned when she was told about it but knew Corrine was right. Everyone needed a morale boost, so a few days before they departed, anyone who could made their way to the palace for a party worthy of the old Viking tales with revelry, music, tales of valor and victory, and food and drink. Lots and lots of drink, which inevitably led to dancing.

Long tables and benches had been set up in the open field adjacent to the palace, fanning out from the stage and providing a clear view to all in attendance. Strings of lights hung overhead from posts set into the ground, although the full moon was bright enough to light the party. Libby and her family were seated at the table closest to the center of the stage. She looked around and was grateful her knights and Ladies were letting their hair down and having a good time.

Corrine did well, as usual. After everyone had been served, Fintan took the stage for an epic tale about Libby's bravery and her many accomplishments. She hated being the center of attention, so was relieved when the band took the stage and tables were cleared away to make room for dancing.

Libby was exhausted, as usual, but when Fynnigan pulled her out on the dance floor she couldn't resist. She loved dancing and he'd always been a great dancer. And it made everyone laugh to see her let loose. She watched him shaking his groove thing, with that shaggy blonde hair falling over brilliant blue eyes and couldn't help but see the little boy she'd once known. He'd grown into a fine young man, a skilled warrior, and was as brilliant as he was beautiful. He had her twirling all over the dance floor until she was so winded, she just couldn't do it anymore. He escorted her, laughing, back to her chair and kissed her hand with flourish and a bow. "Thank you for the dance, M'lady."

She laughed and waved him off to the attentions of all the single ladies. "Get out there to your fan club, Fynn." He flashed her a naughty grin and made his way back to the dance floor. When no one was paying attention, Libby discreetly headed back to the palace to get some rest.

Corrine was happy. She loved it when people enjoyed the events she coordinated. Since she never left Kingdom with her sister, she hadn't seen Libby out on the dance floor since she and Dale were courting. It felt good to see it again. She hoped it wasn't the last time. She knew the strain her sister was under, even if she kept it hidden. A little joy wasn't too much to ask for, and tonight she'd seen Libby's face relax and laugh like the old times.

The last of the stragglers were leaving at dawn, but the field was littered with sleeping people. The kitchen crew was busy preparing vats of coffee and a greasy breakfast to help people make their way home.

Technology existed in the Kingdom alongside magic, but some things must be done the old-fashioned way for tradition's sake. That included setting out on a quest on horseback, despite the modern Kevlar tactical gear and body armor, night vision goggles, and guns alongside swords.

The day before they set out, Libby was shocked into silence to see Fintan arrive at the palace, with his pack and mandolin. Even more shocking was what he was wearing. He was dressed for official travel.

"What are you doing here, Finn?" she finally stuttered, confused.

"Isn't it obvious? I'm going with you," he snarked, rolling his eyes. "All good quests need a bard along to preserve the heroic deeds in song and verse. And as Poet Laureate, it's my duty. I don't trust anyone else to do it properly."

"Are you kidding me?" she asked with a smile that took over her whole face.

He smiled back. "I'm sure I'll regret it, but I can't let you go without me."

"You know it requires horseback?" she asked.

"Yes, and I'll complain the whole way, but I'm going. Plus, you'll need a musician to aid in your healing, and you know there is no one better than me."

"And no one more modest." She chuckled as she watched Fintan head to the stables to pick out a horse, his sky-blue cloak trailing behind him. She'd given him that cloak when he first moved to the Kingdom and accepted the role of Poet Laureate. It matched his blue eyes and seemed fitting for a prize-winning poet, although he was embarrassed and found it pretentious. He hated expensive things, and since he couldn't wear it in the Normal world, it seemed excessive. She'd designed a crest for him, an Irish yew with a quill and mandolin, embroidered in silver thread on the back, and the edges embroidered with ash trees, her crest. She hadn't seen him wear it in years. For the second time since Dale had died, the Queen felt something that reminded her of happiness and hope, and a big grin appeared on her face.

The morning finally dawned when the questers departed on their journey. Libby still fought the urge to curl up and hide from the world, but she had a responsibility to her people, and two realms to save.

Sophia and Krystal remained behind to do their best to protect the force field and assist the Regents.

It was an impressive group that set out on horseback. The knights rode white horses out of tradition. LIWs could choose the color of their horses, although all chose black for an aesthetic contrast to the knights' white steeds. Libby set out on Hoss, the only red horse in the bunch. Leaving him behind after his heartbreak over losing Dale would have killed him. Together, he and Libby found distraction from their grief and loneliness in the mission at hand. They found purpose.

Fintan had selected a silver-gray mare, and it suited him. His silver hair and blue cloak made for a striking figure. *If he's not careful,* Libby thought to herself, *that blue-eyed silver fox will end up the subject of someone else's song or poem.* The rest of the group was cloaked in a deep navy with Libby's ash tree crest embroidered on the borders and their individual crests embroidered on their backs. Libby, Kurtis and Dyanna alone were in the emerald green of the royal family, the ash tree crest sparkling on the back, with a border that included the crests of all the knights and LIWs. Sean hated this since it made it easy to identify who they were, but there was no worry about being singled out as targets in the Kingdom, and Libby believed her people needed to see it. Pomp and circumstance were important to morale. She'd compromised and all three were wearing Kevlar underneath to make him feel better.

Once they got out of sight of the seaside forest city, they relaxed the processional formation. Geoffrey and Scarlett didn't like Libby out front, so after their first break, when everyone packed away their cloaks and Libby stowed her crown, they slowly maneuvered her out of the lead. They weren't alone. The other knights and LIWs had the same idea, and when they saw what their chiefs were doing, it was just a matter of minutes before Libby was safely ensconced in the middle of the group. If Libby noticed, she didn't have the energy to argue. The two heirs were also quickly enveloped by their seniors. Awen rode close to Geoffrey, Scarlett, and the Queen. Fintan picked up the rear.

Days on horseback are tough on even confident riders if they aren't used to it. Except for Kendra and Kurtis, none of them went out on multi-day rides if they could help it. John hated horses, and Fintan was out of practice. Dyanna was the newest to horseback. She liked how tall they were, giving her a better vantage point to see. However, she didn't like how that made the ground a lot further away if she fell. The first day was uncomfortable, but the third day was brutal. She hurt in places she didn't know she had and was complaining almost as much as Fintan.

They'd just arrived on the outskirts of Wexford and knew they were going to get a break from camping. Hot showers and a pub were a lovely break after three nights of sleeping outdoors. They'd avoided Dublin and the larger towns but were all looking forward to a few weeks in the town famous for its opera. Wexford was one of those border towns that made a perfect portal point between the Kingdom and the Normal world. With all of the music magic there, it was also a great opportunity to give Fintan and Awen a break without sacrificing Libby's health.

"My arse is killing me!" Fintan groaned as he slid out of the saddle.

"Mine too," Dyanna chimed in. "Pretty sure the men of Wexford are safe." She patted her horse's mane and gave her a hug before turning towards the stables.

There were a few chuckles, especially after Cristina loudly proclaimed, "Speak for yourself, Dy!"

Fintan rolled his eyes. He couldn't stand the impropriety, but knew he was a dinosaur when it came to etiquette. The laughter ended quickly when Dyanna noticed the look on her aunt's face. Libby didn't often get angry, but the raised eyebrows and frown were an early warning sign of disapproval.

"Dyanna, that's inappropriate commentary for an heir to the throne."

"Whatever, Aunty Libby." Dyanna laughed sheepishly over her shoulder, but she toned it down. She knew that look since her mom wore it often, and she knew her aunt must be on a short temper to correct her publicly. When she noticed Kurtis snickering, she shot him a glare that would have made her mom and aunt proud. *Boys have it so much easier,* she thought angrily. *I wonder if Leia has these problems.*

"Lighten up, Libby," Cristina snorted. "She gets that sass from you." She gave her horse a good brushing. The look shifted from Dy to Cristina, and the LIW let out a quiet, "Well, okie dokie then."

Libby was exhausted and uncharacteristically grumpy.

The entire group got busy unloading and stabling the horses as quickly as possible. Fynnigan had secured a country estate on the outskirts of town that had its own stables and was large enough for their party, although most of them would be doubling up in rooms, including Libby. Not that Larra would have given her the option even if they'd had the space for private rooms.

Libby had fallen into bed fully dressed, without dinner, and immediately fell asleep. She awoke in Maggie's cottage, sitting on the floor cushions. A pot of tea was steeping on the low table next to them. Libby smiled as she realized she could now see Maggie's blue aura easily, and without effort. "Hello Maggie, blue is a lovely color on you."

Maggie smiled. "So, you can see it now? Without effort? Excellent. How is it going with your wizards?"

Libby shook her head and chuckled. "Well, Krystal is trying to teach me how to see the energy from crystals. I'm not quite there yet, but with some concentration I can see all three of their energy auras. It's pretty incredible. And beautiful. It's like a whole other layer of luminescent colors no one has named yet."

Maggie looked at Libby and asked, "What about yours? What color is yours?"

"Mine?" Libby asked. "Why would I need to see mine?"

"It's all about seeing different kinds of energy. You've denied this part of you for your entire life. If you're going to be a complete person, you need to figure out who you are, and this is part of it. You know how most people see themselves differently than others do?"

Libby thought about this. She and Dale had talked about this often. He saw things in her she never recognized and didn't really believe were true. "Yes, is it like that?"

"Not quite. Your energy aura is the same no matter who's looking at it. But you need to see it for what it is, see yourself for you who are. Try it."

Libby looked around for a mirror, and Maggie started laughing. "No child, you don't need a mirror. You're going to use your mind's eye for this one."

Libby bit her lip and took a deep breath. She closed her eyes and focused her intention inwards. She didn't see anything but kept breathing and concentrating. Maggie could see she was struggling, and the soft mandolin began playing in the background. Libby willed herself to surrender, just like she did with the music, and felt herself floating. She realized she was somehow in her heart center. She felt safe, light, and loved. She looked around and saw that she was completely engulfed by a glowing pink light. She smiled when she realized she'd found her core, her magic. This was what she looked like. This was who she was. She started giggling.

Maggie was grinning at her when she opened her eyes, still giggling. "Well dear? What is it?"

"Pretty in pink. Only all glowy and sparkly. And warm and happy."

"Well done, child. You've just taken the first step to recognizing who you are. Whenever you have doubts, especially when you're doubting yourself, this is the place to come back to."

The questers were taking a leisurely pace so Libby could get in lots of training during the day. Although the change of scenery for Libby was the main purpose of their excursion, not far behind was the opportunity to travel the entire length of the force field so Fynnigan could evaluate the strength of the barrier. He'd often saddle his horse and disappear for hours, leaving the rest of the group behind so he could inspect it as methodically as he felt it needed, no matter how long it took. It meant long periods of time camping, so they made the most of any time they could in towns and villages.

They may not have coined the phrase, "work hard, play hard," but they sure put it to the test. Their second night in Wexford, Libby and John hit the local pub, just like they always did. Neither of them counted on the effects her still healing heart would have on her alcohol consumption, and she spent two days throwing up from alcohol poisoning. It was ugly, and painful. The LIWs were livid with John, blaming him for Libby being out of commission.

"That's enough!" John fought back, after Fynnigan started in on him. "Look, I would never do anything to hurt Libby, you know that. She needed a break. She wanted to go out. Neither of us had any indication that her heart situation might have such an effect. I don't need every single one you to explain the Queen's weakened immune system to me. I get it. Until she fully regenerates her heart, we must keep her as far away from whiskey as possible. Just don't forget she's Libby, and she does what she wants. She always has. I was just along for the craic, but I won't let it happen again."

The Queen snapped out of her meditation suddenly, still feeling the lingering gaze of the golden-brown eyes fixed upon her. She'd gone under a healing meditation so didn't know why he was there, but it felt like he was watching her. Whomever he was. In the vision she looked up to see the stranger's eyes staring at her through a black ski mask. She was startled, but not afraid. At first, she thought it was Dale, but no. He had hazel eyes. These eyes were golden brown, like a lion. Or a wolf. Whomever this man was, she knew they were destined to meet. She didn't understand why his identity was hidden, that had never happened before, but she knew he was looking for her, even if he didn't know it yet. She was now wide awake and looked at the clock. Great, she thought. Just midnight. She couldn't shake the sensation of that intense connection, eyes locked. So strange.

Maggie had explained in one of her dream sessions how the visions worked, but that they weren't a training priority right now. Libby couldn't stop thinking about it. There was something about him, a feeling that was familiar.

That night she tossed and turned for hours, unable to fall asleep with those eyes staring back at her from her memory.

"Would you like some tea?" the tiny voice pierced the darkness.

"No, thank you, Larra. I'm sorry if I'm keeping you awake."

"You toss and turn like an elephant," she complained. "Your highness," she added as an afterthought.

Libby laughed as she rolled over and willed herself to sleep, knowing that she needed to train with Michie that night.

Chapter 14

Music, Magic, and Men

It's a motherfucker being here without you
Thinking 'bout the good times, thinking 'bout the bad
And I won't ever be the same

It's a motherfucker getting through a Sunday
Talking to the walls
Just me again
But I won't ever be the same

It's a motherfucker how much I understand
The feeling that you need someone to take you by the hand
And you won't ever be the same
You won't ever be the same
~The Eels, "It's a Motherfucker"

usicians are all magic workers at some level. Some could actually weave spells, and the colors would form patterns that oozed out from the stage into the audience. Music could calm. Music could get them worked up. Music could make them sad, happy, angry, or even confused. There was a reason people were drawn to musicians, even in the non-magic world. They sensed the healing power the music had, no matter what the genre. Most musicians fell into the healer category, but a few used their gift for other purposes.

Libby had always loved music, and she still had a desperate need to surround herself with as much music as possible. Fintan did his best but would get worn out, so each evening they were in a town Libby could be found in the back-corner booth at a local pub or concert hall, soaking up as much music as she could. After full days of fighting practice in the ring and training with Awen, she was always ready for a music break before more training while she was asleep.

With Maggie's continued instruction, and a lot of practice, she could now see energy as easily as she could feel it and was able to experience music in multiple dimensions. She could see the energy originate at the point the music started. Whether fingers on strings, vibrations emanating from a drum, or wind from a flute, it started like the flame from a lit match, flaring out and then softening as it spread out in waves. The effect on her was always the same: her pupils dilated slightly, her mouth opened, and she fell into the music magic like sinking into Dale's embrace. All music had a healing component, even when it came from a person with no magical talent. But when someone with magic was playing, it permeated the soul. That's where she could absorb it, shore up her own energy, and allow her broken heart to heal faster and with less pain than through meditation alone. In those moments, her pain and loneliness were forgotten. Because she was sensitive to the energy, the effects were even more impactful. The stronger the musician, the stronger the response.

She'd tried explaining it to Fintan who, coming from the Normal world, was curious. "It's as if the wall between this reality and the next thins, and I can almost reach through it to the other side. Have you ever looked through a window covered in running rain water? You can see but the water is flowing, and the view isn't quite clear? It's like that. Suddenly there is no sense of up; I'm falling into the other side. It's beyond bliss. I can't explain it properly, but my soul yearns to be there as much as that place wants me to be."

It also worked in reverse, in a strange symbiotic relationship. The musicians were able to absorb the energy their audience gave back. Her enjoyment of the music was powerful. The musicians could feel what she was doing—consuming the music energy they released when they performed and returning it—even if they didn't immediately realize who she was.

Few people knew that the magic each musician created had a different flavor and color, just like the different genres of music. While most music magic had a cinnamon orange sunset glow, others were the vibrant hues of the sky on fire—magenta, purple, gold, and even red. She'd once attended a performance of the Ulster Orchestra and it was like an aurora borealis inside Ulster Hall, all pink and green, bouncing off the green in all the landscape paintings that surrounded the upper seats. She couldn't figure out who was creating it, but she'd soaked it up. She'd gone back more than once and it never happened that way again, so she'd guessed it was the visiting conductor.

Libby was always hungry for more than just their magic. In a pub environment, they almost always came up to introduce themselves at a break. It was then she would get to learn their stories and know them as people. When they didn't, she'd send up a drink for them anyway.

Tonight, the music of the opening band had been good enough, and Libby was tired. She'd decided she was done for the evening and stood up from the table. At that moment the room started to spin. The Queen reached out for the table to steady herself, but it was too far away. She felt herself falling and was mortified. Before Libby hit the floor, hands reached out to grab her. She looked up into dark eyes that were smiling back at her. She was embarrassed and croaked out a pathetic, "I don't normally fall for handsome strangers" line.

By this time her escorts were on full alert, but Libby only had eyes for the handsome musician, who was smiling bemusedly back at her and still cradling her head in his muscular arms. Fynnigan stepped up to them, hand on his holster out of habit more than a perceived threat, and said, "Thank you, we'll take it from here." Fynn and Leia got the Queen seated until she could catch her breath. Once she'd recovered, they escorted her out of the pub and back to the estate where they were staying, leaving the musician watching with a confused grin on his face as he finished setting up. He was the final performance of the evening.

Libby's training continued daily, both during waking hours and when she was dreaming, but her chakra healing wasn't progressing fast enough. Awen had been dreading this conversation, but finally had to share the instructions Maggie and Michie had given her.

Goddess help me, she prayed to herself. "You're making good progress, Libby. We just need to step it up."

"Step it up? What the hell? I'm pushing myself every day! And every night when I'm asleep! What could I possibly do to step it up?" Libby demanded, instantly defensive.

"Well, in order to be at full power when you face Jasper, you need to clear and balance your chakras. With your daily yoga and meditation exercises, your energy is clearing, but you still have some chakra blockage. With everything that happened, I'd expect that. Although your heart chakra is doing well, as are your upper chakras. It's your lower chakras that are still blocked. Your fear is not helping you. We can work on some of that with continued reiki, but other things only you can fix."

Libby pouted in silence. Of course she was afraid. Who wouldn't be? She decided she'd work on her red root chakra and try to meditate through the fear, so was surprised by what came next.

"I see a lot of orange today, but it's muddy. What's going on?"

The Queen looked sheepish. "Orange, huh? That's a surprise. Well, I sort of met someone. Well, not exactly met someone. I felt attracted to someone for the first time since Dale. Is that weird? Is it too soon?"

Awen fought back the huge grin that threatened to take over her face. She knew she needed to proceed cautiously. "No, that's great. And human. I hate to break it to you super woman, you are as human as the rest of us, and you need to experience physical pleasure if you're going to fully open your sacral chakra. Clearly music and good cooking aren't enough. Tell me about him."

"I don't really know anything about him. Not even his name. I was at the pub last night and on my way out, I got dizzy and fell. This gorgeous man caught me before I hit the floor. I was so embarrassed. And then confused. I'd turned that part of my life off when Dale was injured, like flipping a light switch off. Not a second thought.

This was the first time I've felt attraction to a man other than Dale. It's strange." Libby had been unconsciously cracking her knuckles, a nervous habit she'd had since childhood. Awen hated that sound and let a look of disgust and revulsion cross her face before recovering her calm demeanor.

"Listen Libby, I'm not going to give you advice here. Goddess, only knows how messed up my love life is, but I will say it's a good thing. You're young and healthy, heart--regrowing aside, it's normal. Just remember to be safe."

"Oh, for fuck's sake," Libby snapped back, blushing. "I don't need a safe sex lecture. And what's up with your love life? What's going on with you and Geoffrey?"

"Nice deflection. I'm not going to talk about it with you. But as your wizard I *need* to hear every dirty little detail about yours so I can best take care of you."

They both burst into laughter at Awen's naughty grin and her eyebrows bouncing up and down like a drunk letch at the local pub. When Libby started blushing the laughter got even louder and uncontrolled. At least laughter was good medicine.

The rest of the day was pretty typical for Libby. Morning Yoga. Lessons with Kurtis and Dyanna. Physical training, usually a run with whomever was around. Meditation. Magic practice with Awen. Weapons training with Will. It was a grueling regimen for someone with a full heart, but Libby never complained. She always reminded herself that there was music to enjoy at the end of the day, and she could put her feet up and relax and let someone else do the work for a change.

That night Libby headed back to the pub for more music. There was nothing out of the ordinary about that, but her sharp-eyed friends noticed she took a little more care with her appearance. Even the knights noticed she had a spring in her step she hadn't had in a long time. *Is she wearing lipstick?* John wondered. Something was up, and they wanted to know what it was. So instead of her normal pair of escorts, this time, everyone went. If Libby was annoyed, she didn't let it show. They all deserved a night of fun.

When they arrived at the pub, she nodded at the owner and headed to her normal booth. The handsome muscle man from the night before was already on stage singing. When he saw her come in, he gave her a dazzling smile and she smiled back. She got up to order a round of drinks for her team, sending one up to Galen McIntyre and his band. From her booth, she could study him under the guise of appreciating his music. His music magic was an unusual color, a deep brown like melted chocolate, and for a moment she wished she could taste his music. Damn, he was a sexy, brawny, bear of a man. If you put a buffalo plaid flannel shirt on him and an axe in his hand he'd be on the cover of a Men of Lumberjacking calendar or a roll of paper towels. Surprising body type for a musician. She was blushing now, and it didn't go unnoticed.

Leia frowned and began her own study of the musician. Anyone they didn't know was a threat, and they knew nothing about this man Libby was making googly eyes at.

On his break, Galen came over to inquire if she was feeling better.

"Good evening, m'lady. I couldn't help but see you back tonight and wanted to make sure you were fully recovered."

Libby blushed and laughed, "I'm quite recovered, thank you. And please, none of that m'lady nonsense, Galen. It's Libby."

After her rapid departure the night before, he'd figured out she was important enough to warrant an escort, piquing his interest. She'd just introduced herself as Libby. There was only one Libby who would warrant an escort and be this awkward. This had to be Libby McGregor. Everyone in the kingdom knew their widowed queen was traveling while she was still in recovery and training. This had to be her. He felt himself smile as he realized the Queen was flirting with him. He could see her friends hated it, and that made him like it even more. So he made it a point to sit a little closer, and after his gig he stayed. He got her out dancing to the music of the next band, something he never did.

By this point they were all on alert. Scarlett hadn't seen Libby blush like that since the night she'd met Dale. John, Awen, and the two juniors were the only ones who seemed genuinely pleased the Queen was having fun. She seemed happy, and they'd missed that. Fynnigan didn't have any strong feelings about it; he'd known Libby long before she'd met Dale, but he quickly picked up on the concern of the others and decided to do something about it. So, he headed out on the dance floor to cut in. Cristina used the opportunity to get her hands on Galen and see if he felt as muscular as he'd looked from the stage. John, who couldn't stand anyone having fun without him, cut in on Fynnigan. Fintan couldn't stand to be outdone by John and was having none of that, so he made his way out on the floor and tapped John on the shoulder.

"My turn, Morgan. Beat it."

"Whatever you say, Grandpa. Libby, I'll be back when O'Toole needs to go take his nap."

Fintan rolled his eyes but expertly had Libby on the other side of the dance floor in no time.

"What the hell, Finn? What is going on? No one ever dances with me, let alone everyone, and never you."

"Why Aisling, I'm chagrined. We're on a quest. Why wouldn't I want to dance with one of my dearest friends and my queen?"

"I dunno, maybe because you never dance?" Although as the words were leaving her mouth, she realized what a smooth dancer he was. "Where did you learn to dance?"

Before he could answer, Galen was twirling her away from the group, despite Fynnigan and Cristina dancing their way closer. By now Dyanna and Kurtis had also hit the dance floor with the awkward enthusiasm of teenagers who have never danced with the opposite sex before but were trying to fit in with the rest of the group.

"Wow. You're the belle of the ball tonight. What's the occasion?" Galen said, his hand firm on her waist.

"Oh, we're just traveling together and it's been a while since we've had some fun. Apparently, they took my smack-talking a bit too seriously and it became a challenge," she lied.

He raised his eyebrows, flashed a smile at the group that watched them like hawks, and turned his attention back to Libby. "I like a good challenge," he said.

She laughed and blushed at the same time. "Who says I'm a challenge?" she flirted back. Libby could hear the words she was saying and the giggling that followed. She didn't think she'd had that much to drink and was unnerved by her brazen behavior. She never behaved this way when she was in the kingdom. That was always saved for her time out in the Normal world. Any concerns she had were quickly replaced with the rush of infatuation that flooded her every time Galen smiled at her.

"Uh oh," whispered Scarlett. "I know that look. What do we do?"

"We do nothing," said Awen under her breath. "This needs to happen."

Libby swooned for Galen. He was tall, dark and handsome, and an intense free spirit. He was also a hot mess of a tortured artist who drank too much and always seemed to be drowning in angst and drama. The exact opposite of the kind of man the King had been.

The attraction was immediate and intense. The same way she felt falling into a poem, or soul-moving music, she couldn't quite breathe when she was near him. Everything got shimmery as if she was looking at life through the rainbow edge of a bubble before it popped. Warm. Swooning. Magnetic. When one would breathe in, the other would breathe out. Synchronous orbit. She'd never felt that way about a person before. Not even the King. Their relationship was different. Strong, built on friendship and trust and mutual respect. This was... magic. She was on the edge of the cliff, peering over the edge to see how far she could go without falling.

Galen wooed her with poetry and songs of chivalry and love. He described her the way he would the object of desire in one of the love songs he sang, calling her 'Pet' and 'Sweetheart' and 'My Darling.' She was lonely for male companionship, and she ate it up. Once upon a time the corny lines would have made her laugh with derision. Now, when she heard him tell her that she brought joy to his heart like the sun on a dreary Irish day, she found it romantic. When he caressed her hair, looked deep into her eyes and told her she needed someone to love and take care of her, she instantly forgot that she knew how to take care of herself. After being alone, and in so much pain for what felt like an eternity, he made her feel special. He made her feel beautiful.

The knights were concerned. Fintan hated him instantly, but no amount of warning would slow her down. Even John was doubtful, and he was usually the first one to encourage questionable behavior. The knights began to have offline discussions about the risks of this relationship. They wanted Libby to be happy again but there was something about this man they just couldn't trust. Fynnigan was torn, but finally contacted Sean to see what they could find out about Galen McIntyre. It felt like an invasion of Libby's privacy, but as point on field security, he just couldn't take the risk.

The LIWs were less suspicious of him. A few knew that Libby trusting herself and finding happiness with a man was a critical piece in the Queen's healing. But how to balance that with their fear that he was going to hurt her? There were no easy answers. Add in the fact that Libby was smitten with him, and they wouldn't have been able to get her away from him if they wanted to. They knew how stubborn she was, and the more she was advised against something, the deeper she'd dig her heels in. Even if she knew the warnings were right. They wanted to tread lightly to avoid pushing her in the wrong direction.

"Libby. Wake up."

"Yes, Grandmother. Is it time to train?" Libby realized it wasn't Michie, but Maggie who was tapping her foot impatiently as she appeared in Libby's dream. Libby had been out at the pub with Galen until the wee hours of the morning and hadn't left much time for dreaming.

"No. It's time for us to have a conversation. You need to be careful."

"Of what?"

"The music magic is necessary to help you heal, but too much of a good thing is dangerous. You are at risk of addiction. It happens sometimes, and that's what I see when I look at you and the musician together. Once addicted, it's difficult to reverse it. You must find a new way to get your music. Stay away from that man."

Libby's voice rose as her temper flared, all the anger and frustration of her loneliness for Dale boiling to the surface. "What? But why? I like him. He makes me happy. Am I supposed to be alone the rest of my life?"

"No, Libby, but he isn't the one. He will only drag you down. There is something not right about him. The one for you will be there and will love the real you. But in order for that to happen you must accept who you are and love yourself first."

"What does that even mean?" Libby shouted, but it was too late.

Libby woke to the soft sounds of Maggie's repeated, "Stay away from him," fading away. Groaning, she rolled over and tried to go back to sleep, quickly realizing that it was too late. She was wide awake. Despite the months she spent sleeping in the bedroom next to Dale's, it was still so strange to wake up to an empty bed. She didn't know which would be worse, waking up reaching for him only to realize he wasn't there, or the day she would no longer reach for him at all. She decided both were horrible. She felt her heart clench and the tears well up from deep within and fought them back. She focused on her breathing to regain control. Once she felt the tears back off, she sighed and got out of bed to search for coffee. She'd have preferred a breakfast bourbon but the wizards were pretty clear that wasn't a good idea. "Coffee it is." She needed to get up anyway, since she had an early morning session with Awen. She sighed, wishing she could go back to bed and sleep for days. "No rest for the weary," she muttered to herself, stumbling off in search of coffee and her wizard.

After she was appropriately caffeinated, she and Awen got to work, but not before she asked her the question that had been burning in her mind after Maggie's warning.

"I was wondering if it was possible to get addicted to the music magic," Libby said.

"How would I know?" Awen absentmindedly replied as she referred to the scroll she was holding in one hand and reordered a healing crystal grid with the other.

"I just figured as one of my official court wizards you might actually research it," Libby snapped back.

"What? Oh, sorry. Yes, of course I'll research it. Why do you ask?"

Libby was still a bit indignant about her conversation with Maggie, so replied, "I was just curious. I feel different when I'm that close to the magic, skin on skin close." She blushed. "Different than when someone is playing for me."

When Awen started laughing, Libby clarified, "I'm not talking about sex, that hasn't happened. I'm talking about him putting his hand on my arm or around my waist. The other night, he brushed the hair out of my face, and when his fingers grazed my cheek it was like music magic on steroids. And when I'm in the moment of the high, all I want is more. I crave it. I can't think about anything else."

"Interesting, ever thought maybe you're just craving physical touch in general?"

"Forget I brought it up," Libby huffed, eager to change the subject.

"Don't get defensive. It's a normal response, Libby." Awen changed the subject to get Libby focused on her training but made a mental note to ask Maggie in her next visit and to have Sophia and Krystal research it.

It was the team's last night in Wexford, and Libby was back at the pub with Galen. They were dancing and laughing and as the night progressed, they snuck off when no one was looking. The Queen woke in the middle of the night to find Larra speaking to her from the foot of his bed.

"Get up, it's time to go," Larra repeated. "Hurry."

She rubbed her eyes and blinked in confusion. Galen was gone, along with all of his things.

"Where is Galen?" she hissed.

"I don't know. But we have to hurry before anyone else notices you are gone."

Why would he just disappear? Libby wondered as she quickly dressed and made her way to the door. Something was wrong. She started to panic that she'd made a terrible mistake, but then reminded herself of how much he cared about her, and about all the things he'd said. There was no way he could have faked all that.

She quickly got dressed and headed back to the estate, hoping no one else had missed her. She was grateful Larra didn't try to talk about it. She was humiliated. This wasn't proper behavior for a Queen, let alone a grieving widow. Where was Galen? Why would he have left without saying good-bye?

The two women got settled back into their room without incident, and Libby rolled over towards the wall and quietly cried herself to sleep.

The next morning began early and with a few raised eyebrows. Libby had clearly been crying, and Larra quietly informed them that Galen had departed the night before, leaving out the embarrassing details. The knights and LIWs were never really sure of him, and they needed to leave anyway, so most viewed their leaving as a good thing, even though they knew Libby was taking it hard. It was an awkwardly silent start.

Chapter 15

Sometimes Life Is Shit for No Reason

Dale stood there in silence, glaring at the man as he rode out of town. He was glad Galen was out of Libby's life, that would have ended badly, but this just took a turn for the worse. He wanted to kill this man for daring to touch his wife but didn't have control over his form yet. He'd wanted to warn her that this man was manipulating her and that he was bad news but had promised Kokichi and the others that he wouldn't attempt to contact Libby again without their permission. So, he just seethed.

Sean was relieved to learn from Fynnigan that the musician was gone, but as head of security he couldn't take any chances, so he discreetly continued the search for information on Galen. Being Security Chief meant staying on top of all of it.

A week after he disappeared, Sean received the report that Galen had been found. He'd been located on his family farm in a far side of the Kingdom. He had a reputation for taking advantage of vulnerable women, especially widows, and was even heard describing himself as a Widow Hunter. After he'd have a few drinks at the local pub, he'd explain how the grieving were more susceptible to music magic, because they were sad and lonely. He'd laugh as he talked about leaving them wanting more, making a joke about the addictions he'd created. At least he'd had the common sense not to tell anyone about

Libby. Yet. Sean was disgusted that these men existed at all. The security chief knew Libby abhorred violence or would have taken measures to ensure Galen never did it again. For now, he let it go.

He sighed as he called to tell Geoffrey and Fynnigan so that they could inform the Queen. This was going to be messy. For once he was glad he didn't have to deliver the news.

Libby was meditating in her tent, a sheen of sweat covering her brow. This business of growing back her heart was hard work, but she was making good progress. Her concentration broke when the tent flaps opened and Geoffrey and Fynnigan entered.

"Apologies for the interruption," started Geoffrey.

"None needed, I'm due for a break." She took a closer look at them and saw Fynnigan shift his weight from foot to foot. "You have news?" she prompted.

"Yes. I'm not sure how to tell you this."

"Just spit it out, Fynn. The days of niceties are far behind us."

"Of course. Um, Libby, Sean has had trackers out looking for Galen since his disappearance. We wanted to make sure he was okay after his sudden departure. And we can't risk letting strangers get too close to you."

She felt herself hold her breath, and then forced herself to breathe. Breathe in. Breathe out.

"This is really awkward." He paused. He'd always been direct with her, but this was still hard. Fynnigan knew it would hurt her, and that he was the one who was going to deliver the blow. "Galen was found at his home. With his family. Libby, he's married with a wife, a truckload of kids, and a reputation for using magic to seduce women. You were too tempting and too convenient for him to pass up. I'm sorry."

Libby stood up shakily. She'd stopped listening once her brain processed that Galen had lied to her. He knew who she was. He had deliberately manipulated her, then left her. She felt like a fool, and her weak heart was screaming in pain. She headed outside the tent.

The two men hightailed it after her, but she waved them off. "I'm taking a walk," she shouted, "alone!"

She stumbled into the woods that surrounded the lake and made her way to the water's edge. It was here she fell to her knees. "Why?" She screamed at the sky. "Why would you give him to me only to take him away? Is this some colossal joke? Or punishment? Haven't I suffered enough?" She howled and screamed out her pain and her shame. The LIWs came running, Larra at the forefront. Geoffrey reached out a hand to stop her. He and Fynnigan had followed the Queen but kept a respectful distance. This was so horribly awkward. They'd have preferred to be heading out on horseback to give Galen an epic beat down, but they didn't have time for that.

Larra glared at Geoffrey but slowed her pace. Scarlett caught up and Fynnigan quietly gave her the update.

"Galen is married with a family," he reported. "He lied to her about everything. He's a self-described Widow Hunter. We had to tell her. She would have found out eventually and still had her heart broken. This way she has time to get through it and focus on regrowing her heart before she has to face Jasper."

"Are you fucking kidding me?" she demanded. "How much can one person take? This isn't fair. Please bring Awen up to speed, but let's try to be discreet about this. Next time make sure I'm there if you have to deliver shitty news like this. What the hell were you thinking?" she shouted as she head-slapped the young knight.

As Fynnigan returned to camp, rubbing the back of his head, Scarlett took a deep breath and made her way to Libby's side.

"Hey, Sweetie." She wrapped her arms around the Queen. "I'm so very sorry. I wish I could make it better." She made eye contact with Geoffrey and motioned for him to leave. This was going to be hard enough without everyone standing there watching her melt down. The LIWs would take it from here. They set up a subtle perimeter where they could aid if needed, and Geoffrey headed back.

"Why? What did I do to deserve this? I know it's stupid, but I honestly thought Dale had sent him to me. Why would he do this? What's wrong with me? It's too much!" Libby sobbed.

"I don't know." She stroked Libby's hair and let her cry it out. When her sobs quieted down, Scarlett rocked her like she would have her granddaughters, and brushed swaths of blue hair out of her face. "Sometimes life is shit for no reason. All I know is we are rarely given a choice, and there is nothing wrong with you. Being vulnerable is human, Libby. He played you."

The Queen looked up at her through her swollen eyes. "I lose either way," she sobbed. "If I win, I still lose because I'm alone and nothing I do will bring Dale back. If I lose, everyone dies."

Scarlett nodded. "No matter what, I love you my friend. No matter what, I know you will have done your best. That's all that matters."

"Why did Dale have to die and leave me all alone? What if we only get one chance in life to have that epic love? What if I'm doomed to spend the rest of my life alone?"

"I don't know, Sweetie, but I have to believe that our hearts, yours in particular, are big enough to love more than one person. Don't forget, you knew love before Dale. You're regrowing your heart. That means that you'll have room for as much love as you want."

Scarlett slowly stood up and helped the Queen to her feet. Larra materialized as if from thin air, with a flask of uisce beatha. After a good swig, Larra swapped it out for one of fresh water. "Here, this is what you really need. The other was just to take the edge off."

They headed back through the woods. Every few feet another LIW would fall in. By the time they made it to camp, Libby was surrounded by all six of her LIWs who escorted her back to her tent. Geoffrey wondered if Galen knew how at risk he was now that the Ladies-in-Waiting had found out he'd deceived their friend and Queen. The knights would be angry, but a group of furious LIWs would be deadly.

Scarlett and Harley got Libby to bed and had Awen help her with a sleep spell. Then she went to meet with Fynnigan and Geoffrey.

"She'll be okay, but this is really bad. What the hell happened? Why didn't we know this about him before he'd magicked his way into her bed?"

"He did what?!" Fynnigan sputtered, shocked. "I will fucking kill him!"

"No, you won't, Fynnigan. She's a grown woman. No matter how vulnerable she is right now, she can do whatever she wants. But we need to make sure we perform background checks on everyone who crosses her path, and sooner rather than later. There will be other people out there looking for a way into her world. It's our job to make sure that doesn't happen. Although, knowing Libby, she'll never again let anyone close enough to try, and that's not good either."

After seeing Libby safely to her tent with the rest of the LIWs, Dyanna had made a beeline to Kurtis and jerked her head towards the path in the woods indicating he should follow her. He jumped up and tried to look nonchalant as he hustled to catch up with her. As soon as they were out of ear shot Dyanna told him what had happened.

"You can't tell anyone else about this or I'll have to kill you. If Aunt Libby doesn't kill me first."

"I heard Geoffrey and Fynnigan shouting about something but couldn't hear what they were saying. Spill it. Is Aunt Libby okay?"

"I don't know." Dyanna pulled her blue hair out of her face and started pacing back and forth. "I don't know! I've never seen her like this. I mean, I know we're the youngest and all, but that jerk face Galen was a lying creep and seduced her and then disappeared. She's a wreck."

"What?" Kurtis shouted in disbelief. "What do we do? How dare he. Do we challenge him to a duel? Can we just kill him?"

"Don't be such a boy," Dyanna chided him, although she was furious for her aunt and thinking the same thing.

"We'll figure something out later, after Aunt Libby has battled the dragon. I'm just in shock. She's one of the smartest people we know. And I've never seen her like this… like a regular person who can get her heart broken. How could this have happened? I heard Scarlett say he used magic. If it can happen to Aunt Libby, how do we defend ourselves against something we can't even see?"

Kurtis shrugged his shoulders. He didn't know, but he was going to figure out a way to make it right. "Until we figure it out, we just have to be extra careful to watch anyone new that comes close to her."

Dyanna looked up at him. "Thanks for keeping it a secret. It's nice to have someone to talk to who doesn't look at me like I'm a kid who shouldn't be here."

"I know what you mean. I'll let you know if I hear them talking about anything else."

She gave him a quick hug, then yelled "Race you!" as she took off down the trail back to camp, Kurtis hot on her heels.

Libby was humiliated. And hurt. And angry. Not just angry, full of rage, an emotion she'd never really dealt with before. How dare he lie to her? How dare he gamble his children? Her healing heart was bruised, but not broken, and she set about the repair work like she did any other project. It was easier this time because it was only a patch job and she'd gotten used to the pain, although it took a while for his music magic spells to wear off. She was surly and short with everyone until it was out of her system. She vowed never to let herself be manipulated that way again. Could she be more of a cliché? The vulnerable lonely widow who gets sweet talked by the first jerk she meets. Un-fucking-believable. Maggie had been teaching her how to set protection spells. Despite the risk to her chakras, she set a ward to protect herself from opening her heart to anyone else.

Libby decided she needed some advice, so she called her sisters. They always treated her like their sister, before they treated her like a Queen. Right now, she needed to feel like a regular person.

"How are things going?" Libby inquired.

"Fine, although we miss you," Ava assured her. "How are you?"

"I've been better. To be honest, I don't have a clue what I'm doing. I'm making mistakes, and the loneliness hurts more than re-growing my heart. A heart that just got broken again. I feel like the Universe is punishing me for every bad decision I ever made. Maybe I deserve it. Corrine, do you remember that time after University when I almost left it all behind for a man?"

"The Viking. How can I forget? I almost had a heart attack since I was next in line. I didn't want that responsibility. That was your role.

I was happy just being a teenager while you were out traversing the globe. I never had that desire to leave the kingdom, but sure as heck didn't want to rule it."

"I know."

"Wait, what are we talking about?" asked Ava.

"You were probably too little to remember, but years before I ever met Dale, I fell madly in love with a guy I'd met on my travels. A Normal who had no idea who I was or that magic even existed. I was young and naively believed love could conquer all. But even before I could tell him who I really was, it all fell apart. That's when I came back to the Kingdom, tail between my legs to suck it up and do my duty. But, for a time, I was willing to turn my back on everything I was supposed to be, for him, for a chance at a life with him. Now I feel like the Universe is punishing me. Now I'm afraid my responsibility to my people will cost me anything resembling love."

"That's not true," Corrine jumped in. "The right man won't put you in a position to choose. It will just be."

"Yeah. I know. I married him. And now he's dead and I'm alone." Libby spared herself a self-pitying sigh, and then said, "At any rate, I wanted to tell you I love you two. I'm doing my best, even if it rarely feels good enough."

When the call ended, Corrine looked at Ava. "I'm worried about her. She's different. Resigned instead of resolved."

"It's just the grief," Ava assured her, although she was at a loss. She didn't know how to help her big sister, so she just told herself everything was fine. Her mind was spinning, though. It had never occurred to her that her eldest sister may not have wanted the throne. As the youngest, she'd been spared the bulk of the burden of family duty. Or was, until now.

Chapter 16

Firing on All Chakras

Fear can keep you safe and at the same time
kill off parts of you that are most alive.
~J.M. Storm

A few days after the bombshell about Galen, Awen finally told Scarlett about the need for Libby to keep trying with men. The two women were on an easy morning jog in the woods near their campsite. As full as their schedules were with meetings and training sessions, this was a way to kill two birds with one stone. She explained that clearing all of her chakras would be necessary for Libby to have a chance to defeat Jasper, and that involved opening her heart to a man.

"Are you joking? You saw what just happened with Galen. This is Libby we're talking about. There is no way she'll let another man close enough to even try. What the hell are we going to do?" Scarlett's head buzzed.

"I don't know. Somehow, we have to help her. I think we're going to need to tell the other ladies. It's going to have to be a team effort."

"You realize she'll kill us both."

"She can try," Awen laughed. "It's for her own good. It's for all our good. No matter how stubborn she is, she will always do her duty."

Scarlett sighed. "Okay. I'll meet with the rest of the team and we'll figure it out. You're going to have to work on convincing Libby."

"What? Why me?" Awen demanded, coming to a sudden stop

Scarlett continued jogging down the trail and shouted over her shoulder, "It's your idea. Besides, you're the wizard. Magic something up."

John was passing Libby's tent when he was startled by the sound of Libby angrily shouting at someone.

"No! Out of the fucking question! Get out! I want to be left alone."

John heard a woman's voice softly respond, but he couldn't make out the words. He waited, hand on his holster, to make sure Libby was okay.

"I will do no such thing! I don't give a flaming fuck if I die fighting that dragon. I will not do that again!"

John quickly realized it was probably Awen or Scarlett, and that Libby wasn't in danger. He didn't want to interrupt her if she was in that bad of a mood, so he continued on to the other side of camp.

Libby sat fuming after Awen had left. The universe had a twisted sense of humor if this was what she really needed to do.

"No fucking way!" she shouted to no one.

"Are you sure about that?" Michael's voice came from behind her.

She turned around to see the sweet boy smiling at her. "Hello, Michael. I'm afraid I'm not in a good mood right now. Perhaps you can come back later?"

"Nope. You need me now," he said as he plopped down on one of the cushions on the floor of her tent.

Libby took a deep breath and tried to get her emotions under control, taking the cushion opposite Michael.

"Mom, you know what you need to do," he said gently.

She looked into his eyes, and shook her head.

"You can do it. I'll help you. Just like last time. Mom, you have to take the wards down you put around your heart. It hurts you."

Libby shook her head again, unwilling to speak lest she start sobbing.

"Mom, you need to try. There has to be something good in what happened. Think hard. Find something to be grateful for in meeting him. Find something good in him. Then, forgive him. It's much harder to forgive someone who has wronged you, so you'll need to reach into your heart center. It will have to come from love. Once you've done that, you need to forgive yourself. I know that's the hardest for you. But you need to forgive yourself and trust yourself. You need to take down the wards. To deny yourself the possibility of love again only hurts you. I love you, and I don't want to see that. You deserve better than that. You deserve joy and happiness."

Libby would no longer make eye contact with him. He sat, staring at her a while longer.

"Okay, I'll go. Just please think about what I've said. Search your intuition. You know I'm right."

He stood up, leaned over to give her a kiss on the cheek and then was gone.

John noticed Libby was increasingly tense. They'd go for walks and regular battlefield practice, but she wouldn't talk about it and he wouldn't pry. It wasn't until he saw the growing concern and near panic in the wizard's eyes, and the fact that Scarlett's eyes never left the Queen that he decided it was time to take action. He'd observed the repeated attempts on the part of the LIWs to introduce her to men while they were out at the pubs. Libby would sometimes chat them up, but for the most part she'd get up and walk out of the pub frowning. Something was off and he wanted to know what it was.

He'd finally had enough waiting and decided to take Libby out on the town for classic John-and-Libby-shenanigans. He figured they'd have some fun, let off a little steam, and maybe he'd get her to talk. He'd waited until everyone was distracted and under the guise of one of their longs walks he snuck Libby away across the force field into Belfast to their favorite pubs.

They'd always managed to end up at Harp Bar whenever they went out, and tonight was no different. It was wall-to-wall people, as usual. No matter what day of the week it was, Harp was always packed; it was one of the reasons John and Libby liked it so much.

After a few drinks, and twirls around the dance floor, he looked at her. "Okay, Libster, what the hell is going on with you?"

Libby stopped laughing and downed her drink. "Well, John Leonard Morgan, whatever do you mean?"

He stared at her. "I'm serious Libby, I can see something isn't right. You're stronger than you've been in months, but something is fucking with you."

She burst into hysterical laughter. "Oh my Goddess, you have no idea how funny that is. It's the nothing fucking me that is what is fucking with me." She howled with laughter until tears streamed down her face, drawing the attention of those at the tables closest to them.

John burst into laughter and started teasing her. "You're horny! That's what's wrong with you! Libby, that's normal." It was a relief to see her laughing, really laughing.

"No, you don't understand. It's not that. I *have* to get some soon if I'm going to have a chance to defeat Jasper. This is the most fucked up thing I've ever heard. Pun intended." She collapsed in a fit of laughter once again.

"I don't get it."

"I'm not getting it either," she shrieked.

More laughter. By now they'd drawn the attention of most of the bar regulars and the bouncers who wanted in on the joke. Fortunately for the pair, most found watching the two of them laughing until they were crying funny enough to keep them from joining the conversation.

Libby finally stopped laughing long enough to wipe the tears away and get the words out. "Awen tells me that in order to defeat Jasper I must have all of my chakras unblocked and clear." She continued explaining at his confused expression. "There are seven chakras, or energy centers in our bodies. Each has a different color and qualities. Well, since Dale died, I've been working on healing all of them, but the one that pertains to getting busy. After the disaster with Galen I shut that down."

"And do others know?"

"Yes, Awen and the LIWs."

John roared. "Oh, Dear Lord, now it all makes sense." His stomach was starting to hurt from laughing so hard.

"Yeah, no matter how many men they push in front of me, I just can't. I don't find any of them remotely interesting, and all these first dates are painful."

"What? Dates? Sweet Jaysus, that's why they've been giving us all the extra nights off? For fuck's sake Libby, literally, if all you need is the Big O, you're looking at it wrong. You should have come to me in the first place. My God, leaving a group of women in charge of this was a horrible idea."

"What do you mean?"

"You just need to give yourself permission to have a good time, *without* worrying about a relationship. I know how you are; you think it has to mean something. It doesn't."

John ordered another round of drinks and proceeded to give her his advice. He told her to find a guy, but not get attached. "Libby, just make sure to totally bin him afterwards though. Shag 'im and ghost 'im. Save all the sloppy emotional stuff for the absolute one. Act like a dude. No attachments, no guilt, just fun. It's allowed. Whatever you do, don't fall in love."

"This coming from the guy who is so sentimental he carries an ancient suitcase because it belonged to his grandmother. And you needn't worry about my getting attached. After…what happened I set wards around my heart to prevent that."

"Touché. I'm impressed you remembered that story. But Geez, Libby, wards? I know I said don't fall in love, but it's you we're talking about. Didn't you say you had to experience the joy of it all? You have to open up your heart in order for this to work. Take those stupid wards down."

Libby stared into her glass and sighed. "Now you sound like Michael. I know. I figured I could do this without letting anyone get close. Fine then. I'll take the wards down and let full naughty mode commence.'"

"Yes, this pirate approves of full naughty mode. You have good badness about you Libby, as all girls should. This is totally okay. But maybe it's better if you stick to guys here and not the Kingdom. Here not as many people know you."

"Righto."

"And don't make it so complicated. The less talking the better."

"Sweet Jaysus, you're romantic. Tell me again how you convinced your wife to marry you?"

John didn't get to answer because at that moment both of their phones started ringing. Their absence had been noticed, and not appreciated.

While no one could say much to Libby, John incurred the wrath of Sean via phone, Fynnigan, and Geoffrey. They were all yelling at him, when he cut them off. "She wasn't in any danger but needed to be off the grid. And before you start again, I know what she needs. You need to mellow the fuck out and let me do my job as Queen's Knight Grand Champion." He stormed off to his tent.

Scarlett and Awen were secretly relieved, and finally shared this bit of information with Geoffrey. It was understandably awkward for him, but he also laughed. Dale would have found this hilarious. He was also relieved that John was, in fact, exactly what Libby needed in a Champion. He'd figure out a way to get Fynnigan and the other knights to back off.

Meanwhile, Libby finally followed her son's instructions. Maggie had told her that when she felt doubt, to return to her heart center. So that's what she did.

"Here goes nothing," she whispered to herself.

She grasped the talisman that Krystal had given her before they'd departed, and let the pink glow wash over her, washing her clean of the pain and guilt of her encounter with Galen. She searched for, and found, reasons to be grateful for Galen. He'd reminded her that she was still alive, and what she'd been missing, even if it wasn't real. She realized his behavior reflected his own pain and suffering and had nothing to do with her. She decided that it wasn't a mistake, but a learning experience. Digging deep into her heart center, she found love and forgave them both. And though she was still hesitant, she released the wards she'd set around her heart.

She felt rather than saw Michael smiling at her.

Chapter 17

A Belfast Break

A fter making the decision to take a few weeks off in the regular world, Libby settled down to her favorite activities: hanging out in pubs and listening to music. John had come with her. Scarlett was dead set against her going out on her own, but even she knew she'd be safe. Libby definitely needed a break from training and the reminder of what she still had to do. And though Libby had forgiven him, any opportunity to erase the memories of Galen McIntyre would be worth it. She begrudgingly let her go. *Funny*, Libby thought. *I figured it would be Sean and Fynnigan who'd give me the hardest time.* She left them all to take some well-deserved time off with their loved ones.

She grabbed a table in the back of the pub and waited for the evening's musician to arrive. It took a while to realize that this was the first time she'd been at the Duke of York since the night Dale was injured. She was sitting alone since Dee wasn't able to make it on short notice and John hadn't arrived yet. Not a big deal. She'd shown up unannounced, and this was Belfast. It was safe, and with her bartender friends keeping an eye out, no one would bother her. She looked around the pub. It wasn't crowded yet, so there were still a few copper-topped tables available. The sheer quantity of whiskey memorabilia on the walls and ceiling was overwhelming to someone with minimalist taste, but the music, whiskey, and people were what kept her coming back to the Duke every time she was in town. When tourists had a vision of an Irish pub, this was it.

They didn't say who was playing, which wasn't unusual. Irish musicians were often loosey goosey about time and showing up, so most pubs had back-ups on deck as needed. As she nursed her whiskey, she noticed him come in the side door. Long dark hair, golden eyes, and a disarming smile. He was tall and trim but had the swagger of a man who knows he's got it all and can have even more. As he was setting up, she realized she recognized him. He was a big name in American Country music and currently lived in Nashville. Nashville and Belfast were sister cities and shared a long musical connection. She remembered reading he was originally from Ireland but wondered what he was doing there in the pub that night.

As famous as he was for his chart-topping music, he was equally infamous for his womanizing. The confirmed bachelor and self-described lovable rogue had a thing for the ladies. Confident, charming, and a smooth talker, it wasn't about the conquest. It was all about the challenge. He ignored the groupies who threw themselves at him. No, the more unavailable or uninterested a woman was, the more he dialed up the charm. If he was a hunter, he'd be bagging big game somewhere. It was the thrill of the chase for this Belfast boy who'd made it big.

Despite his regular road crew, when he played back home, he did his own set up. He never charged the pub for the performance, just made them promise to keep it a secret until he took the stage. It kept him close to his roots, and he loved the intimate venue. He could see more from the stage in places like this than he could in the large arenas. He came from a long line of music men. Generations ago one of them had married a wizard. His great-great-grandfather didn't know it, but that union would infuse musicians for generations with the ability to unknowingly create magic when they played. It may have been one reason he'd been so successful. His latest album, *Brash as Fuck*, had hit triple platinum in record time.

He'd noticed her watching him as he was setting up and wondered who she was. She was pretty enough, but not what anyone would describe as beautiful. A hint of exotic, perhaps? You didn't see too many multi-ethnic women in Belfast, and it made her stand out. And then there was the whole blue hair bit. It was her confidence he found attractive. She had bearing, even sitting alone, that warranted further investigation.

He lost her attention when her male companion arrived. Rohan wrinkled his nose at the sight of them together. They didn't look like they belonged together at all. He continued to observe while he finished setting up. They were obviously close. They were sitting closer than business associates and had an intimacy that was apparent as they leaned into each other. But, perhaps not a romantic one. He was a tall man, so his arm around her seemed a practical way to spread out rather than a romantic gesture. Friends? Relatives? He wondered.

She felt him watching her and looked up at him in time to meet his gaze. She smiled, and something about that smile issued the challenge. A fun one. He'd never let a man stop him from going after a woman he wanted.

So, he watched her. *Tonight just got interesting*, he thought to himself as he flashed her one of his famous smiles and started to play.

Her eyes widened as she saw the familiar sunset glow emanating from his fingertips. *For fuck's sake*, she thought. *Tonight just got interesting*. She got up and ordered another round of whiskeys and had the bartender send down a pint for Mr. Rohan Fitzpatrick. "What are you doing here, magic man?" she whispered into her glass.

While he was playing, Libby tore her attention away and took the opportunity to talk to John.

"I appreciate your willingness to come with me but think you should use this break to visit your family."

"What are you talking about? You want me to leave the party early?" John demanded, pretending to be wounded.

"We both know that time could be short. Neither of us knows what will happen. Spend this time with your wife and son. You know I'll be fine here. It's Belfast." She insisted.

John ran his fingers through his long blonde waves while he thought about it. It was a nervous habit whenever he was deep in thought. He knew she'd be fine, and that she was right.

He broke out into a grin and said, "Well, there's no time like the present."

He drained his whiskey, leaned over to kiss her on the cheek and stood up to leave. "Catch you in a few Libby. And thanks. Don't be good while I'm gone."

She blew him a kiss and motioned him away as he turned and loped out of the pub into the night air and home.

Rohan rocked the house until it was time for his break. By now social media channels had let out that he was in town and playing on his old turf. He was mobbed by old and new fans alike. He shook hands, posed for photos, and eventually pulled away and made his way to where she was sitting.

"Thanks for the pint," he said as he slid into the booth beside her, pulling his shoulder length dark hair back into a ponytail. "Where's your friend off to?" motioning to the empty space John had filled just moments ago.

She just smiled, ignoring the question. "You're welcome for the pint. Least I could do. Your music isn't half bad. Duke of York was one of my first Belfast pubs and I always visit when I'm in town. I'm addicted to live music, and Belfast has the best out of everywhere I've been. Maybe tied with Nashville."

He smiled again and said, "Well, I play there too sometimes."

"I know who you are, magic man."

"Magic man? Well, I do have magic fingers."

She almost spit out her drink laughing at that one. She knew what the local musicians meant by that.

"Classy," Libby snorted.

"That still doesn't tell me who you are," he said.

She extended a hand. "I'm Libby McGregor."

"Rohan Fitzpatrick," he replied as he took her hand in his. "The pleasure is all mine."

"Is it? Pity. You didn't seem like the one-sided pleasure kind of guy," she replied, laughing.

He laughed, too. She was funny.

They exchanged a few more inappropriate one-liners, and then he got up to retake the stage.

"Hey, Cowboy," she called after him. "Play well. I'd hate to be disappointed."

He shrugged his shoulders in mock disbelief but chuckled all the way up to the stage. Yes. This was going to be fun.

She sat there in the pub, feeling that familiar warm glow begin as the colors around his hands changed. She quit wondering what his magical lineage may be and let herself close her eyes and fall into the music. The energy of each musician was different, like a magical fingerprint. As he played, she savored his. It was warm, comfortable, familiar, like she'd felt it before. It was also sexy. *What?* her eyes popped open. That had not happened in a long time. Was that right? She felt something she remembered...desire. While she'd been attracted to Galen, it had been loneliness more than desire—the need for a physical connection to another human being. His use of magic had manipulated that, which meant it wasn't real. This was different. This was fun.

Well, she thought, *if I have to do this anyway, I may as well enjoy it. This is unexpected.*

She heard Maggie in her head, telling her to shut up and not to overthink it. So, she took a deep breath and a swig of her whiskey, and just let the music wash over her. *Yes,* she thought, *definitely sexy.*

He kept glancing her way. Her reaction to his music was unlike anything he'd ever seen. He wondered if she knew what she looked like, with her eyes half-closed and that blissed out smile on her now rosy-cheeked face. For a split second he envisioned that face in bed next to him. Content. Satiated. Sexy as hell.

He was into his next song when he noticed her stand up to leave. She winked at him and nodded as she turned and walked out of the pub.

He rarely let himself get distracted by a woman, but suddenly couldn't think about anything else. He was in it for the hunt now. She'd practically dared him to find her. There wasn't a woman alive who could resist his charms. Not even a queen.

Especially if that Queen didn't want to resist.

It had taken a few pints after the show to get Paul, the bar manager, to tell him what he knew about this American woman, Libby McGregor. He was able to figure out the building she was staying in, not far from the pub. After that it was pretty easy to get flowers and a note delivered to her flat. Belfast was still a small town and he had enough connections to get what he wanted. When he saw the American number ringing through on his phone, he knew it had to be her.

"Thanks for the flowers, Stalker," the voice on the other end began.

"Stalker? I'm chagrined. More like an admirer."

"Admirer? Of what?" she laughed. "And how did you know lilacs were my favorite flower?

"I can only tell you that in person. Have dinner with me tonight."

"I have plans," she lied," but thank you for the invitation."

"Break them. You know you want to. I saw you watching me sing. I've never seen anyone want to have dinner with me more than you. I'd hate to have to show up and knock on your door like the pizza boy."

There was silence on the other end. He wondered if he'd pushed too far. American women were a lot more sensitive than their Irish counterparts.

"What do you have in mind?" broke the silence.

He grinned. "Dinner at my place."

"Wow, forward AND cheeky," she replied.

"Now hold on, you know who I am. There isn't a restaurant in town we could have a meal and enjoy some peace and quiet."

Libby laughed. "Wanna bet?" she challenged. "I know just the place."

Later that evening his taxi pulled up at the address she'd given him on Antrim Road.

"This can't be it. Are you sure this is the right place?" He leaned forward to ask the taxi driver.

"311 Antrim Road is what you told me, and that's where we are," he retorted with a shake of his head.

Rohan looked at the address again, and then around to see if there was anything else close by that might fit the bill. When she walked up to the taxi and knocked on the window, he realized they would in fact be dining at Walker's Chip Shop and finally got out of the car.

"Really? A chip shop?" he snorted, clearly disappointed.

"Best fried chicken on the planet. And no one here cares who you are. Emphasis on the no one."

He laughed and draped his arm around her shoulders as they entered the shop, "We'll see about that."

After they got their order, they sat at the edge of the bar on the wall away from the window. Fish and chips are hardly romantic date food, but she was right, the food was excellent. And, disappointingly, no one did seem to notice or care who he was.

"Alright, spill it, Stalker." Libby demanded. "How did you find my flat, and how did you know lilacs were my favorite?"

A grin crossed Rohan's handsome face. "You were wearing lilac perfume the night we met. That's not a common fragrance. I don't think I've ever even seen lilac perfume before. I took a chance ordering them. As for finding your flat, that's my secret."

"Why do you like lilacs?" he asked, wanting to get her to talk about herself.

Libby shrugged. "I always have. My mother always had them planted in the garden, and they remind me of her. There is something about them that makes them a beautiful contradiction. Lilacs are wild and delicate at the same time. They are sweet but incredibly sturdy. Totally reliable, but easily out of control. And they are survivors. Do you know anything about gardening?" She asked.

She continued when he shook his head. "Well, lilacs, along with roses, can survive almost anything. If you ever come across an abandoned cabin or farmhouse, you'll likely find the lilacs and roses have taken over. They are a force of nature."

"Sounds like a perfect choice for a woman like you, Libby McGregor." She rolled her eyes, and he made a mental note to have fresh lilacs delivered to his house the next day. He wasn't going to leave anything to chance.

He was funny. He made her laugh, and he made her feel good about herself. More than that, he made her feel sexy and desired. She was still young and wasn't meant to live a life alone. Hell, Awen kept on her about it. She just hadn't found anyone interesting enough. Rohan persisted, and succeeded where others had failed. The first morning they were together, she could actually feel the energy blockage in her chakra shoot out of her feet. As she lay there purring like a mama kitty, her feet felt like they were on fire. She could see the orange energy pulsing around her. And she couldn't stop laughing.

Libby was almost ready to fight the dragon.

One afternoon, white cotton sheets tangled around them, Libby asked Rohan about his life as a musician. He'd told her about his first nice guitar, a Gibson. Back then, early in his career, he'd saved every cent he earned. Most of the money went back to equipment, and as things got more high-tech they also got more expensive. He loved that guitar; it represented that he'd made it to where he'd always wanted to be. He'd bought it after his first big album success, *I Am Trouble*, hit the charts. He was heartbroken when it was stolen a few years later. He looked at her, feeling a bit sheepish. "I know it's silly, but I'd even named her. GiGi, short for my Gibson Girl."

"I think it's sweet, Rohan," she assured him.

Talking like that, alone, wrapped in each other's arms, his guard was down. She noticed that his face changed. His tone changed. He was confident and relaxed but without any strategy. He was an authentic, less guarded version of himself as opposed to his normal state of being "on," with constant calculation and adjustments he had to do from the stage. It wasn't a performance. He was relaxed and he trusted her. It made no sense. Just like her trusting him was totally illogical. He trusted her with who he was.

They talked for hours. She loved learning things about people, what they did, what they found interesting, and how it all worked. He answered all of her questions without hesitation, no matter how silly some of them must have sounded.

At some point they realized they were hungry. Libby got up to make them each a sandwich, leaving Rohan in bed, strumming his guitar.

When she returned, he leaned the guitar against the bed while taking the tray from her hands, setting it on the nightstand while she climbed back in next to him.

"I trusted you today, Libby. When we talked."

"I know. And I get that you don't know me well enough to."

"I still do, you know. Trust you," he said as he rolled over towards her.

As he gazed at her, something in his eyes changed. He suddenly seemed feral. Like the wolf tattooed on his forearm, the one she loved to run her hands over or kiss. Then the bolt of recognition hit her—the golden eyes. He was the man from her meditation, the one looking for her. What could this mean? This intensity was new. It was intimidating and exciting at the same time. Maybe she'd misjudged this. They weren't supposed to get serious. Just a fling. Libby had needed him, and she knew he'd needed her. She wasn't sure why, but it worked out. She'd come a long way. With his help, she finally remembered that the joy was worth the risk of more heartbreak.

She wasn't afraid of him, but she was starting to fear that they might feel more for each other than was good for either of them. Libby tried to force herself to turn off her thinking brain and just surrender to the intensity. As she felt the familiar magic energy tingle when he ran his fingertips down her back, she made a mental note to ask Awen again if she'd learned anything about the risk of addiction. It sure felt like a drug and she couldn't get enough. Then, she didn't care anymore.

Rohan saw everything from the stage. He had a front row seat to the clumsy courting attempts. He witnessed the games. He saw the sad eyes, the drunks, and the silliness. He also saw the joy his music brought, providing an escape from everyday life. Much of what he observed from the stage ended up immortalized in one of his songs.

That night, her last night in Belfast, was no different. He'd scanned the crowd until he found the face he didn't realize he was looking for. He wasn't sure when she'd slipped in, but once she was there, she was impossible to miss. She wasn't so different from everyone else, but she had a presence that demanded his attention. Even though she tried to be nondescript, there was no hiding the fact she was, like her lilacs, a force to be reckoned with.

She's changed, he thought, as he flashed back to their first meeting. Was it just a few weeks ago when he first saw her? He'd seen someone with kind eyes who looked like a fun challenge. She'd bought him a pint when he took his break. They'd chatted, and she had a sense of humor. Something about her laugh made him want to hear it again.

Since that first meeting, each time he saw her out in the audience, she was a little different. A little more confident. Sexier. Tonight, he saw her holding court from her favorite booth in the corner. She was relaxed, and happy. Genuinely happy. She loved the music, and despite the men who tried to get her attention, she only had eyes for him. That smile almost made him forget the lines to a song.

He knew she was leaving. That was all part of the plan: No attachments. But in that moment, when he watched her tilt her head back and laugh deep and true, suddenly her happiness mattered to him. What started as a game had become something he was no longer in control of. He knew he was going to miss her. He realized life was never going to be the same. They could never be together. He knew part of his success meant maintaining a single playboy image, and he knew she was committed to her job and had to leave. She would always be the "what if," the one he'd unconsciously be looking for in the audience. The one he'd think about every time he sang her favorite song. *Damn. This is going to hurt.*

Despite having already said their goodbyes, she ended up coming home with him again. One last time. He dreamed about her that night even though he was lying right next to her. He was on stage at their favorite pub. She was sitting there listening to him, smiling. Only in his dream he was playing GiGi, singing to his real-life Gibson Girl and they were alone. It felt perfect.

Rohan woke up reaching for her and knew immediately she wasn't there. There was still a hint of her lilac perfume on the pillow next to him, but the warmth and light was gone. He rolled over and sighed. He'd known this day was coming. It felt like an eternity ago that he'd looked forward to it. No attachments, no relationships. This lying in bed missing her was not "Brash as Fuck." "Get your act together, Fitzpatrick," he admonished himself. He laughed out loud, got up and moseyed into the kitchen for some coffee. He was half asleep and after hitting the button on the machine, he turned around to lean against the counter while the coffee brewed.

That's when he saw it. The guitar case leaning against the dining table, with a small white card attached.

"What the hell? Tell me she didn't buy me a present."

He opened the guitar first. "Oh my God. Can it be?" As he picked it up, he realized that it was his guitar. Not just the make and model, it was *his* guitar. His Gibson Sunburst. He knew it the minute he held her in his hands, but he did a quick inspection to confirm and saw GiGi, engraved into the neck. How? He'd spent years looking for it before finally giving up. He ran his fingers across the strings as a smile took over his face, coffee forgotten. His mind wandered back to that afternoon, her in his arms, telling her about GiGi. "How the hell did she find her?" he wondered.

He looked over at the card, loathe to put GiGi down after finally being reunited. He held the card in his hand for a few minutes before finally putting the guitar down and opening the heavy white envelope.

> *R,*
> *Remember me, sometimes, when you play her.*
> *Thanks for everything,*
>
> > *L*

He laughed. "Oh, my Darling, remember you? As if I could ever forget you." He shook his head and returned to GiGi, the beginnings of a song percolating in his brain about what if's, a girl, and a Gibson guitar.

Libby smiled through the tears as she felt him open the card. Maggie had continued teaching her magic during her break, and she'd left a little magical delivered-read notification on it. She hated to say good-bye to him but knew that they weren't meant to be together. She could have loved him, hard and far too easily, but he had good things waiting for him, and she would only hold him back from that. Besides, she had a job to do. She sighed, pulled her hoodie up and turned down the deserted alley behind the Duke of York to meet John and go home.

Chapter 18

Back to Business

After their short interlude out in the real world, John and Libby returned to the Kingdom and the palace. John knew something had happened in Belfast, something more than just getting laid, but Libby wasn't ready to share, and he didn't feel like it was the right time to pry. She was different. He wasn't magic, but he knew people, and he knew her. She was stronger. More confident. Relaxed. And something else. Sexy? Weird to think that about one of his best friends, but it was there. She was putting out a completely different vibe.

Great, he thought. *Now when we go out, I'm going to have to get in a fight because some dumb ass is going to make a wrong move.* Then he grinned as he remembered their last bar fight, and that it was Libby who caused the most damage, including to herself when she decided to head-butt her way out of a fight, fracturing the maxilla bone in her face in the process. "Sweet Jaysus," he laughed to himself. "I feel sorry for the poor sap who falls for her. He won't stand a chance." He shook his head, feeling strangely proud of his friend and Queen.

He knew how terrified she'd been to open her heart again, but she'd faced that fear anyway. He also knew returning to the palace would present its own challenges. John hoped that their time away was enough to help Libby deal with the memories that were waiting for her at home.

Libby immediately went to Awen to get back to work on her training. In addition to her dream lessons with Maggie, she'd been doing daily energy work, and she'd been trying to work on the sight when she could, but the big focus was her heart growth.

Awen began her usual examination with instructions to "spill the dirt," and then stopped. "I don't understand." She said, incredulous. "You've only been gone three weeks."

"What's wrong?"

"Nothing. Quite the opposite. I just don't understand. Your heart, it's grown back. It's weak... like tender pink tissue after a burn, but it's there. Just how much sex did you have?"

Libby blushed and started laughing. "Well, quite a bit, actually, but he wasn't a regular Normal. He had magic although he didn't know it. And he sang to me. A lot." She paused. "And he drew magic on my skin with his touch. It's hard to explain."

"Hmmm. I'll have to make a note of that for future equations."

"Really? Is that necessary? I don't need a written record of that."

"Theoretical, of course," Awen chuckled. She was curious, but also optimistic for the first time in almost a year. This could work. This crazy plan could actually work. She silently thanked Maggie who had coached her on how to help Libby.

Libby opened the door to the bedroom she and Dale had shared, the one he'd died in. It had been cleaned since, but she hadn't stepped foot in it until today. She felt the pain well up in her chest, threatening to overcome her and remembered Maggie's lessons. She closed her eyes and took a deep breath. In a moment she was back in her heart center, surrounded by a cloud of pink. Once she felt centered, she opened her eyes. She saw Dale standing at the window.

"It's about time," she said quietly.

Dale turned around to look at her and smiled. "I've been here the whole time, Ash, I just wasn't ready to talk to you yet. I wanted to, but after I screwed it up and almost killed you I couldn't."

"What are you talking about?"

"Shortly after I died, I was yelling at you not to take any more sleeping potion. You thought I was encouraging you. That night you died, and the force field almost collapsed. It was my fault."

"No, it wasn't," she said loudly, shaking her head in disbelief.

"Yes, it was. I was forbidden to attempt to communicate with you again until I got permission, but I've been here the whole time. I've heard you talking to me."

Libby suddenly flushed with embarrassment. "Wait, you've been watching me the whole time?"

Dale laughed. "Yep. I've seen it all. But I've been a gentleman and respected your privacy. Trust me, I don't need to see my wife with another man."

Libby felt sick to her stomach. This was a horrifying thought.

"We have a lot of things to talk about, but that's not one of them. I need to know why you never told me about Michael. Ash, we weren't supposed to have any secrets from each other, and you deliberately hid this from me. For years! What gives?"

Libby felt her eyes well up with tears. She took a deep breath and sat on the bed, their bed, hugging a pillow while she talked. "I knew it would hurt you. But mostly it hurt me to think about, let alone talk about. My heart was broken, I loved him the minute I knew he existed, and then he was gone. When the doctor told me I'd never be able to have children, I felt defective. Incomplete. Dale, I was grieving. I wasn't thinking clearly. You had a right to know, and I should have told you. For that I'm truly sorry. It's almost funny now. I thought that was the worst pain a person could endure. I was wrong."

"Oh Ash," Dale sighed, taking a seat next to her. "This wasn't our plan at all. We were supposed to grow old together. I wasn't ready to leave you. It's not fair."

"No, it's not," she said quietly.

He shook his head. "Ash, you're going to be okay. I'll always be here with you, and for you, but this is a path only you can walk. And I don't want you to walk it alone. Do you understand what I'm saying?"

The Queen clenched her jaw before snapping, "I'm not having this conversation with you right now."

"Fair enough. But we're not done talking about this. I love you, Ash. I want the best for you, even if I can't be the one to give it to you."

Chapter 19

Heroes

So if anybody thinks I'm a hero
When they watch me walk right into the flames
I'm just marching to the sound of her heartbeat
Yeah, I'm a soldier but if I'm a soldier
She's an army.
~Lady Antebellum, "Army"

With Libby firing on all chakras, and back at full fighting strength, her confidence began to return. She still struggled with her fears and the awful sadness, but they no longer controlled her. She trained hard, every day, both in magic and combat, and Fintan sang to her every night.

While sparring with Fynnigan one afternoon, he continued a conversation he'd started a few weeks ago about the engineering of the force field. He was fascinated by it, but it was also a deliberate attempt to distract her during battle. "Libby, I've been thinking more on the force field. After you defeat Jasper, you'll need a way to support the energy required on your own. I know you're doing it now, but at some point you'll want to get away from the musicians and wizards."

He glanced over and saw Fintan frowning at him.

He grinned. "I mean, my God, can you imagine being stuck with O'Toole every day for the rest of your life?"

"Fuck off, Van der Linden," he heard Fintan mutter. Since Libby called them both by their shortened names, it sometimes got confusing.

Was she referring to Finn or Fynn? They both hated sharing her term of endearment, so would only refer to each other by surnames

Fynnigan laughed and continued. "I've been doing some additional research. I think if you permanently anchor the kingdom on a ley line, that will provide enough steady energy that you won't have to do all the heavy lifting by yourself. It may even be possible to remove your link to the force field altogether. You already drew some power from the ley lines when you anchored outside of Belfast, so we know it's theoretically possible."

He didn't let up on his sparring efforts but could see Libby thinking and pressed harder.

"Permanently anchor it? I don't know. What a crazy idea." She thought about it. The ability to move the kingdom wherever it needed to go was one of the best things about it. Any dangers could be avoided, and she could travel easily back and forth whenever it suited her. But life had changed. Maybe anchoring was what was needed now. "Where would you recommend? And how would that work? And how on earth did you even think of this?"

He blushed. "It just came to me one night. We're already in Ireland, I'd keep it here. The ley lines here are some of the strongest and oldest in the world. Plus, you seem to like it here. I don't know why though, my country has so much more to offer."

Libby burst into laughter. "Oh, Fynn. I do love your country very much, but there is no place on this planet that can offer what Ireland does. And the less I know about what comes to you in the night the better. I don't think I've ever seen you blush before. Good Lord."

He ignored her, but his cheeks got redder. "As for how it would work, I've been talking to Awen about it. I think it's as simple as creating a sort of graft or tether to the ley line. I've got most of the details worked out, and the science behind it works. It's different from the heart graft, but basically you are connecting the force field to the ley line which is the life force of the planet, sort of weaving them together. I'm working out the engineering, but it is theoretically possible. Probable, even."

He left out the details of how he came up with the idea since it involved a lot of whiskey, and a crazy night with Larra. She'd threatened to kill him if he told anyone, and he took that seriously. To be honest, he couldn't quite remember how it came up in conversation, but the topic did come up and they got into a surprising amount of detail given the circumstances.

Libby realized Fynn was distracted by what she assumed was the engineering of it all and went in on a full attack and finally knocked him on his ass.

She reached down to help him up and quickly found herself on her back, Fynnigan laughing at her expense, much like he'd done when he was a child.

"Never let your guard down, Libby. You taught me that."

They both lay there, winded, laughing. "Yes, grasshopper, I did. I wouldn't have if I'd have known you'd use it against me."

Fynnigan got up and helped Libby to do the same, taking a seat on the low stone wall as they both caught their breath. He knew her physical strength was back by how hard she'd pushed in their sparring session. He also knew her well enough to know that she was still struggling with self-doubt. They'd known each other for more than half his life and he knew her as well as, and in some ways better than, the rest of her team.

"Do you remember that time when I was little?" he began. "When we were out on that winter walk in the woods?"

"How can I forget?" She laughed somewhat hesitantly, nervously tucking her hair behind her ear.

Fintan's ears perked up. He hadn't heard this story before.

"I remember it like it was yesterday," Fynnigan continued, brushing the blonde hair out of his face. "You were on one of your extended visits. It was lightly snowing, and there was a few inches of snow on the ground. Highly unusual for us and I wanted to play in it, even though you thought we should stay indoors until my Dad got home. I wasn't going to wait, so you came with me. We were on our normal path near the lake, the one we always took. You saw them first, the wolves. I didn't know what was happening. I just remember you stopping and pushing me behind you. You pulled a big-ass knife out of your boot, without taking your eyes off the wolves. At the time I'd never seen anyone carry a weapon. No one did that in my country.

I was terrified. Of you, to be honest, until I saw the wolves. I think I may have started crying at that point."

"You somehow found a big stick," he continued, "and you called me your brave Fynn and told me to get face down on the ground and not look up, no matter what. I felt you stand over me. Then I heard you talking. To the wolves. You told the wolves to leave. You told them I was yours. You demanded they recognize you, that you would be their Queen. You told them they could not have me, and that they needed to leave or die. I was only twelve, but I thought you were insane. Why the fuck were you bothering talking to a wolf? And what was this Queen nonsense? You were an art buyer, for God's sake. And did you really think you could fight a pack of wolves with a knife and a stick? I wanted to run, but something made me trust you, so I remained face down in the snow. Then I heard a low voice reply, saying you were a cub and no Queen yet, and to step out of the way or face the consequences. You know, for years I told myself I'd imagined that part. Then I was invited to the Kingdom and learned magic was real."

"After a while I heard my Dad's voice shouting from the other side of the lake. I looked up and could see him in the distance. He'd heard about the wolf sightings in town and come looking for us. I'd never seen him look afraid before, but there was a look of terror on his face. He was running towards us. Then I heard the crack of that stick, a wet thud and the wolf cry out. I heard the snarls and you yell, 'No!' I remember the feel of the snow clumps falling on my back as you jumped over me to attack. Then more whimpering. I was definitely crying by then, with my face buried in the snow, hands over my head. It felt like an eternity but was probably only a few minutes. Then there was only the sound of my dad's voice, still far away, and you reaching for me asking me if I was okay.

"By the time Dad got there the wolves had run off. I was still crying like a little girl and dove into his arms. It wasn't until he let me go to look me over that I finally looked around. You were standing there covered in blood, some of it your own. There was a dead wolf lying in the snow a few feet away. Your black hair was blowing in the light breeze and the snow covered it like white lace. The sun had come out behind you and you were glowing with a pink halo like a warrior Goddess in one of those comic books I liked to read. I already loved you as my grown-up American friend because you never treated me like a kid, but that was the day you became my hero. I believed then that you were fearless and could do anything. For fuck's sake you fought wolves and won! You saved me. I now understand you were afraid, but you did it anyway. You're still my hero, Libby. I know you're afraid, but this is just like the wolves, only now you have me and everyone else. You aren't fighting this battle alone. You are still that warrior Goddess I saw that day. I believe in you."

Libby smiled through the tears that were now falling freely. She reached up and brushed the hair out of his face, resting her hand on his cheek.

"My brave Fynn. My Fynnigan. It has been my honor to be part of your life. I've been blessed to watch you grow up into the amazing man you are. The day you agreed to join the knighthood was one of the happiest in my life. I still sometimes see that thoughtful sweet boy who stole my heart with those pink cheeks, brilliant blue eyes, and endless questions. I don't know anything about being a hero, but I will do anything to protect those I love. And I love you too, kiddo."

She paused a few moments, replaying the memories, running her fingers over the faint bite marks that scarred her forearm, lasting reminders of that day in the woods. "Do you want to know a secret?" she asked.

"Always," he answered, blue eyes sparkling.

"You know my name means Dreamer, but did you know I sometimes dream about the future?"

"I've heard talk," he said cautiously, wondering where this was going.

She sighed, deep in the memory. "I dreamt about you before I ever met you. Before I even met your dad. The first time your dad introduced us, I recognized you immediately. It was always the same dream. The two of us at the lake in the woods, with the wolves in the winter. It's how I knew not to let you go alone that day, and how I knew to go armed. Well, at least as armed as would be allowed in your country. You loved those walks, and with the added enticement of the snow, I knew you'd go without me if I didn't go with you. It was safe back then, and your dad never worried when you went off on your own. But that day was different because I knew what was coming. Since I couldn't talk you out of it, I went with you. Truth be told, I treasured our daily walks. Those woods are still one of my favorite places. Leaving you to return home was one of the hardest things I've ever done.

"For fuck's sake! You knew? Really? Damn, Libby! You just leveled up to superhero status. Although you should maybe not tell Dad about the dreams. You know how he is about the stuff he can't science. He *never* spoke of that day again. I'm not sure what freaked him out more, you standing there covered in blood after killing a wolf, the fact there were wolves that close to home, or that I could have been killed."

"Oh my God, can you even imagine?" she laughed. "Poor Bas, his engineer brain might explode. I have a hard enough time accepting the dreams and they've been part of my life since I was a child."

They both started laughing and he pulled her up off the wall to walk back to the armory. When he was a boy, she could rest her arm comfortably on his shoulders. He was small for his age back then. Now he was a head taller than she was and burly like a Viking. He reminded her a lot of his dad when she'd first met them. Now it was reversed, and he was the one with his arm on her shoulders, and she had her arm around his waist. Like Kurtis and Dyanna, Fynnigan was one of those young people who were as close as she'd ever get to being a mother. She hated physical violence but would do whatever it took to protect those she loved. Just like the day she stood over him facing off against a pack of wolves. He was right. She would face Jasper no matter what, and this time she wouldn't be alone.

For the first time in years, she didn't fight back against the rest of the memories that went with that story. The anger and fear from Bastiaan. The realization he would never accept her for who she really was; who she was meant to be, and the tears as she packed up and left shortly thereafter. They'd kept in touch, mostly about Fynnigan, and would run into each other off and on over the years on their travels, but things would never be the same again. Libby examined the pieces of those memories. She realized she no longer resented Bas for how things ended. In that moment, she also forgave her younger self for the choices she'd made. She smiled as a flood of pink light and love washed over her. She couldn't really explain how it all worked, but she liked it. She wondered if this was what Maggie and the other spirits meant by figuring out who the real Libby was, and that acknowledging the past was part of it. She knew Michael would be proud of her for figuring it out on her own.

Libby didn't know that Bas had witnessed her leaping over his son to defend him from the wolf. He was at a distance but had seen it all. He saw the wolf attack the woman he loved, and then saw her kill it. He also saw the flash of blinding pink light that seemed to shoot out of her. His brain couldn't process it, so he refused to acknowledge it.

Fintan remained seated on the other side of the stone wall, deep in thought. Sometimes he struggled to wrap his mind around the magic-filled life that Aisling led. But the imagery of Van der Linden's story was burned into his brain, and he knew he had to find a way to incorporate it into Libby's story. His friend, Libby, the Queen of Wolves? Wolf Queen? Something with wolves needed to be included. That line about the lace snow veil; he'd never admit it to the young knight, but that was a great line.

Chapter 20

Dragons, Duels and Duty

ibby woke up to the sun streaming through the open window and the sound of the waves crashing on the shore below. She rolled over and reached for Dale, before remembering he wasn't there. That he'd never be there again. That was enough to wake the rest of her brain and remember where she was. She was in her top floor suite at the Caisleáin Óir Hotel in Annagry, one of her favorite places in Donegal. The owners always took great care of her, and in this case all fifteen of their traveling party. This was always her first choice when she came through town. Annagry was one of those border towns that made a perfect gateway between the Kingdom and the world outside the barrier. With a population of just a few hundred people, and off the beaten path of tourists, they didn't have to be as careful coming and going. She wanted a comfortable place to rest before confronting Jasper.

She got out of bed to stand at the balcony and admire the view. The McDevitts' ancestors had done well selecting this location to build their bar and then later the hotel. Nothing would ever come between them and the view of the North Atlantic. She noticed Awen and Harley on the rocks below, doing their morning yoga. Several others were already out on a morning run. She could see the uninhabited island she'd requested for the duel off in the distance but knew that's not where the duel would happen. That was still a good two days' ride away, but this was on the way and preferable to camping.

The poet in her loved the meanings behind names. The literal translation of Caisleáin Óir was Palace of Gold, but that could also be stretched to mean building palaces in the sky or to have dreams that seemed impossible. Since Aisling meant Dreamer, it seemed like a good match and an appropriate place for her to set out from for her impossible duel. Her real-life poet agreed, and Fintan was practically drooling when he'd made the observation himself.

A soft knock on the door was her morning coffee being delivered. She smiled, grateful. The McDevitts knew her well, but they took great care of all of their guests. Anticipating guest needs was one of their talents, and the level of service and care they provided gave visitors the feeling of being a guest in someone's home. Despite the fact they'd filled the hotel so there were no other guests, she also knew that at least one of her team was hovering close by in the hallway. She opened the door to find Will was on duty. "Join me for coffee, Will?" she asked.

He smiled, "How can I turn down a beautiful woman inviting me to her room for coffee?" he joked. She laughed. She was already wondering what Anita was cooking down in the restaurant. Her food was famous, and Libby would be sad to leave it behind for yet more campfire cooking. Oh, and there was still the matter of battling a dragon. She wasn't in a hurry for that either.

The day of the duel dawned bright and sunny. It was surreal to think this was it. It had been over a year since Dale had been cursed, and almost a year since he'd died. Jasper thought he was giving himself an edge by choosing the duel location at the site of Skarra's camp and the beginning of Dale's long slow painful death. The location was harder on Geoffrey and Hoss than it was on Libby since they'd been there, but the timing was rough on the entire group. Libby had made amazing progress, but the pain of the anniversary hit her hard, and Awen and Fintan were working overtime to keep the Queen's energy clear and her strength up. Both were exhausted.

Geoffrey's stress level was even higher because of the private conversations he'd had with Awen. She'd explained that she was the back-up plan. That should Jasper fail to honor the terms, she'd use magic to destroy him before he had a chance to kill Libby. While she wasn't strong enough on her own, pouring her life force into the spell would make it work. Just like Skarra did when she killed Dale. They couldn't allow Libby to die. The part of him that was Senior Knight knew it was a sound plan and may be necessary to save the Kingdom. The part of him that loved her, refused to accept that she'd sacrifice herself, even if it was the heroic thing to do. Damn it!

Geoffrey and the knights had set up a perimeter patrol, secure in the knowledge that nothing would get through the LIWs. It had been weeks since Libby went anywhere without a full security detail. No matter what Michie had said, they didn't trust Jasper to honor the terms of the deal. After Galen, they knew that they couldn't leave anything to chance.

Libby was deep in meditation in her tent when Michie came to her. Today she was dressed like Libby, in modern tactical gear. Even her hair was cut short in a cute modern bob. It was a dark blue, not too different from Libby's. Outside of the body armor, she could have been any young person cruising the streets of Tokyo, but with the gear and blue hair she was almost an anime.

"Well Mago-chan, this is it."

"Do you think I can do it, Grandmother?"

"Of course. You are stronger than I ever was, since I didn't have magic. I also didn't have the benefit of me as a teacher." She winked.

"Thank you for everything."

"Don't thank me yet. You still have to defeat the dragon."

"Any last minute tips?"

"Yes. Do not forget who you are. You are the Queen. The only force in this universe powerful enough to stop you, is you. Remain confident. Remember we are all here with you, and more importantly that we believe in you."

With that, the rest of the Spirit Council appeared, along with one extra.

"Dale?"

Before he could answer, her father spoke. "Aisling Elisabeth, you've been preparing for this moment your entire life. You'd always believed you'd married a king, but you were the one who was destined to rule the Kingdom, just like Michie. Never forget who you are."

Dale jumped in. "He's right. You gave me this life. You were my Queen only because you made me King. You can do it, Babe; I know you can."

"I love you," she said. "I love all of you. I do this knowing I have all of you at my back. I won't let you down."

"Don't worry about us, young one," Michie encouraged. "We love you. No matter what."

Maggie chimed in, "And it's all about love. At the end of the day, love is all that matters." Maggie placed her hand on Libby's heart center. "Whenever you feel doubt, you know where to return to; to who you really are."

Libby nodded and opened her eyes as she heard Awen and Scarlett talking outside.

With a big sigh, and a "Let's do this," under her breath, she stood up, straightened her crown, and stepped outside.

As Libby emerged into the sunlight, her team gathered around her. This was it. There was no more preparation to be done. There was nothing else for them to do but wait. It was all up to her now.

Will looked at her closely and nodded approvingly. She'd come a long way in the last year. It was hard to remember the broken shell of a woman who couldn't stand without help and needed a machine to breathe. The wounded woman who could barely hold her sword and shield was now a fierce warrior—one who had a real chance of defeating a dragon. He was proud of her, standing tall in her enchanted tactical armor, blue hair blowing in the breeze, sun behind her creating a glowing halo that you didn't have to possess magic to see.

Fintan noted all of it as well, already mentally composing the tale of her epic victory. He was scared for her, of course, but felt surprisingly hopeful. She was ready. He felt the excitement in his soul that comes when you can feel you're at a pivotal moment in history. It was up to him to make sure the future knew what happened here today.

Dyanna and Kurtis were nervous but in awe of their aunt Libby. Dyanna was memorizing every detail about her stance, and the words that she was saying. Libby was always good at words when it counted. *This is what it is to be a queen,* she thought. *To face your fears and do whatever it takes to protect your people, no matter how much it hurts. Aunt Libby is so badass!*

Kurtis thought about how proud their uncle Dale would be if he could see her right now. The two young people had matured over the course of their journey. They were both scared but stood tall in their matching body armor and emerald cloaks emblazoned with the royal ash tree. Libby had selected them, instead of Geoffrey and Scarlett, to accompany her to the duel. She'd received a lot of flak about that decision, but it was hers to make. They felt proud. Excited. And scared.

Libby looked around at the group assembled. She loved them beyond description. She nodded at Fynnigan who set up a video conference call from his phone back to the palace so the knights and LIWs left behind, the Co-Regents, and wizards could be part of this.

"There's no precedent on how to address your bravest warriors, fiercest friends, and your family on the day you're supposed to fight a dragon." She smiled and nervous chuckles made their way around the group. "I can't thank you enough for your loyalty. Without your love and protection, I wouldn't have survived losing Dale. You've not only saved me, you've saved our kingdom, and both the physical and spiritual realms. Now it's my turn. I would gladly lay down my life for you, but that's not how this works. Today I will live for you, for our people, and for the rest of the world."

The small group burst into applause and cheering on both sides of the video link. Libby nodded at her niece and nephew. It was time to go. They'd been working with Libby daily for months, and knew they had important roles to play. They weren't going to let her down. Kurtis wordlessly extended a hand to help Dyanna into her saddle, before mounting his horse. Then they headed out to confront the dragon. Following protocol, the rest of the party followed a short distance behind.

As the Queen and her escort arrived at the clearing, they finally got their first look at Jasper. He was huge and took up the entire clearing where not long-ago Dale had confronted Skarra. Dyanna and Kurtis were terrified, but took their cue from Libby, controlling their breathing and facial expressions. There was no way they were going to embarrass her, or themselves. Fintan's eyeballs almost popped out of his head but he had a job to do and started writing, even though his hands were shaking. The sun reflected off Jasper's black scales, which rippled with excitement when he saw Libby approaching.

If Libby felt fear, she didn't let it show. She remained mounted, her hair and cloak blowing slightly in the breeze. She was grateful Hoss didn't show it, although she knew he was nervous. He was still as a stone—majestic, just like his rider. He'd be immortalized in Fintan's poem as the horse of all horses.

John looked at his friend with a hint of awe. As many times as he'd seen her both out on adventure and at court, he'd never seen her look so regal. "I want to remember this moment forever," he said under his breath. "My Libby, badass Libby McGregor, is staring down a fucking dragon like it's no big thing."

Libby's voice rang out clear and strong. "Jasper of Shenyang. I am Queen Aisling Elisabeth McGregor, ruler of the Kingdom of the Talking Trees. You are trespassing on this land. You've accepted the challenge of a duel to the death. Are you ready to begin?"

The low rumbling of his laughter was so loud it made her teeth rattle.

"No, Queen." He sneered. "A fight to your death would destroy me as well. I challenge you to the previously agreed upon duel of wit and skill. Once you accept the terms it becomes magically binding. Cheating or lying isn't an option, and results in an automatic forfeiture of the round. The winner is the one who wins the majority of the five rounds. The loser will remain the lifetime prisoner of the winner. Do you accept my terms?"

Libby paused as she thought about his offer. She realized this was the best possible outcome should she lose. With Michie's coaching she understood that if she survived, the force field would also survive. This was the only way to ensure her people would survive until Dyanna or Kurtis were old enough to be installed as ruler, or Fynnigan figured out how to sever her attachment to the force field and attach it to the ley lines.

"I accept the terms." Libby dismounted, leaving her green cloak and crown on Hoss, who walked backward until he reached the other two horses, never taking his eyes off Jasper. She tied her blue hair back in one fluid motion and proceeded to approach the dragon, hand on the hilt of the katana at her hip. As the words left her lips, a scoreboard of light magically appeared on the edge of the clearing. Magically binding, indeed.

Dyanna and Kurtis also dismounted, flanking their aunt. Kendra was holding her breath at the edge of the clearing, hands clenched until she realized her fingernails were cutting into her palms and willed them to relax. Harley came over and put her arm around her. The kids looked so grown up, and fierce. There was nothing more they could do to protect them. In fact, they no longer looked like they needed protecting. After months of hard physical training both now sported fit muscular physiques, despite their young age. It's difficult for parents to look at their kids, no matter how grown they are, and not see them as the little ones they once had been. They were proud and terrified at the same time. Back at the palace, Connor and Corrine were holding hands and praying for the best. They would have to watch from afar. They'd have to wait to see if Libby won, if they survived.

The first part of the duel, per Michie's initial instructions, was the battle of wits and skill. That made no sense, but Libby trusted her. Libby locked eyes with Kurtis and motioned for him to begin. They'd been practicing and were ready. Fynnigan noticed the scoreboard and adjusted the angle of his phone to include it so those back at the palace could see.

"First challenge," Kurtis shouted, his voice cracking a little. "Science." He didn't need to shout for Jasper to hear him, but it made him feel better.

So began the duel. There were five challenges total. Kurtis and Dyanna took turns announcing each round, and Libby and Jasper each had the opportunity to either ask a question or issue a skill challenge in the subject matter. If they both answered correctly, or incorrectly, the round was a draw. The first two rounds, science and music, were answered correctly by both. Back at the edge of the clearing, Geoffrey began to wonder what would happen if each round was a draw.

"Third challenge," Kurtis yelled. "History."

It was Libby's turn to go first. She had no facial expression at all as she asked, "Name another reigning Queen to have survived the death of her King."

Jasper burst into laughter. "There was no such Queen. You are one of a kind Libby. And even your survival is still in question."

A small crooked smile tugged at her lips.

"That is incorrect. In 169 A.D. Queen Mori Michie, of what is now Southern Japan, not only survived the death of her King, Mori Ryunosuke, she rose to become King."

"That's not possible!" he sputtered. Jasper was stunned. He knew it was true the minute it left Libby's lips, he just couldn't believe it. Duels left no room for lies, so he knew Libby wouldn't be able to make it up if it weren't the truth. He glanced at the scoreboard and saw a large glowing red zero for his third round.

This was Jasper's first wrong answer. Dyanna looked closely at him, wanting to pump her fist and scream at him, "Take that you tiny-handed freak!" but that was inappropriate behavior for an heir to the throne and the Queen's personal escort. So she stood still, one hand resting on the hilt of her sword, and the other on the holster of her pistol. She hoped her expression was neutral. If she lived long enough, she'd have to master how to do that. He seemed smaller. Maybe she was just getting used to being so close to him? *No*, she thought. *I can see the ocean through the gap in the pine trees. I couldn't even see that cluster of trees before. He is definitely smaller. How is this possible?* Libby had also noticed his decreasing size and felt her confidence increase. It was working. Michie must've known this would happen and that's why she emphasized confidence. She had to keep Jasper on the defense without allowing her confidence to waiver.

Jasper was furious, but he still had a chance to draw the round if she got the question wrong. He decided on something obscure. "Who invented the Zhuge Nu, and why is it significant to Chinese history?"

From the other side of the clearing Will yelled, "Yes!" Before remembering Jasper could hear him and lowered his voice to a whisper. "Girl, you know this one! Please remember this. I taught you this. You laughed at me, remember? You told me it was like algebra, useless in life! I told you one day it might come in handy. You know this!"

Libby couldn't hear Will, but the rest of the assembled knights and LIWs jumped when Will started playfully punching John, who was closest to him. Outbursts like that were unlike him.

"What the fuck, Will?" John was annoyed and motioned for Will to be silent so he could hear.

When Libby started smiling, they did too. They knew she remembered Will's long-winded historical weapons lectures. Hope is a beautiful thing, and it's contagious.

"The invention of the Zhuge Nu[3] is often credited to Zhuge Liang, but that is incorrect. It was invented by Qin Chu in the fourth century B.C. as a self-defense weapon to be used by scholars and women. It quickly became the weapon of choice of female assassins and changed the course of warfare and assassination in China for centuries."

Jasper saw the glowing number one appear on the score board and howled with rage that she'd gotten the answer correct. *This was not happening! That weapon had disappeared from use centuries before Libby had even been born. How could she possibly know that it was Qin and not Zhuge who'd invented it?*

Libby watched him get even smaller, as her confidence continued to grow. "I can beat him in our physical battle if he continues to shrink," she thought. For the first time since she stepped into the clearing, she had the vision of Jasper in a small cage.

Fynnigan slapped Will hard on the back, causing the Weapons Master to take an involuntary step forward. "Nice work, old man. I promise not to give you a hard time about your boring facts ever again. Well, at least until they get boring again."

---

[3]   Wikipedia

Scarlett grabbed his face and kissed him on the lips, making him blush. "Good job, Will!"

But there was no time to celebrate; the duel continued.

"Fourth challenge," Dyanna called out, "Magic."

Jasper was unaware that Libby had been working on this skill, or her abilities. Outside of her wizards, Scarlett, Geoffrey, and the Spirit Council, no one knew. Maggie and Michie had wisely advised Libby to keep this bit a closely guarded secret. Maggie was so nervous she could barely stay in phase. This was it. They'd see if all their coaching was enough.

Libby challenged Jasper to cast a healing spell on a dying tree at the edge of the clearing. It was next to impossible for an evil heart, even in a magical being like a dragon, to create something so selfless and good. So while he could craft the mechanics of the spell, he was unable to get it to work. A second red zero appeared on the scoreboard next to his name. His second failure. But he was less concerned about this one since he knew it would be a wash. It was common knowledge Libby couldn't do magic.

Jasper knew about Libby's love of music and couldn't wait for the red zero to appear next to her name. "Okay, Pet, I challenge you to make music magic." He laughed at the irony that what she loved so much would be her failure. He was smug, knowing that only a musician gifted in magic could do it. He knew Libby was neither.

"Fucking hell!" exclaimed Maggie. They hadn't studied this. At all.

Libby gritted her teeth at the sudden and unwelcome reminder of Galen, who was the only one who had ever called her Pet. In an instant she was taken back to the anger, self-loathing and self-doubt she'd endured. She forced herself to breathe, and Maggie's words made their way through the fog of the pain that had resurfaced with the memories. Libby fought to regain her center. The pain on her face was clear, but Jasper misread it, assuming he'd already won the round.

The group assembled had fallen into anxious silence. Fintan didn't know what to do, so in an uncharacteristically brave move, he unslung his mandolin off his back and started out into the clearing to give it to her. He wasn't sure why; it wasn't as if she could even play, but it was the only instrument they had. He stopped when she turned and motioned for him to go back. Back at the palace, eyes glued to the large monitor in the council chambers, Krystal and Sophia had instinctively reached out for each other. "This is it," Krystal whispered. The wizards were terrified. They could only hope that Maggie had been teaching Libby this since neither of them could make music magic.

Libby turned her gaze back to Jasper. She fished her rose quartz talisman out from where it hung under her shirt and held it in her left hand over her heart center and closed her eyes. She reached deep into her heart chakra, took three deep breaths, opened her mouth and began to sing. As she sang the words of "Feeling Good," her favorite Nina Simone song, words that held so much meaning for her, she poured her life magic into them—a magic that came from pure love. Rose-colored light came pouring out of her into the clearing, drawing pictures of galaxies and flowers and rainbows and trees in the air, creating the back-up music for her song. She opened her eyes. The light of her magic filled the clearing with the faces of everyone she'd loved and lost—of Dale, her parents, her ancestors, and her baby Michael.

During her time with Rohan she'd watched him closely. She'd observed how he wove magic despite never receiving any training or even being aware he had magic. She let her intuition guide her hands, and they wove the stories of those who rode with her and those she'd loved along the way, her friends and family, and the beauty of her Kingdom. Her music magic told her tale, a tale of love and loss and sadness and hope—the one that Fintan would later put into words.

They could all see it, even those who had no magic. Awen made a mental note to research that, but for now she was too busy crying and trying to memorize everything she was witnessing.

Fintan was stunned, his jaw hanging open like the village idiot. He wasn't alone. Except for Larra, who had occasionally heard the Queen singing in the shower, only her immediate family knew she could sing. She'd never had the confidence to sing in front of anyone else, including Dale. The poet was mentally logging all of it, his terror about being so close to Jasper forgotten. *Way to go girl*, he thought to himself.

"Fucking hell," came out of John's mouth. "Where did that voice come from?" He'd only ever heard her drunk singing along with pub bands, and that was nothing to write home about. "Who is this woman?" She never ceased to surprise him.

Shocked silence and tears filled the council chamber. Sophia and Krystal were stunned by the magic they were witnessing. It was intuitive, untrained, and beautiful. They were both crying.

"What's happening?" demanded Ava. "What's wrong?"

Krystal whispered, "Sophia, she's doing it. She's making magic. Maggie was right. Oh my Goddess, it's so beautiful! I've never seen anything like it. Are you seeing this?"

Sophia didn't hear her as she had her fists pumping in the air, screaming, "Yes! Good girl, Libby! You've got this! I knew you could do it!"

Corrine and Ava looked at each other slightly confused, but hopeful. They could see a pink glow surround their sister and fill the clearing but couldn't see what Krystal and Sophia could see. Unlike the rest of the group in the clearing, the non-magic users on their side of the video link couldn't see the images that surrounded Libby, but they knew by the wizards' reactions it was good. They hadn't heard their sister sing in years, but remembered she used to sing to them when they were little, years before she was Queen.

When the song ended with pink fireworks filling the clearing, Libby turned back to smile at her closest friends waiting on the edge of the clearing. She winked, shrugged her shoulders, and turned back to Jasper for the final challenge.

A glowing red one appeared on the scoreboard. By now Dyanna and Kurtis couldn't help themselves, both were wearing the giant toothpaste-commercial grins they shared in common with their aunt. The look on Jasper's face as he realized he was now as small as a Toyota only fueled their excitement.

"What just happened?" demanded Cristina from the edge of the clearing.

"Our Libby just won," said Fynnigan, running his fingers through his blonde curls. He hadn't realized he'd been holding his breath.

"Not yet, she didn't," said Scarlett, still anxious about the fighting to come.

"Oh, yes, she did," countered Fynnigan quietly. He knew she could do this.

"Fifth and final challenge," Kurtis called out. "Combat."

Libby looked at Jasper closely. She could see him for what he was, a small being who made himself bigger by cutting others down. He was still bigger than Libby, and his tail was his most dangerous weapon, but she knew she could defeat him. "It's not a fight to the death," she reminded herself. "I just need to get him to concede."

Jasper didn't wait. He charged, tail on the attack.

Libby dodged the first swing, but only just.

Jasper laughed, and came in for another attempt. This time Libby was ready. She jumped over his tail to land on his back. Jasper couldn't attack without risk of stabbing himself. He shook her off. Libby rolled and got to her feet quickly. Now she knew the weakness of his tail and had a strategy. She just needed to stay out of the way until she could make her move. She wasn't counting on tiring him out. She'd normally be winded by now, but the music magic she'd created had unexpectedly made her stronger. She'd need to remember to ask Awen about that. Music magic was supposed to be symbiotic, feeding the listener and their response feeding the maker. She'd never heard of a musician healing themselves.

Jasper was both angry and full of fear that Libby may actually defeat him, and he was getting reckless. Her father had always taught Libby not to rule with emotion, that emotion caused you to make mistakes. Logic and strategy were what kept you alive in a fight, but pride and fear go hand in hand and Jasper was making foolish choices.

Libby finally saw her opening and ran at Jasper, cutting off the end of his tail with a smooth upward slice of her katana, all of her muscles moving with the memory of Michie's battle skills. His howls could be heard for miles, and he continued to shrink in size.

"Do you concede?" Libby demanded.

Through the tears, Jasper bellowed, "Never! It's a fight to the death."

"No. Those were not the terms we agreed to."

"I will never concede!" screamed Jasper defiantly.

"Don't be a fool," Libby chided him. "You are weaponless. Concede."

"Never!" Jasper ran at her with his jaws open to tear her apart.

Libby raised her sword. "So be it," she said as the hilt of her sword caught him on the jaw, knocking him out cold. He was now the size of a large dog. Libby looked at Kurtis and nodded, and the young man quickly hogtied the dragon so that he'd be secure when he came to.

The cheering on both sides of the video link was deafening, as the glowing red one appeared next to Libby's name. Dyanna and Kurtis grabbed each other in an embrace before rushing to their aunt's side.

Libby stood there, still covered with Jasper's dark blood, sword hanging from her limp arms. For Fynnigan it was déjà vu, seeing her just as he had when she'd saved him from the wolves. "Still my goddamned Warrior Goddess," he said aloud to himself as he ran to her. Kurtis and Dyanna were ecstatic, but both could see she was close to collapsing. They each grabbed an arm to support her while she caught her breath. The rest of their group came running, whooping and hollering, into the clearing. Libby took the brief moment alone with them to quietly say, "Well done, you two. You've made me very proud."

She looked up at Hoss who had come galloping her way. He was smiling at her as she leaned against him for support, releasing her heirs to celebrate with the rest of the group. They'd done it. She'd done it. She'd defeated the dragon and saved the Kingdom. While Jasper hadn't killed Dale, in a weird way, by saving the Kingdom, they'd won a victory for the man they both loved.

Fintan finally made it to her and looked her over closely. She still had that rose glow around her, although he could tell she was exhausted. "You know, I've never performed as a duo before. If you ever get tired of queening, I could probably tolerate you for a few performances before firing you."

She smiled at him. "Fuck off, Finn." After a brief pause, she said, "And thanks. I love you too."

He smiled at her. "We'll have to continue this conversation another time."

Kendra finally caught up with Kurtis. She grabbed her son and held him tight. She was openly crying and kissing him to the point where he let out a, "Mom, seriously, all the guys can see."

"I don't care!" she told him. "I'm so proud of you!"

Cristina and Harley, who had overheard this exchange, looked at each other laughing and joined Kendra in the kissing until he was so red in the face he had to run away.

"I need a shower," interrupted Libby. "This stuff is disgusting. Oh, and Awen will you please take care of Jasper's tail? We need to stop the bleeding."

Scarlett laughed at her and agreed, "Yes, you smell awful. I wasn't going to say anything, but this dragon's blood is horrid. Let's get you cleaned up."

Chapter 21

Taking Flight

After getting cleaned up, Libby sat alone in her tent meditating. She wanted to talk to the Spirit Council one last time. Now that the crisis was over, she knew communication would have to change and would require more effort on her part.

She opened her eyes and found herself in her grandma's kitchen. It looked just like she remembered from her childhood visits. The Council was seated around the old chrome-edged dining table. She smiled at them as they stood up to greet her.

"You did well, child," Teruyo said while giving her a big hug.

"Thank you, Grandma. Thank you, all of you, for your help. I know you will be leaving me soon."

"Actually," Maggie interrupted, "the Council will officially dissolve, but we are always here for you. You now know how to contact us. You should have faith in your abilities and never be afraid to seek us out."

"Thanks for teaching me."

"Teaching you? Girl, you do things I never imagined possible. You'll be the one teaching in the future. I'm so proud of you." She grabbed Libby's face in her hands and planted a big kiss on her forehead.

She looked at her dad, who just wrapped his arms around her. "Aisling Elisabeth, I'm so proud of you. I knew you could do it. Know you're not alone. I will always be here for you if you need me. Trust yourself. Trust the decisions you make. You were born to be Queen."

"Thanks, Daddy. I miss you so much."

Libby felt a tug on her hand and looked down to see Michael holding it, swinging his arm as he spoke. "I'm proud of you, Mom. You found your love for yourself, and because of that you were able to share it. Always remember that forgiveness and love go hand in hand."

She knelt down and took the little boy in her arms. "I love you so much. I wish we'd had a lifetime together but am grateful for what we have now."

Michael laughed and reached out to put his hand on her cheek before shimmering away.

When Libby stood back up Michie was the only one left.

"Mago-chan. You've done a lot more than save the kingdom. You have given me hope."

"Hope?" Libby was confused.

"Yes. It's time you know the rest of our story. Are you ready?"

"Of course, Grandmother."

Michie reached out and gently touched the center of Libby's forehead.

Libby was instantly transported back to Michie's memories. She could see the sun glinting off the river below. She could make out the arches under the stone bridge. She felt the breeze in Michie's hair as she stood on the white castle walls. She heard the oni's final curse, as Michie's knights executed him next to the bridge below. Michie—struggling to survive and keep the force field intact—watched from her hillside castle in silence. "You will never be together, Michie. Not in this life or the next. You won't be reunited with your King until a queen can tame the black dragon." Libby felt Michie's anger and her pain as she watched the oni die, pennants flapping in the wind, white dragon emblazoned on a black field.

"Wait, is that true? Do you mean to tell me that all this time you and Ryunosuke have been apart?"

"Yes, Mago-chan. Do you remember when I told you that I didn't know why you experienced my dream memories as your own? That somehow we were linked?"

"Of course."

"Well, I think this is it. I believe you are the one who will break the curse."

"How do I do that?"

"You must tame the dragon."

"What? How? What do I need to do? I'll do anything."

"I'm afraid I don't know. But, based upon how you use your magic intuitively, how you have defeated Jasper in battle, how you've saved the Kingdom, I have faith you will figure it out. I am proud of you, my young queen. In many ways you remind me of me, only so much more. No matter what, I will know you have done your best and will love you for eternity. Thank you for giving me hope again. Thank you for honoring our family with your courage. Thank you for trusting me."

Tears were running down Libby's face. "I will do this for you, Grandmother. I will figure it out so that you and Grandfather can be reunited in the spirit realm. I promise."

Michie smiled, gave a deep bow, and faded out with the rest of the Spirit Council.

Jasper woke up and immediately knew something was wrong. He wasn't in pain, but he couldn't feel the end of his tail. The memory of Libby's sword making contact came flooding back and he started wailing. When he realized he'd not only lost but had to live with that loss, he shrank even further. He was now about the same size as a Labrador retriever nestled in a cage in Libby's tent.

"Why didn't you just kill me?" he demanded. "I'd rather die than live with this humiliation."

"I didn't kill you because those weren't the terms of our duel," Libby replied. "The terms were lifelong imprisonment."

"No!" he cried, mortified at how high-pitched his voice was now that he was so small.

"Jasper," Libby continued, "I have no intention of harming you or humiliating you. This can be as easy or as difficult as you make it."

He snorted, turning his back to her. He'd continued to shrink and was now the size of a large lizard. His bite and scratches would be painful but wouldn't be life-threatening unless he managed to sever an artery.

Libby sighed and stood up to leave. "Jasper, you have my word. No one will harm you. My team knows you're under my protection and will leave you be. You've been through a lot so perhaps you should rest."

He turned back to face her again. "Under your protection? How dare you! I will kill you."

"So be it," Libby said as she walked out, letting the tent flap drop behind her. She paused at the entry and looked at Fynnigan. "Fynn, he isn't to be harmed. See to it that he is kept safe."

Fynnigan shook his head. "I don't like it, Libby. He will kill you the first chance he gets. We need to take care of him now. Keeping him alive is a mistake."

"I don't need you to like it Fynn, just do it. I'll take care of Jasper. Don't worry about me." She leaned over and kissed him on the cheek as she walked away from camp.

Libby thought while she walked. *What do I do now?* She realized that she liked life on the road and wasn't sure she wanted to return to palace life, which was still heavy with memories of Dale. She decided she wanted to take some time off and go exploring while she figured out how to tame the dragon.

"What the hell am I going to do about Jasper? How will I tame the dragon who wants to kill me? If I'm going out in the Normal world, I can't just take a dragon with me. What to do? Michie said to trust my intuition. Maggie says my magic is unique and has no guidance for me other than to trust myself. Okay. So, I always need to keep Jasper with me, but invisible."

She laughed when she thought about how small he was, and how easy it would be for him to just ride on her shoulder like a parrot on a pirate. *Wouldn't that be hilarious,* she thought to herself. *Although he's small enough now he could wrap himself around my arm like one of those Egyptian snake bracelets.* She stood up straight as she had a vision of a dragon tattoo around her wrist. "That's it. He'll always be with me, but hidden so I can protect him. Trust myself, huh? Hope this works."

While everyone was celebrating Jasper's defeat, Libby snuck out of camp. Announcements had already been made that Libby was safe and uninjured, so the entire kingdom was breathing a sigh of relief. They'd make their way back to the Caisleáin Óir tomorrow, and then back to the palace.

She'd made her way to the shore and sat on the stone wall watching the waves come and go from shore in an endless dance. The heels of her boots bounced off the rocks as she kept time to the music softly emanating from her headphones. It was one of the songs Rohan had picked out for her playlist. He'd never know how much he'd taught her. He'd never know that he'd helped her save the world. She smiled as she thought about him and listened as John Spillane crooned out "All the Ways You Wander." Tonight, it spoke to her. She felt like a wanderer in her own life, like she didn't belong, and Libby felt the need to roam free from royal responsibilities.

She did her best thinking on the water's edge. Any water, really, but the sound of water lapping or crashing was her favorite, and John knew that's where he'd find her.

"What's up, Libby?" he asked as he eased his long frame down beside her.

She looked up at him. Even seated he towered over her. He was one of the few who'd dare to interrupt her solitude.

"Just thinking," she replied.

He let her sit in silence.

"Do you think I can do it?" she finally asked.

"Do what?" he responded, although he knew what she was asking.

"Do you think I can start over? Find happiness without Dale?"

"Libby, I don't just think you can, I know you can. You're an incredible girl. And you truly deserve good times. I'm rooting for you, Libs."

"I'm scared. I don't know who I am anymore."

"I know you don't. But I know who you are. You're Libby McGregor, the badass Queen who defeated a dragon. I know you because we're friends! Kindred spirits. As a bona fide descendant of Captain Morgan, I'm very capable of steering through choppy waters.

Just like you, Libby. You're not a passenger on this crazy ride anymore. You're the fucking pilot."

She looked up at him and gave him a small grateful smile. He was right. She wasn't going home, at least not to stay. If she was going to be both King and Queen of the Kingdom, she needed to figure out who she was supposed to be as a person. She had no idea what that looked like, but a little adventure was always good for the soul, so it seemed like the right place to start. Then there was also her task to tame the dragon.

"You're jealous,'" she retorted.

"Fuck yes, I'm jealous. You know I can't stand it when people have more fun than I do. And despite my extreme FOMO, I'd offer to go with you but I know you well enough to know you need to do this on your own."

"You're right, I need to do this on my own. However, I expect you to meet up with me sometimes for updates and shenanigans."

"I'd be hurt if you didn't invite me." He put a long arm around her shoulders. They sat there until the sun set and then began a slow walk back to camp. She'd let them celebrate tonight. She wouldn't tell them she was leaving until they got back to the palace. They all deserved this victory, a chance to celebrate instead of grieve. For her, it was bittersweet. She was thrilled at her victory, and so sad and lonely over Dale at the same time. He'd have carried her around on his shoulders, bragging to anyone who would listen what a badass his Queen was. The pain of missing him was a dull constant ache, like the scar tissue on her heart.

After walking back to camp, Libby returned to her tent, sending everyone away to enjoy the party. She said she was tired and didn't want to be disturbed. Since there was no threat, she didn't get any push back. She'd just defeated a dragon; who wouldn't be tired?

She sat down on her bed and stared at Jasper. "How do we make this work?" she asked him.

He just stared at her with hatred in his eyes, refusing to speak. He coiled up even tighter. If it weren't for his wings, he'd look like a small snake. He was snake-like enough that the idea of touching him made her skin crawl. Her revulsion was mildly funny, considering she'd just faced off against him as a house-sized dragon.

"Well, okay then. Here goes nothing." She wove a tranquilizer spell and opened his cage. She grabbed him by the neck before he could bite her. He fought her until the tranquilizer took effect. "Jasper, you and I are going to be spending a lot of time together." She wrapped him around her left wrist, winding what was left of his tail up and around her arm. She could feel the softness of his scaly skin, and the ripples of his muscles even though he was asleep. She had to fight the urge to fling him off. She kept a firm grip on his neck, just in case he was tricking her. She closed her eyes and opened her heart chakra, releasing the same pink glow as she had in the clearing. This time she wasn't singing. She focused her intention on Jasper and willed their joining into reality. She had no idea what would happen but was trusting her intuition and heart magic.

She wasn't sure how long she'd been there but woke to Awen and Geoffrey yelling for her to wake up. She opened her eyes and knew immediately that it had worked. She could feel Jasper slithering on her wrist and could hear him in her head. It was a bit distracting. "I will kill you! What have you done?!" he screamed at her.

"Be silent," she commanded, muting him.

"What did you do?" demanded Awen. "Tell me exactly what you did. I felt the magic like a beacon and everyone could see the glow coming from your tent."

"I did what needed to be done."

"Where is Jasper?" Geoffrey had noticed the empty cage and had his sword in hand, ready to take action.

Libby lifted her left arm. They could see the glittering black dragon tattooed around her arm, bright blue eyes scowling at them. If they looked long enough they could swear the tattoo moved.

"Oh, for fuck's sake!" Awen screamed. "Libby, what did you do?"

"Jasper is safe. I am safe. You are to tell no one about this. That's the only way this will work. We will tell the world that Jasper attacked me and was killed in self-defense. His body was burned by a spell and there is nothing left to prove he existed." Jasper stopped moving as he digested this bit of information. That was actually a good strategy to keep opportunistic trophy hunters off his back until he could figure out how to separate from Libby and kill her—and he would figure out a way.

Awen and Geoffrey looked at each other. Both knew she was right about the need for secrecy. The world was better off thinking Jasper was dead. But with no information about how this worked, they were concerned for her safety.

Awen nodded at Geoffrey and sent him out to have everyone stand down. "What did you do, Libby?" she asked, much calmer now. "I need to know."

"I have no idea. I just willed it to happen and poured my energy into that intention. And here we are."

He was furious and kept tightening around her arm until she had to order him to back off.

"I was wrong about you," Jasper snarled at her. "You're not brilliant. You're insane."

"Perhaps. But now we're in this together.

"Until I figure out how to undo this and kill you.

"And you'll remain silent unless I speak to you first."

"You can't tell me what to do, girlie! How dare you! As if I wanted to speak to you."

He was growling and cursing, but she'd already hit the mute button so it was wasted effort.

Ever since you were a little girl
Your daddy told you, you could run the world
And I knew it when we met that day
When you were sitting in the corner sipping Earl Gray
You had the sweetest dreams in your eyes
But burn with the fire chasing sunset skies
As much as I want to hold you I couldn't hold you back.

There's no stopping you
'Cause your mind's set to
Where your heart says go
Go on go girl go
I hope you find me in a stranger's smile
Hope you hear me in the lonely miles
You gotta do what you were born to do
'Cause there's no stopping you.

~Brett Eldredge, "No Stopping You"

After a triumphant return home, Libby called a council meeting. Corrine and Ava were there as Co-Regents. So were Dyanna and Kurtis, who were now included in all official meetings. Krystal had already returned home to her family. Satisfied that there was nothing more she could teach Libby, Maggie had finally released Krystal from her teaching assignment. Libby was now operating on intuition and working magic they didn't know anything about. Awen and Sophia were more than capable to document it for posterity, but Libby was no longer a student.

They weren't quite sure what to expect when they arrived at the council chamber, but Ava came prepared with financials just in case. Paperwork always made her feel more prepared.

They all stood as Libby arrived, but she motioned for them to be seated. Her blue hair was pulled back in a low ponytail, and she was wearing black jeans tucked into her black riding boots. She peeled off her black leather jacket to reveal a sleeveless navy silk blouse. She looked more like a rock star than a queen. All eyes were drawn to her new tattoo. It was huge, wrapping all the way up her left arm. She'd tattooed Jasper to mark her victory. It was distracting, and shocking. The ink work was beautiful and intricate. As Libby gestured, it almost seemed as if the tattoo was watching them with its brilliant blue eyes. The eyes were reflected in the dark sapphire ring she now wore instead of her wedding ring.

There is way too much glitter on that for it not to have some magic. Corrine thought to herself. *Great, now Dy is going to want a tattoo.*

"Thank you for being here. We have some important things to discuss. First, I want to formally thank you all for your loyalty and bravery in the face of adversity. Our Kingdom, owes you a debt of gratitude, as do I.

"I'll just get right to it then. I'm taking a short leave of absence. Before I assume the role of King *and* Queen I need to take some time to figure out what that means for me as a person. And I have a promise to keep that requires some time away. Awen and Sophia, Fynnigan tells me we've figured out how to anchor the barrier to a ley line, keeping the force field intact, even if something happens to me. I'm assigning Fynn the lead on that project, and we'll implement that immediately. While I don't love the idea of anchoring permanently, I'll do whatever it takes to keep the Kingdom safe in my absence.

"Ava and Corrine, you've done an excellent job as Co-Regents during the quest. You will continue in that role but include Dyanna and Kurtis as well so that they can continue their education on ruling the Kingdom." She looked at her heirs. "You two have made me proud. I expect you to continue to learn. I expect you to be active participants, but to also respect the decisions the Co-Regents make, even if you don't agree with them. When Ava goes on maternity leave, you will jointly take her role but will defer to Corrine's judgement, as well as that of Geoffrey and Scarlett.

Ava looked both shocked and relieved. She was going to get a break with her baby after all. Brilliant. Kurtis and Dyanna looked at each other in surprise. They were nervous and excited, but after facing Jasper this seemed easy. They'd matured a lot over the last year, but those big grins they both wore reminded Libby of how young they were.

She looked at her security chief. "I know that you're already mentally planning logistics for my journey. You can stop. I'll be going alone."

For the first time anyone could remember, Sean stopped typing into his tablet. "You think you're doing what?" he challenged. Sean was already planning out how his spy network could keep tabs on her.

"I'm going alone, and without observation. This is necessary. My decision has been made. I will return no later than one year from now. I promise to stay in regular contact with you. Should a decision require my opinion or blessing, you know how to reach me, either by magic or by phone."

A year ago, there would have been vociferous arguments from the group, but their Queen had just done the impossible. They were uneasy, but there was little they could say to dissuade her.

Libby looked at Scarlett and assured her, "I've already spoken with Larra. She hates this idea but has begrudgingly agreed to respect my privacy on the condition I check in weekly. The day I'm one minute late you have my blessing to set her loose on the Normal world. During my absence she will be doing some travel of her own but will also be accessible."

Scarlett replied hesitantly, "Okay. I guess. Not one minute late. And since we're all here, I want to make it clear that I'm not postponing my retirement plans any further."

"I wouldn't ask you to. I'll be back before then. I have complete faith in all of you to carry on, business as usual, in my absence. I trust the decisions you make. And again, I'll be available to discuss anything you feel needs my attention."

She was already packed, so Libby said her farewells to the group, and rode off with Hoss for the overnight trip to a border town where she had a friend. The Gallagher farm was a peaceful oasis, and the mistress always welcomed Libby with open arms. Libby wasn't staying this time but was leaving Hoss. Hoss was furious, but once she left the barrier, horseback was no longer an option. Hoss was safer here. "Hey Buddy, I promise I'll be back to get you. I love you. I'll be gone a while but will need you here waiting for me when I get back. They'll take good care of you here. I'll miss you. And don't worry, I'll have Jasper with me."

Hoss bared his teeth and snapped at her left arm. He could smell Jasper on her, even though humans could only smell her lilac perfume.

"Hey boy, it's okay. I'll be okay."

She gave him a long hug before turning towards the house to speak with Mrs. Gallagher. After, she headed to the break in the barrier that would take her to Cavehill in Belfast and the start of her adventure.

Chapter 22

Anonymous

Just like she always did when she didn't know where to start, Libby began in Belfast. While she had friends there, she was happy with the anonymity. With the exception of Dee and Mark, people here didn't know who she really was, and no one had met Dale. She could be anyone. Meet anyone. Do anything—go dancing, kiss handsome flirty men in pubs, do crazy things—and no one cared.

There was no one giving her the look of pity, and no one was looking over her shoulder, trying to protect her. That was probably the hardest, and the biggest surprise. Dale had full faith in her abilities but tended to be overprotective and treated her like a fragile china doll. It had been annoying at times, but she realized now she missed it terribly. She didn't need anyone to take care of her, but she missed having someone want to. She missed not having to be strong all the time. She missed having him to lean on.

It was liberating to have no one looking to her to save them or lead them or do anything for them. She didn't miss that feeling of everyone wanting something from her, and the sense of obligation that came with her role in life.

Still, the loneliness was overwhelming. She willed herself to fight through the waves that threatened to drown her. There was no way she'd dishonor Dale's memory by failing to live the most out of every minute of this life she'd never planned on, even if it hurt. So she threw herself into it, dragging Jasper along for the ride.

Belfast had always been good to Libby. So had Dee. The two women picked up right where they'd left off, which always meant Friday nights at McHugh's Pub to see Dee's husband, Mark and his best friend Gary play. On this Friday night, the one Libby would later recall changed everything, it was wall-to-wall people. Dee was tall, beautiful and regal; exactly what you'd expect from a direct descendant of the ancient Irish King Brian Boru. Since Libby was short, it was sometimes a challenge to elbow her way to the bar on nights when it was this crowded. So while Dee headed off to get the first round, Libby looked around to find them some seats. She managed to find two, conveniently located next to the most beautiful blue eyes she'd ever seen. She gave their owner a big smile and he motioned for her to come over.

When Dee finally made her way to the table with their drinks, Libby and the handsome red-haired man were deep in conversation. The music and the crowd were loud, giving them an excuse to sit even closer together so they could hear each other. Dee caught Mark's attention from the stage, and made a motion as if to say, "Are you seeing what I'm seeing?" Mark blew her a kiss and grinned through most of his next set. Libby McGregor only had eyes for the handsome man next to her and was oblivious to all of it.

The next morning, Dee grilled Libby over tea.

"Well, tell me everything!"

Libby grinned in spite of herself. "What's to tell?"

"You were practically sitting in his lap, and it was like the rest of us were invisible. Spill it."

Libby laughed. "We used to know each other a long time ago. It's been years. He's smart. And funny. I enjoyed talking to him. And, damn, time has been good to him. He wants to see me again, but I'm not sure I'm ready to think about anything else."

"Libby, we never know what we want—"

Libby interrupted and finished Dee's favorite bit of advice, "We just learn what we don't want. I know."

"How will you ever learn if you don't try?" Dee paused to drink some tea. "Just have fun and see what happens."

"We'll see."

"Hmph. Well, what have you learned you don't want?"

Libby sighed. Dee wasn't going to let this go. "I don't want someone married. I don't want someone that makes me feel like an afterthought. And I sure as hell don't want someone who thinks they have to compete with Dale.

As for what I want? I don't exactly know, but the bar has been set high. I'm not looking for a replacement for Dale. That's not even possible. But even if you take Dale out of the equation, the other men in my life have set the standard, and that includes my fifteen-year-old nephew! They have my best interests at heart. They love me for who I am, not who they think they can fix me to be. They pull no punches, but still care about my feelings. They believe in me and remind me of my worth when I forget. They check on me, despite knowing I can hold my own. They let me figure out how to make my own decisions, even if it means maybe making a mistake. So I don't know what exactly it is that I want, but I at least want that." Libby's voice had gone up an octave with the emotion behind her words.

Dee just sat there sipping her tea, feeling proud of herself for getting Libby to put some thought into it. Now that the conversation had lulled, Libby was lost in thought. Every now and again a smile would cross her face. Since Libby wouldn't even volunteer his name, Dee was forced to give the mystery man a nickname. Redman seemed to fit his red curls, and was easier to say than "Friday Night McHugh's Guy." She smiled again as she calculated how long she'd have to wait to start digging for information on Libby's past with Redman.

Tender is the ghost
The ghost I love the most
Hiding from the sun
Waiting for the night to come
Tender is my heart
I'm screwing up my life
Lord I need to find
Someone who can heal my mind
Tender, Blur

She woke up and, for a few minutes, thought she was back in the palace. Then Libby realized she was in the flat she'd rented in Belfast a few weeks ago. She should have just bought one years ago but had kept dragging her feet. Since she could come and go through the portal it had never seemed like a priority. She got up to pull open the curtains, and quickly dove back into the warm bed. She felt she was being watched and sat up quickly, rubbing her eyes awake. She saw Dale sitting at the foot of the bed, like he used to when he was alive.

"Good Morning, Babe," he said, smiling at her.

"Make yourself useful and bring me coffee." She grouched, punching her pillows so she could lean up against them.

"Hilarious. Still a morning person, I see. You know I'd make it for you like always if I could."

"I know. I miss you. Why'd you have to leave me?"

"I'm right here."

"It's not the same".

"I know it's not. That's what I'm here to talk to you about. I think it's great that you are moving forward and still living life, but I don't want you to be alone."

"I'm not alone," she interrupted.

"You know what I mean. I know you have lots of friends. But Ash, it's time for you to take a chance on someone. Don't be alone. And before you say it, that fucking snake around your arm doesn't count."

"Fuck off, Dale. I told you, I'm not having this conversation with you. And you know I've been trying."

"You know damned well that's not what I mean. Chatting up guys in pubs and going on dates is fine, but you have to let someone know the real you. I know John tells you all the time, I like that guy more and more by the way, but you are a diamond. Diamonds don't try to get found. People come looking for the diamond. But when the right guy finds the diamond in you, you have to let him try to love you. I know how lonely you are, and how afraid you are. This arm's length bullshit has to stop. And I'm not going to lie, it will take time to find the one that is strong enough to love you; that is worthy to love you. The real you. You have to keep letting them try. But before any of that can happen, you have to figure out who you are first.

"I know you love it here, but you need to hit the road. Belfast will always be here, but it's too comfortable. Go out into the world again. See beautiful new places, meet interesting people. Go have stupid reckless adventures that you know I'd try to talk you out of. Go have fun."

Libby sighed and pulled the pillow over her head. "If it's that important to you, why don't you just find the right guy and send him my way?"

"Where's the fun in that?" He laughed. "Seriously, Ash, you know that's not how it works. No matter what a spirit may think or try to maneuver, the living have free will. Most guys are intimated by you. Not everyone can be as awesome as I am. As I was," he corrected, shaking his head. "Trust me. These yahoos you keep finding really do care about you; they just worry you're out of their league—which you are—and don't know how to handle it. Nothing I can do about that. In fact, their inability to deal with it makes them all wrong for you, no matter how much you may like them. I know you and Krystal have already talked about this. Why do you waste so much time asking questions you already know the answer to?"

"Where's the fun in that?" she snarked back.

"Babe, just do it. Give them a shot. You'll know if I don't like them. Stay away from musicians, though. You're too susceptible to the music magic and you don't think clearly. And get rid of that dragon as soon as possible."

She could hear him laughing as she flipped him off and rolled over.

"Super helpful, Dale. Thanks for nothing, Fucker!" She fought back a wave of loneliness and fear. "Fine. I guess it's time to go. Where should I go next?"

"If I weren't bonded to you, I'd vomit right now," snarked Jasper. "The least you could do is let me sleep. No. You have to wake me up with that drivel. Whining about a man? I expected better of you, Libby. I'm disappointed."

"Good thing I give zero fucks what you think, Jasper. I thought you weren't to speak to me unless I spoke to you first?"

"You did. You asked where you should go next. I hate the cold here, and the fucking annoying music and happy Irish people you seem to love. Go someplace warm with a beach where I can sun myself and pretend I'm not trapped with you."

"You can't hide here forever," he persisted.

"Wanna bet?"

"You know you won't abandon your Kingdom for a man. Even if you found the right one. I don't even know what to say about your choice in men, other than you clearly lucked out with Dale. Wait, your dad picked him out, so maybe you just need someone else's help."

"Shut up, Jasper." Anyone else would have heard the warning in her tone and backed off. Not Jasper.

"Let's review. First, you find the Widow Hunter. Ridiculous and stupidly gullible. Then, you fall for the famous musician who you know is temporary. Any fool can see that you're choosing men who aren't available because you aren't ready for a relationship. This diversion needs to be over. It's time for us to go."

Libby was angry, but more at the truth of what Jasper was saying than the words he was using. She sighed. She didn't want to admit it, but she'd felt the familiar stirrings of itchy feet. He was right. She still wouldn't trust anyone enough to let them get close. Maybe she didn't trust herself not to make a mistake and chose men who wouldn't put her in a position to make a choice? "Damn it, Jasper!"

While she hadn't admitted it to herself until now, she hadn't been able to stop thinking about the blue-eyed Redman she'd run into that night at McHugh's. Dee's nickname had stuck, and that's how Libby also referred to him these days. She knew he travelled as much as she did, and wondered where he was now, and if he ever thought about her.

She shook her head and stopped that train of thought, and muted Jasper. Jasper felt the loneliness and sadness come rushing back the minute she'd made the decision to leave Belfast. He didn't understand. How could someone like her, a Warrior Queen who'd bested him in combat, be so dependent on another human for love and companionship? *It is their need for love that makes humans so weak,* he thought derisively to himself, *even someone like Libby.* He shook his head and went back to sleep now that he knew they'd be on the road soon.

Chapter 23

Time to Go

I like that you're broken, broken like me.
Maybe that makes me a fool.
I like that you're lonely, lonely like me.
I could be lonely with you.
~Lovelytheband, "Broken"

ibby spent months traveling the globe, as Dale had instructed. She met people, had adventures, went on dates, and even had a few thoughts about trying a relationship. But more often than not she was on her own. Over time, she got used to both being alone and the loneliness that came with being a widow. She still had no idea of who she was supposed to be, or what she was supposed to do with Jasper. Eventually, she got used to that too.

That didn't mean she'd stop trying to connect with someone beyond a platonic friendship. After that night in McHugh's, when she'd reconnected with Redman, they'd stayed in touch. Their old familiarity had eventually won out over her understanding that a future with him wasn't destined to be, no matter how much she'd like it to work. She quickly found herself back in the warmth and safety of his embrace.

But now she knew it was time to move on and felt the wave of loneliness at her decision to leave. Sometimes she wondered if she was destined to be alone the rest of her life, if the universe only allowed each person one chance at an epic love. She always shook that off. She believed that if our hearts were meant to grow and accommodate an unlimited number of hearts to love, then that meant the Universe had designed it to be so. It didn't make the endings hurt any less, and she was struggling to let this one go. She was horrified at the realization that she'd grown to love this man, even though he'd never know the real Libby. She hadn't intended to let him get this close again. She certainly hadn't planned to move in with him, yet here she was.

And then there was Jasper. He was the only constant in her life. He'd sleep for long periods of time, but knowing he was there kept her from being as lonely. She'd found that she looked forward to his snarky commentary when he was awake. Was it possible Jasper filled the void left behind when Dalen died? He'd never admit it, but he begrudgingly respected her. She'd managed to do something only one other person in history had done. She'd survived an unendurable pain and then thrived. She never gave up. That was both her most irritating and endearing quality. Even when her faith wavered, she persevered. She'd have made a good dragon. Well, except for the needing other humans part.

Libby left the little house she shared with Redman and went for a stroll along the river to clear her head. She found a quiet dock and walked to the end before sitting down to meditate for a bit. She was unsettled and anxious. She hadn't felt this sad in a long time. She knew she had to make this decision. She loved this man. He was a good man, and he loved her back, in his own way. Despite their compatibility, it wasn't right for either of them, and she knew it. How could it be, since he'd never know who she really was, and without that she'd always be holding back? Hell, Dale was right. She was only just figuring out who she was, how could any man know her if she didn't know herself? To be fair, while he'd gotten closer than anyone else, she still kept him at arm's length. She felt that doubt creep back in, and the fear that if she left, she'd be alone forever. Dale chose that moment to show up. He always had impeccable timing.

Dale's head bobbed up out of the water in the middle of a paddling of ducks. "Hey, Babe. Penny for your thoughts?"

"Nice of you to duck in." She rolled her eyes. "I'm just trying to figure out if waiting for Mr. Right is worth it or if I should just go for Mr. Right Now."

"Ash, you have to believe me. The right guy is out there for you. The one who will love the real you. But first you need to figure out who you are. The real you. Who you are at the core."

"So you keep saying. You tell me not to quit trying. You tell me to wait for the one. You tell me to have faith, but don't have any answers for me."

Dale pulled himself out of the water and took a soggy seat next to Libby. "Have you ever thought that not having the answers is the answer?"

"Great, Dale. Fucking great. Is that like the sound of one hand clapping?"

"Funny. Babe, please just wait. You need to be okay with being alone."

"Really? The last time you told me to give men the opportunity to get close and not to shut them out. It's hard to learn to be okay with being alone if I'm always spending time with someone. Would you make up your mind? And for the record, I am okay with being alone. Even though I've come to accept being alone, I hate the loneliness. I'm surrounded by people who know and love me and have never felt lonelier in my life. Without you, they only see me as half a person. I didn't just lose my husband when you died. I lost my future. My identity. My purpose in life." She was gesturing and yelling out loud. A passing jogger wondered if he should stop and see if she was okay, then decided better against engaging in conversation with a crazy woman yelling at herself in English.

Dale groaned and covered his face in frustration. "I'm sorry, Ash. I'm still working on my communication skills. I wasn't great at it when I was alive, and it's a lot more challenging now. Clarity is a rarity, as Maggie likes to tell me. What I mean is you need to be okay with who you are. You need to know who you are, and love who you are. Babe. I know you're lonely. I'm truly sorry that I left you alone, but neither of us can change that. This is a time for you to figure out who you are. Until you do, no man will be the right man. Do you understand what I'm saying?"

"I'm working hard to figure out who I'm supposed to be. Growing a heart was fucking easy compared to figuring out who how to live again. Alone. I know in my head I need to wait. I know in my heart he'll never know the real me, and therefore can never give me what I really need, want and deserve. But I also know how good it feels to have someone remember how I like my coffee and have it waiting for me when I wake up in the morning. How having a hand reaching out to hold mine in the dark makes me feel connected to another human. How his arms around me make me feel safe and less alone. How we talk for hours about everything and nothing. How being with someone, even the wrong someone, makes me miss us a little less."

"Ash," Dale started again.

She held up her hands to cut him off. "No. Don't say it. I'm not looking for a replacement for you. There is no way that would ever be possible. I'm not the same person I was. I just want the closeness of having a partner in this shit show we call life, someone to have my back. I can't even let myself imagine what it would be like to find someone who sees me. The real me. The me no one but you ever knew. The me no one else, or at least no other men, seem to want to know. So back to my original dilemma. Mr. Right? Or Mr. Right Now?"

Dale sighed. "Aisling Elisabeth McGregor, please stop. Have faith. I will always be with you. Have faith that it will all work out."

Then he was gone again.

She remained seated at the edge of the dock. Tears were running down her face. She knew Dale was right, but damn, the loneliness was miserable. She wasn't ready to go back yet, so leaned back to stare at the sky. She popped in her earbuds and started listening to music, enjoying the sunshine on her face and the breeze in her hair. Her hair. A week ago she'd made the decision to dye it back to her original color. There was something symbolic in getting back to the red she'd been born with. A visible symbol of accepting her role in life, the one she was born to play. She hadn't told Redman she was going to do that, and when he got home from work, he was startled. She'd laughed when he told her she was like a box of crayons and he never knew what color she'd show up with next. She'd joked that she was only trying to be as pretty as he was. The sweet memory made her miss him already.

Jasper was awake and had heard the entire exchange but had remained still and silent. He knew she was crying. She cried a lot. It disturbed him that it disturbed him. Why should he care if she was sad? Her loneliness and longing for a companion was a weakness. He should be exploiting that. But he didn't, and he didn't know why. He'd have had a fit if he'd known the emotion he was feeling was called compassion. The man she was with couldn't appreciate her fully because he didn't know anything but her Normal persona, but she seemed to love him. Although even a Normal could see they were both holding back. Idiots. Humans were so bad at communicating their true feelings. *She deserves better,* he thought, and then started cursing at himself for caring. He willed himself back to sleep so he could stop thinking about her.

Now he's brought down the rain, and
the Indian summer is through
In the morning you'll be following your trail again, fair lady

You ain't calling me to join you, and I'm spoken for anyway
But I will cry when ye go away

Your beauty is familiar, and your voice is like a key
That opens up my soul and torches up a fire inside of me

Your coat is made of magic and around your table angels play
And I will cry when ye go away

Somebody left us whisky and the night is very young
I've got some to say and more to tell
And the words will soon be spilling from my tongue

~The Waterboys, "When Ye Go Away"

Libby walked to the end of the lane with only the streetlight to guide her path. Her bag slung over her shoulder, she looked back at the house she'd just left. She was torn. She wanted to run back to Redman, running her fingers through his red curls and kissing him awake. He was used to her sudden departures since they both traveled so much, him on business and her on adventures he thought were related to her job as an international art buyer. She'd left him a note saying good-bye and that she would check in with him later. She just had no idea if, or when, that would ever happen. As if he knew what she was thinking, Jasper chose that moment to startle her with a, "Are you just going to stand in the middle of the street all day? You're making everything they say about gingers out to be true." Libby shook herself out of it and turned around, wiping the tears off her face.

"Give it a rest, Jasper," she said as she strode off down the street to hop a train to the airport. She needed to get far away so she wouldn't waiver in her decision. Going to the other side of the planet seemed like a good idea.

A few hours later she was stretched out on an airplane, glass of whiskey in her hand, wondering if he'd found her note. She'd told him the night before she was leaving to go back on the road. She'd just left out the part where she was going and for how long. She knew sneaking out was pathetic, but after saying good-bye to Dale, she couldn't bear the thought of saying good-bye to anyone again. She shook her head. How had she allowed herself to get so attached to Redman?

Jasper, she thought, *I'm taking you home.* She looked down at the sleeping dragon on her arm and wondered how this would go.

After weeks of travel through China and Japan, Libby awoke one night with a start. She'd been dreaming of Dale's death, but in her dream, everything was mixed up. She was both Libby and Michie, and Dale and Ryunosuke were one and the same. She watched Dale take the arrow, and then they were back at the palace, only it was Ryunosuke dying in Dale's bed, and he was about to be devoured by Jasper. It was the first nightmare Libby'd had since the duel. Jasper had been awakened by her fear. When he realized there was no threat, he closed his eyes but couldn't go back to sleep.

Interesting, he thought. He wondered what she'd been dreaming about. He couldn't read her thoughts, but could feel her pain, loneliness, and fear. He could also feel her joy. He'd never met anyone with the complexities of emotions that ran through Libby daily, and was surprised that she could feel joy in the midst of great loneliness, or excitement despite her sorrow.

He'd spent a lot of time analyzing and trying to figure out what she'd done in her joining spell. He'd never heard of such a thing before. In fact, the closest thing he could determine was a royal marriage heart graft. While they weren't sharing hearts, they were definitely connected. He'd begun to worry whether the spell would be reversible without killing them both. Her power and survival instinct were incredible, that was true, but they were also totally wild and mostly untrained. Although even he was unclear how she did what she did, he began to theorize that her lack of instruction was a benefit, kind of like when someone learns to play the piano by ear or feel rather than read music. He snorted. It always came back to music with her. He just hoped they could figure it out, so they weren't stuck with each other for the rest of their lives. He was uncertain whether he would survive her death, despite the near-immortality dragons enjoyed. At some point he'd run out of time.

He was stunned by the realization that he no longer wanted to kill her. He analyzed his feelings for her and knew that the jig was up. Somehow, after helplessly feeling her feelings for so long, he'd grown to care for her. Care about her. *How did this happen?* he wondered. *Damn her magic.*

The two had arrived in Iwakuni-shi in the late morning. Libby took a deep breath in and smiled. She was back in the Motherland, and it felt great. It was hard to explain to her friends who had never left their home countries. Despite not growing up in Japan, it was the land of her ancestors and returning would always feel like coming home. It was in her blood, and every cell recognized the energy of the land, water, and air and celebrated her return. The same thing happened every time she visited Ireland. She wasn't born in either place, but both were home.

Something in Jasper changed. This place felt...familiar. He couldn't explain it. Maybe after all this time with Libby he was channeling her homecoming response. He was almost giddy.

Libby felt the change, and jokingly said, "Down, boy."

"Shut up, Libby," he said but he was smiling, and pulling her by the arm towards the castle on the hill.

After dropping her bags at the traditional Japanese ryokan they'd be lodging at, they took a taxi to Kintai Bridge, which was now a famous landmark. Libby had spent a lot of time there in her youth, decades before she'd learned the connection to Michie. It was just as beautiful as she remembered it. The last time she was there it was cherry blossom season, and she'd enjoyed the traditional hanami[4] party with her friends and cousins along the river bank. The memory faded as she was distracted by Jasper, who was practically shaking with excitement.

"What's gotten into you?" Libby demanded, laughing.

"I don't know," he replied honestly. "But I'm supposed to be here."

Libby strolled across the bridge, merging the view she was looking at with Michie's memories. The river had changed a bit, and the city wasn't there in Michie's time, but overall it wasn't too different. When they'd rebuilt the iconic bridge, they were careful to keep it the same. She looked up at the gleaming white castle on the hill. It would have had archers patrolling the walls, and pennants would have been flying everywhere, but it was still there. They walked up the path to the castle. Libby was grateful it was a weekday and not very crowded. Talk about double vision. Seeing through two sets of eyes was disconcerting and made for tripping hazards. Libby wasn't allowed to access the entire castle, which was now a museum and tourist attraction, but did manage to find one section of wall that was open. As she stood there, she relived Michie's memories of the oni's curse.

She looked down at Jasper on her arm. Maggie had told her to trust herself and her decisions. Libby felt a moment of anxiety when she realized it was time to let him go. She'd be alone again but knew this was what she needed to do. With a big sigh, and a surprising

---

4   Hanami is the traditional Japanese cherry blossom viewing picnic held in the spring.

wave of sadness, she made her way back down to the river. Along the bank, she ducked under one of the dry archways of the bridge to have some privacy.

"Jasper, it's time for me to release you."

"What? How?" he demanded.

"Please let me finish. It's time. I can't believe I'm saying this but I'm going to miss you. You've been a pain in my ass from the beginning but being with you has made me less lonely. I'm grateful for the time we've spent together."

"Are you sure you know what you're doing?" he asked.

"Of course not. When do I ever know what I'm doing? But this feels right. It's time to set you free. It feels like it must be here. I expect you to leave my people in peace. If you can do that, you can always visit me. If you want to."

Jasper observed her in silence. He wasn't going to volunteer any information, but he was going to miss her too. She took insane risks, but was also highly intuitive. He admired her bravery.

"Just do it," he replied, holding his breath.

Libby sat down and closed her eyes, taking a deep breath. She opened her heart chakra and let it fill with love and light. She directed that love at Jasper. She created her intention to release him and filled it with her love magic.

Jasper was intently watching every move she made. He started to glow pink when he felt the graft release, and uncurled from Libby's arm. This time the feel of his scaly coils didn't make her skin crawl. She felt him stretch out for the first time in almost a year, and he took off flying low over the river. He picked up speed, circling back around and through the arches like a dog on an agility course. Then he dove into the river, speeding under the surface before bursting straight up in the air, higher than the castle walls.

Libby watched him and noticed that he was changing. He was growing, yes. But he was also getting lighter in the sunlight. As Jasper slowly spiraled his way down to the river bank where Libby was standing, he continued to fade until he was no longer black, but glittering white, like a pearl in the sun. A white dragon just like in the pennants from Michie's dream memories. Jasper landed lightly and came up to Libby.

Oh, my Goddess, thought Libby. *When the oni cast his curse, he must have sent the family guardian away and wiped his memory.* Libby assumed that the white dragon on Michie's crest was a family guardian, a spirit protector of their family and kingdom.

Libby was only half right.

"You've honored your word, Aisling Elisabeth McGregor. You've kept me safe and have now released me of your own free will. You would have made a good dragon. I can't believe I'm saying this, but I'm going to miss you. Although if you tell anyone you've tamed the dragon, I will kill you without a second thought."

Libby didn't have time to respond to what he'd unknowingly admitted because Jasper started to shiver and shake at those words.

"What's happening?" he screamed in pain, terrified, as his hide began to bubble and split open.

He burst open, and before she knew it, Libby was standing face-to-face with the man she knew only from her dreams.

"What just happened?" Libby whispered, although she already knew the answer.

"Libby. Mago-chan," the man smiled. "You did it. You broke the curse. You tamed the black dragon and freed me."

"Grandfather? All this time you've been Jasper?"

Through the tears, Libby willed Michie to appear.

Michie was mid-greeting when she saw him, and cried out, "Ryunosuke!" She ran into his open arms. "It's you! I've looked for you for so long. Beloved, is it really you?"

"Yes, my Queen. It is really me."

She stepped out of his embrace and turned to Libby. "Thank you. Thank you," she said dropping to her knees. Libby knew that it was an honor to receive such a deep bow from an elder, and returned it, even though the river rocks cut into her knees.

Michie and Ryunosuke fell into each other's arms once more and disappeared.

"Goodbye. I'll miss you." They were gone by the time the words had left her mouth.

"Alone again," Libby sighed as she got back to her feet and turned toward the taxi stand. She was spent. The gorgeous view no longer held her attention. She wondered if the ryokan had any Japanese whiskey on hand that she could enjoy while taking a long hot soak in the natural hot spring, or onsen, that the ryokan was built on. "What a day, Libby. What a day."

Her task completed, Libby returned to Europe on the next available flight out of Tokyo. Her arm felt naked every time her eyes caught a glimpse of bare skin. Like a weird tan line, there was a faint outline of where Jasper had been. Life without him was strangely quiet, but not sad. She felt lighter without his weight, but also lonely again. Knowing that she'd played a small role in Michie and Ryunosuke's love story made her smile. At least one of them got a happy ending. It gave Libby hope. She knew that she'd be reunited with Dale again someday but didn't want to wait til she died to find happiness again. She realized that Scarlett had been right, that day on the banks of the lake. Her heart was large enough to accommodate as much love as she wanted. She was surprised to realize that she was ready to try again. She was ready to get back to living her life. A whole life.

Libby made her way back to the man she'd left behind when she decided to take Jasper to Asia. She'd missed Redman, and he'd been waiting for her. They quickly settled back into their comfortable routine. It was peaceful and quiet, and she loved it. They'd go for walks, talk for hours, and she was content to just snuggle up with him in silence in front of the fire. Life with him was the opposite of adventure. More than any place she'd ever been outside her palace, he felt like home.

One morning, she woke up and realized that she had nothing left to learn about herself by traveling, and that while she had people she cared deeply about here, she missed home.

"Dale, I don't know if you can hear me, but I think I'm ready. I've made peace with being alone and found beauty in the loneliness. I've found love and happiness despite that. I'm ready to come home. I'm ready to be King. All by myself. And not because it's my duty, but because I want to. It's who I was born to be. It's who I am. It's the real me."

She paused, waiting for a response. When she didn't get one, she sighed and rolled out of bed to start making arrangements for her return, careful not to wake the man sleeping next to her. The one she had to leave behind, for good this time. It was time. Despite her penchant for leaving when things got too serious, she'd never stopped loving him. Even though he loved her too, Redman didn't know who she really was. She knew him well enough to know he'd never be able to accept that magic was real or love her as King Libby. She decided that was okay, and that she was grateful for what they'd shared. She wanted the best for him, even if it wasn't her. It was time to go home.

She was in the middle of booking her train tickets online when her phone rang, causing her to jump. The ring startled her since she rarely received phone calls on the road. She picked it up when she realized it was John.

"Hey, John. What's up, my friend?"

"Hey Libby, are you okay?"

"Yeah, I'm fine. Why?"

"Okay. Ugh, this makes me really uncomfortable. You know how I am about this stuff. I just can't take it anymore."

"John Leonard Morgan, what the hell is going on?"

"Okay, I know this is crazy. It's Dale. I've been dreaming about him. Same dream every night. I'm fucking exhausted, so taking a chance I'm not actually losing my mind. I'm supposed to call you and tell you that, and I quote, 'He's a good guy and loves you and I know you love him, but it's not right and you know it. The right one will know the real you. Don't settle.'"

Libby was silent.

"Are you still there? Libs, I'm sorry, I didn't know what to do."

John couldn't see her shaking her head, but he was relieved when she started laughing. "It's okay, buddy. Thanks for delivering the message. If it makes you feel better, even though I wish it weren't true, I already knew. Just so you know, Dale likes you and it's a compliment that he visited you with this."

"Sweet Jaysus, that's a relief. Well, the part where you already knew. I don't need him to like me or ever visit me again. You'll have to fill me in later on the details, which will include discussing why I didn't know about this mystery dude in the first place, but Dale's right. Don't fucking settle. You're a goddamned diamond Libs, no settling."

"Love you, John, I'll talk to you later. I'm on my way home."

"Love you too, Libby."

She sighed and looked up at the ceiling. "Well, Dale, I guess if that's your reply that it's time to go home, I'll take it. For fuck's sake, next time don't make me go through the whole relationship process before waiting for me to figure out he's not for me. It would save me a lot of heartache and tears, and I think I've cried enough of them for one lifetime."

Later that morning she told Redman that she needed to return home to her responsibilities there and wouldn't be back. Ever. He wasn't one to show his emotions, so she wasn't sure he even cared that she was leaving. No, that wasn't fair. She knew he was disappointed, but they'd had a unique on and off again relationship. This was par for the course. Libby knew it was permanent this time, even if he didn't fully believe it yet.

'Tis better to have loved and lost
Than never to have loved at all.
~Alfred Tennyson, "In Memoriam"

Libby opened her eyes to find the sun streaming through the window. She stretched out like a cat until she realized it was moving day and the smile faded from her face. Travel days were always sad for her. She hated goodbyes and the longer she stayed anywhere the harder it was. She loved meeting people, so it wasn't hard to make friends wherever she went. Anything longer than a week and she'd have favorite pubs and cafés and people that it hurt to leave. She'd already been here far too long. She rolled over and hugged the empty pillow, fighting back the tears. She knew this was necessary, but damn, why did it have to hurt so much? Redman had left the day before on business, so there was no awkward goodbye, just a last look at the cozy house they shared when she was in town. It was the closest she'd gotten to feeling like a home since she'd left the palace almost a year ago. It was hard to leave.

She laughed to herself and wondered what the afternoon talk shows would say about her abandonment issues. "On today's *Dr. Phil*, the Warrior Queen who defeated a dragon but has anxiety attacks when she says good-bye, so runs away before she forms strong attachments to people despite her overwhelming loneliness. News flash: She sucks at it and falls in love with everyone in her life. Back with this Catch-22 after this word from our sponsors."

She sometimes wondered if her new friends knew how quickly they took up residence in her still-fragile heart, and how important they became to her. While she never showed it, those good-byes almost always ended in private tears when she was alone. She wanted so desperately to stay with them. Tennyson said it was better to have loved and lost than to have never loved at all. She'd met other grieving widows along the way who railed against that theory, but she believed it and worked hard to keep her heart open no matter how much it hurt to lose again.

She'd said her goodbyes to the people who mattered the night before, so a few hours later she was watching the world speed by outside the window. Once the train got out of the city, she felt her heart pang with wistfulness at how beautiful the countryside was. She'd miss the windmills and tulips and forests, but it was time to begin the trek towards home.

Who knows? she thought, trying to cheer herself up. *Maybe someday life will bring me back this way again.*

An American girl
Whiskey in the jar
Watches the world go by in an Irish bar.
An American girl
A Gibson guitar
Watches the world go by from an Irish bar.

And I know she'll be gone
Yeah, I know she'll be gone
At the end of this song.

An American girl
Chases a star
Watches the world go by in an Irish bar.
An American girl
The road is long
To watch the sunset
She made me write a song.

And I know she'll be gone
Yeah, I know she'll be gone
At the end of this song.
~Rohan Fitzpatrick, "An American Girl"

Libby was apprehensive about going home. For the first time since they'd become friends, she didn't tell Dee she was coming back to Belfast. Instead, she immediately made her way up to Cavehill, to the opening in the barrier discreetly tucked away. She could have easily taken the emergency portal behind the Duke of York, but she needed to get Hoss, and wanted to meander back across her Kingdom. It gave her time to savor the landscape and really prepare herself for how much her life was going to change. She stepped up to the edge of the rock face and ran her hands over the wall.

She hesitated a moment. This was it. She was really going back. Home.

"Aisling Elisabeth McGregor, you grew yourself a new heart, defeated a freaking dragon, and broke a centuries old curse. You can do this. Put your big girl panties on and pull yourself together woman," she whispered to herself. "It's time to go home."

She fought the urge to run to Dee's. The barrier shimmered, and with a deep breath she stepped through, back to her Kingdom for the first time in a year. She wasn't the same person she was when she left. She wondered how much the Kingdom had changed. She wondered if it would be weird.

Chapter 24

Homecoming

Times have changed and times are strange
Here I come, but I ain't the same
Mama, I'm coming home
~Ozzy Osbourne, "Mama I'm Coming Home"

Her first stop after crossing the force field was the farm where she'd left Hoss. He'd heard her walking up the gravel path before he saw her and came galloping over to greet her. Prancing with happiness but also voicing his displeasure at being left behind.

"Hey, old boy. I've missed you," she said and buried her face in his neck, wrapping her arms around him. "I know, you've missed me too. You've put on some weight. Farm life making you lazy?"

He snorted in response and tried to bite her hair. She was prepared for it, and nimbly stepped out of the way.

"Nice try, buddy. I'm only kidding. You're as beautiful as I remember. Like the hair? Now we match, although I'll never look as beautiful as you. Are you ready to go home?"

Hoss stopped and sniffed at her arm, giving her a questioning look.

"Yes. He's gone. See?" She raised the sleeve of her dark green sweater so he could see her Jasper-free arm.

He nuzzled her arm a bit and then raised his head to smile at her. This was excellent news. And yes, he was ready to go home.

The mistress of the farm had seen her approaching on foot and quickly got to steaming Libby's cloak and getting her travel pack ready. By the time Libby reached the front porch, Ruby Jane Gallagher was waiting with a single malt and a hug.

"It's so good to see you again, Libby. Will you be staying with us awhile?"

"Thank you. No, Hoss and I will be heading home immediately."

Ruby looked her over like she would one of her kids or grandkids. Libby looked good. Fit. Relaxed. Younger? The Queen's time out on her own had done her good. She'd come in to her own. After the pain and suffering she'd endured, it made Ruby happy to see her Queen so well. She'd known Libby for years, since she and her daughter, Harley, had become friends at University. They were both so grown up now, but not so much that Ruby Jane couldn't still feed and nurture them, at least as much as they'd let her.

"Food first. Come on in, the table is set. You've a long journey ahead."

"Yes, ma'am." Libby laughed, allowing Ruby Jane to guide her in, arm about her waist.

After their hearty late morning meal, Libby went for a walk in the nearby woods. She'd grown to love these woods years ago. There was something magical about them. She was sure the tree spirits liked having her visit, because the woods felt happy every time she was there. This visit, however, was different. For the first time she could see the energy of the trees. Everything shimmered green and gold. Grinning, she hugged as many trees as she could. She could feel them call to her and she obliged. She breathed in the sweet smell of the woods and listened to the birds sing and the wind rustle through the treetops. She felt Dale fall in beside her and looked up at him.

"Hi," she said. "I was wondering if I'd see you again."

"Hey, Babe." He looked at her and smiled. "You did it, Ash. I'm so proud of you. I know it's been so hard, and you've wanted to quit. You've faced your fears head on and come out on top. You finally know what the rest of us do, that you are a total badass. You are a survivor. Beyond that, you've thrived. I've loved watching you grow, even though I've had to do it from afar. Nothing brings me more joy than to see you happy again."

"I never wanted you to be alone. I know that taking a chance on love has been the hardest fear for you to face, but you did it, even when it didn't work out. The thing about love is that it has to be freely given with nothing expected in return. I promise you the right guy is out there looking for you." Dale grinned at her before continuing. "He's looking for you right now. The one who will love the real you." He continued as she rolled her eyes at him. "Don't give up. And don't you dare set those wards on your heart again. Promise me you won't."

"I won't," she promised, although her heart still ached for the embrace of the man she'd left behind in the Normal world.

"Babe, I know you're scared to go home, but it's time. You've accomplished what you wanted and needed to do. The Kingdom needs you, and you need to remember that the old you and the new you are still you. You've grown, and you've changed, but you're still Queen Aisling Elisabeth McGregor. It's time to be the whole you. I love you so much, and will never leave you, but it's time for you to go live life without me."

He stopped walking and as she turned around, she could see him smiling at her. She was surprised she didn't feel sad as he faded out. She knew he was right. She smiled, wondering how heavy two crowns would be as she walked back to the farmhouse to get Hoss and head home.

"Thanks again, Ruby Jane. For everything. Feel free to send word that I'm on my way. I know your daughter has probably already ordered you to do it anyway."

Ruby Jane laughed. "That girl can't tell me what to do. But Harley would never let me hear the end of it if I didn't, so thanks for the blessing to do so."

After riding a few hours, Libby left the grassy plains and slowly crossed into the high desert country. She pulled Hoss to a stop so she could breathe in the grandeur of the mountains in the distance, still capped by snow, wrapping around the hot sand glittering across the valley below. The desert valley was separated by a narrow band of sagebrush and the blue green of the river snaking its way to the sea—to home.

She'd forgotten how beautiful it was. It was rugged. Different from the beauty of Scotland or Romania, but just as strong. It was the kind of ruggedness that dared you to make it your own. It still felt untouched by humans. Wild.

Hoss turned to look at her, wondering how long they were going to stay here. She leaned forward in the saddle and stroked his mane. "Hoss, old boy, did you ever think we'd see this view again? I didn't. Truth be told, I didn't really want to. But we're nearly home, and I'm ready. What do you say, keep going?" Hoss started down the trail into the valley. They still had another day of riding if the weather cooperated. His rider may not care about the rain, but he refused to walk in it unless he had to.

The next morning, they were up with the sun. Tonight, they'd be sleeping in their own beds, and both were excited to get started.

The valley gave way to rolling green hills. The sagebrush was left behind and the green pines that took their place grew taller as they made their way further west. As Libby and Hoss climbed the last of the hills, they could begin to smell the salt air of the sea. The sea! It made her giddy to think about it.

Off in the distance she could make out the seaside city surrounded by crystal blue water. She could see waves crashing on the dark gray rocks, and boats coming and going from the harbor. Up on the far hill was the palace surrounded by a grove of ash trees, royal pennants billowing in the wind. Home. She looked down from the top of the hill and for a moment wanted to turn around and run away again. Hoss could sense it and turned his head and snorted at her. He was ready to be home. She was too. She'd probably already been spotted by the knights. She leaned over to hug Hoss. "Thanks, Buddy. Thank you for waiting for me, for being so brave, and always protecting me.

It's been scary and sad and fun and happy. But you're right, it's time to go home. Want to run for a bit?" she asked.

He'd already started at full gallop before the last word had left her lips.

That's what the knights on duty saw from their Tower: Libby and Hoss flying down the side of the hill at full gallop, long red hair flying out behind them. At first glance it would have been easy to mistake them for a centaur, since Libby's new hair color wasn't too different from Hoss's red mane and tail. Libby was wearing her emerald green cloak, though and they'd have known it was her, even without Mrs. Gallagher's phone call. They'd been on the lookout for the last two days. From the top of the Knights' Tower the call went out, "She's back!" By the time she'd reached the outskirts of the forest just outside of town, they were waiting for her. All of them: her knights and Ladies-in-Waiting, her friends.

After the phone call from Mrs. Gallagher, Ava and Corrine sprung into action, getting Libby's quarters ready and putting the kitchen on alert for the return of the knights and LIWs, and the feasting that would commence once Libby was back at the palace. They'd also let Fintan know that she was on her way back so he could be there when she returned. Mrs. Gallagher was two--days ride out, so they'd had a little time. Today's call from the Knights' Tower said she was close, just an hour away. They notified the steward of the new timeline and went to get ready to meet their sister. Before they separated, they high fived and hugged each other with the relief that their sister was alive and back and their duties as Co-Regents were about to come to an end. There was no time, but they'd soon head to the private palace bar for a whiskey to celebrate. For now, there was work to do. Corrine had a party to plan: the coronation of their new king—King Libby.

Libby pulled the reins to slow Hoss as her team waited for her in a clearing. The minute Ruby Jane's call had come in, Sean and Catherine had notified the knights and LIWs, who had returned to the palace immediately. They wanted to be there to welcome her home. Larra came riding in a few paces behind Libby.

Libby looked back without much surprise. "I should have known you'd be right behind me," she said, pleased.

"Where else would I be?" asked Larra.

Together, the two women entered the clearing.

"Well, this is a bit much," she said, "It's almost like you missed me or something." She dismounted so that she could hug them all. Through tears she let them know how much she missed them. Kurtis and Dyanna had morphed from the hesitant teenagers she remembered into confident young adults. She took their faces in her hands and looked them over approvingly before kissing them both on the forehead.

"Damn Libster, you're looking good!" John said far too loudly as he picked her up and spun her around. "Shenanigans just haven't been the same without you. Say, I've been wondering what happens to the Queen's Knight Grand Champion when you become King?"

Libby laughed, and grabbed his ponytail to pull him down so she could kiss him on the cheek. "We can figure all that out later, my friend. I have some work to get caught up on. I can only imagine what the pile of paper on my desk must look like."

After all the hellos were done and everyone was convinced she was okay, Scarlett grasped her friend's shoulders and met her eyes square on. "Are you ready? Are you ready to do this?"

"Ready as I'll ever be," Libby replied and swung herself back up into the saddle. "Let's do this."

Scarlett pulled Libby's crown out of her bag and handed it up to her. "Might want to comb that hair first," she suggested. "Looks great, by the way. I can't remember the last time you wore it this long."

John started singing the Aerosmith song "Back in the Saddle" in his loud and unabashedly off-key voice, and laughter made its way around the group. She was back alright.

Libby took her place at the head of the line. They all fell in, knights on white horses on the left, LIWs on black horses on the right, and began their processional back through the streets of town to the palace. It was quite the sight, and the perfect bookend to their departure a year and half earlier. Their Queen was home.

Word spread quickly and the closer they got to the palace, the more crowded the path became. Fintan was waiting on top of the fortress wall, taking it all in as he mentally composed the final verse to *The Tale of Queen Libby: How the Queen Tamed the Dragon, Saved the Kingdom, and Became King*. He didn't realize he was wearing a big grin on his face, the kind of toothpaste-commercial grin he used to tease her about as being too American. He'd missed her.

Libby wasted no time getting back to work. She'd been absent almost two years including her recovery time after Dale had died, and she needed to re-familiarize herself with her Kingdom. While a lot of that was spent touring and welcoming new additions, most of it was spent in mind-numbing meetings.

She delegated specific duties to Dyanna and Kurtis permanently, and formally relieved Corrine and Ava of their Co-Regent responsibilities. The heirs took up permanent residence at the palace, just as they would have if they had been Libby and Dale's children, to continue to grow into their roles and responsibilities.

One of the duties of the King was to welcome each new addition to the Kingdom, whether one joined by birth or relocation from the Normal world. One of the newest additions was Ava's son, Luke who was born while Libby was in Japan with Jasper. Libby wanted to hold him every chance she got. So, while Ava was getting accounting reports ready for yet another meeting, she left Luke with his aunty Libby. When Ava left the room, Libby reached out to the Spirit Council members for an introduction. It didn't take long for them to appear.

"Meet the newest member of our family, Luke Kenjiro Roberts. Dad, I think he looks like you." Kokichi was beaming, but all of them were thrilled. Spirit may not have much emotion about death, but they were enamored with births and all the power and possibility of a new life. Dale kept making funny faces at him, and Luke fell into a fit of giggles. Babies, and sometimes small children, can see Spirit, although most outgrow it.

Maggie examined him closely, and then looked quizzically at Libby. Libby just smiled and nodded. She could see what Maggie saw, a soft purple glow surrounding her nephew. Magic. She'd keep all this to herself until he was older, and when Ava was ready to hear it. Now wasn't that time. It would be hard enough to explain what the baby kept staring and laughing at. Maggie laughed. Even though he wasn't Libby's child, he was going to carry on both their family's royal lineage as well as its magical gifts.

Libby couldn't stop cooing and kissing him, which is what she was doing when Ava returned. Ava wouldn't know about the little family reunion that just happened for years to come.

A few weeks before the coronation, Libby set out on Hoss to visit Fintan. He was pleased she seemed so much better than when she left. Like everyone else, he could see that she'd changed, but he also recognized the sadness that she carried within. He saw it every day in the mirror. With a whiskey in hand, Libby asked him if he ever thought about taking a chance on love again.

Upon seeing his horrified expression, she told him about the man she'd fallen in love with while she was away, and how much it hurt to leave him behind. She'd confessed it was the second time in her life that she was tempted to abandon her responsibilities to follow her heart, which wouldn't be true to who she was. She knew she had to leave him, that he could never truly love her if he didn't know the complete her. She knew Dale was right, and she needed to wait for the right man. She confessed that she was afraid she'd be alone the rest of her life,

"Twice?" He asked gently. He hadn't heard this story before, and she shared more with him than most.

She stared intently at the whiskey swirling in her glass "Yes. Twice. When I came of age, I traveled outside the Kingdom. A lot. Sowing my wild oats, I suppose. I knew that the day would come where I'd become Queen and have too many responsibilities to spend extended periods outside the barrier. In my travels, I met someone. He was smart and funny and beautiful inside and out. I fell in love. I was young. I was ready to walk away from all of it. The Kingdom, the throne, my life as the heir. But in the end, I couldn't do it. I couldn't abandon my responsibilities. I just had to have some help making that decision."

She paused to take a swig. Fintan waited in silence for her to continue.

"One day something happened, and we got in to a horrible fight. I left a few nights later while he was sleeping so I wouldn't have to say good-bye. I knew if I had to look into his eyes and tell him I was leaving that I'd change my mind. I was also terrified that if I did tell him face-to-face that I'd see relief in his eyes and learn he really didn't love me at all. So I chickened out and just left him a note. I returned to the Kingdom and did my job. Then, when Dad announced he was going to retire, I knew I'd have to marry. I was still lonely for this man that no one but my best friends knew about, and even they only knew of him by a nickname, The Viking. Stupid, I know. When Dad chose Dalen, I gave him a fair shot, and I fell in love with him to a depth that I didn't know was even possible. Yet, here I am. Alone. Again. Maybe I'm just meant to be alone."

For the first time since Sheila had died, Fintan opened up about the loneliness. He told Libby that losing his beloved was heartbreaking, but it was the loneliness of life without her that nearly broke him. He joked that poets make their living on pain, but it was too much to even write about. The reason he'd accepted her offer to move to the Kingdom was because being lonely in a new place was easier to bear than being lonely in a place where everywhere he looked, he saw a void that was shaped like her.

Libby nodded in understanding. The loneliness was somehow easier when you weren't at home. At home it was oppressive.

"Libby, you're young and have plenty of time. No matter what, trust your heart. When it's meant to be it will happen." He thought about what he'd just said and snorted in disgust. "Sweet Jaysus. I sound like a damned greeting card."

After a period where the only sound was Libby tapping her sapphire ring against the whiskey glass, Fintan cleared his throat.

"May I ask you a question?"

"Anything."

"This topic makes me uncomfortable. But I know you can see ghosts. Spirits of those who have died." Fintan got up and started slowly pacing.

Libby nodded, pretty sure she knew what question was coming next.

"Have you ever seen Sheila?" Fintan asked, looking her right in the eyes.

Libby looked away and paused, before looking up at him again. "Yes. Twice."

Fintan drew in a jagged breath as his eyes filled with tears.

"Tell me." he pleaded.

"I've denied this all my life, Finn," she started. "So, understand that I didn't keep it from you deliberately, even though you wouldn't have believed me if I'd told you." She blew out a deep breath to give her a little more time to figure out what to say. "Sheila visited me about six months after she died, in a dream. She told me that she was worried about you. That you were too alone, despite having your kids and grandkids nearby. She asked me to invite you again to live in the Kingdom. She politely asked me to force you, if necessary." Libby snorted at the memory. "Normally spirits are so bossy, but she was just as polite in the afterlife as she was in life." Libby looked directly into his eyes. "She told me we needed each other, that fate brought us together that night in the pub in Killarney all those years ago. More importantly, she said I'd need you in a way I couldn't possibly understand at the time. She was sure right about that. I don't think I'd have survived any of this without you."

The old poet looked away as a tear rolled down his cheek. "And the second time?" he asked.

"The second time was after you'd moved to the Kingdom. Do you remember the first time I came to visit you here? I had a horrible headache and got a nosebleed? I told you it must be allergies to whatever the flowers were that were growing on the river bank."

"I'd forgotten, but yes. Now that you mention it, I remember that. It was strange."

"It was her. Back then, before I learned how to control or accept it, I fought it. So whenever a spirit came to visit me while I was awake, I'd suffer. She was here. She thanked me for convincing you to move here. She thanked me for being such a good friend to her in life, and to you. She told me, one day if you ever asked about it, to tell you how much she loved you and how she hoped you'd take a chance on love again. That she wanted you to remember what it felt like to be happy and loved."

"What!" he roared at her.

"Hey, I just take the message. Normally, I'd force myself to ignore them still, but on that day, I argued back with her. I told her I loved her and missed her terribly, but nothing like you did. I told her I was your friend and there would never come a day where you would ask me about this, and that if you did, I couldn't possibly figure out how to give you her blessing to find a woman to love and to love you." Libby suddenly sat up straight. "Oh my Goddess! But that's what I just did. Somewhere she's laughing at me. At us. Damn it, Sheila! Sometimes spirits are annoying as fuck."

Fintan sat there, deep in thought. Libby let him sit in silence. She'd learned that spirits had no sense of time, at least not like the living did. For them "now" could mean the action you took yesterday, or making a decision, now, to do something next year. "Soon" could mean now or five years from now. It could get confusing. Add in human interpretation and messages could get cloudy. Clarity is a rarity, as Maggie O'Brien would say.

Since Fintan was lost deep in memories, Libby returned to the palace. She knew she'd hear from him when he was ready.

Chapter 25

King Libby

ost of the Kingdom had gathered in the palace courtyard, much like they had for Dale's funeral. This time, however, Libby wasn't hiding on the balcony. She was front and center. She wore a formal gown of dark gray silk. She was draped in her formal robes in the same emerald green as her travel cloak but of heavy velvet. Her crest was embroidered in silver on the back, and the crests of all of her knights and LIWs made up the border. Fintan had made a small suggestion to modify her crest, and now the silver ash tree was in a halo of rose gold. She carried no scepter, but her katana was strapped to her side. She wore her red hair up in a simple knot, unusual for her since she normally liked the freedom of wearing it down. But then, nothing about this was usual.

She stood tall. She stood alone.

Dyanna and Kurtis as heirs to the throne were nearby, just behind her. Each held a crown, the one that would one day be his or hers. For now, they belonged to Libby. Both of them. The Royal Wizards approached the heirs. Kurtis was first, offering Dale's crown, a simple gold circlet designed to look like tree branches and roots to Sophia. Dyanna offered Libby's crown to Awen—a silver diadem, of equally simple branches, but with tiny emeralds that made up the leaves of the Tree of Life. The two wizards took the crowns and the heirs stepped back to stand with the rest of the family.

Sophia and Awen fit the two crowns together. There was an audible click as they interlocked, as if they were always made to be worn together. It reminded Libby of her wedding and engagement rings, a pair that wouldn't be separated. Krystal took the two-become-one crown in both hands and presented it to Libby, instead of placing it on her head. Libby had done this on her own. She didn't need anyone else to grant her the title or authority of King; she'd gone out and taken it for herself. Libby accepted the crown, holding it high for everyone assembled to see. Then, with her heart racing, she placed it on her head, without saying a word.

The crowd erupted into cheering: "Long live the King! Long live the King! Long live the King!"

Libby watched all of this in silence, a small smile on her face. She'd noticed Dale appear, beaming with pride.

Libby started laughing at the victory dance no one else but Krystal could see, and waved to everyone, motioning for them to proceed to the celebration feast.

Epilogue

ife as King continued more or less the same for Libby with a few notable exceptions. Scarlett transitioned into retirement, and Catherine took on the responsibilities of Senior LIW. She joined Libby in meetings and on tours around the Kingdom. This particular morning they'd set out on a tour of the force field with Fynnigan and the engineering team.

Before she'd left on her solo adventure, Libby had put Fynnigan officially in charge of force field security, a direct liaison among the engineers, wizards and Sean. He had free reign of this project and had recruited a new engineer. He was practically giddy when he told her.

"Libby, things are going well. Everything we theorized about tethering to the ley line worked perfectly! And we're still learning about more options. We should be able to remove your bond to it in the near future."

"Are you really that excited about the force field or do you have something to tell me?"

"What do you mean?"

"You look like the cat that ate the canary. Spit it out. Oh my Goddess! You're getting married?"

"What? No! Bite your tongue, woman!" Fynnigan started laughing. "I've recruited a new engineer to the team! A Normal."

"That's what has you so excited? She must be hot," Libby replied, unwilling to relent in her teasing. "I trust your decisions, Fynn. Tell me about this Normal engineer."

"Well, I don't know about hot. It's my dad! He'll be arriving later today."

Libby's mouth gaped open. "Wait, what? Bas? What does he know? Does he know who I am?"

"He knows about the Kingdom, not about you. Although I did tell him the King would welcome him personally, that it's kind of a tradition. I thought that would be a fun surprise. He's been in a funk

227

since he broke up with his mystery girlfriend. Talk about a regular disappearing act. I never met her, but all he's talked about for the last year was this woman he'd met on his travels who traveled as much as he did which is why I couldn't meet her. At any rate, I guess she left him once and for all and he's been mopey and ready for a change. He is intrigued by the engineering of the force field."

"What? Oh Fynn, I'm not sure this is a good idea. I don't question your judgement on the team you've put together, but your dad...I don't think he's going to be happy to see me." Libby was practically squirming.

Fynnigan looked confused. "But, Libby, you've been friends since I was a boy."

"It's complicated." Libby stopped and reached out to put her hand on his shoulder. "No worries, Fynn. You've done amazing work here, and I'm so proud of you. I've got some other meetings to attend but will formally welcome your dad to the Kingdom this afternoon. Would you like to be there?"

"Of course! I can't wait to see the look on his face when he realizes King McGregor is none other than you!"

"Great," Libby said. "I can't wait." She turned on her heels and headed towards the palace, Catherine right behind her.

"What was that all about?"

"Nothing, I'm just tired."

"Bullshit. But if you don't want to talk about it that's fine too."

Libby struggled to focus on the remainder of her meetings. She felt the apprehension in the pit of her stomach. She knew in her head that this had to happen. As King it was her duty to greet all new Normal residents to the Kingdom. However, the fear was strong enough that it triggered her fight or flight response, and in this case it was flight. Catherine took one look at her and announced, "I'm coming with you."

"No, that's unnecessary."

"Oh, I think it is. I've known you long enough to recognize when you get squirrely, and there is no backing out of this, Libby. If you were anyone else, I might let it slide. But you're you. You're the freaking King, for Goddess' sake. You can be mad at me all you want, but I know you'll thank me later. You're too much of a professional for this. Besides, you know you want to see him."

"No, I don't! And I'm fairly certain he doesn't want to see me. I can't believe Fynn talked Sean into recruiting Bastiaan to the engineering team."

"Libby, he is a qualified engineer. The fact that he's Fynnigan's dad shouldn't be that big of a deal. You're overreacting. Normals move into the Kingdom all the time. They get used to it. Even ones as... engineer-y as Bastiaan Van der Linden. It was important to Fynnigan, and you give that boy anything he wants. It's not like you and his dad aren't friends. You've known each other for years."

Libby cringed and felt her cheeks get warm.

"Wait just a minute." A cat-like grin spreading across Catherine's face. "Just how well do you know each other, exactly?"

Now Libby's face was as red as her hair. "Um, well. Oh, this is embarrassing. Remember the mystery woman Fynn was talking about? The disappearing act? Yeah, that was me. We, uh, sort of reconnected when I ran into him in a Belfast pub last year. No one knows, not even Fynn, that Bas and I were an item before Dale came into the picture."

"Holy fuck! Fynn's dad is Redman? Wait! What? Oh my Goddess, Redman is The Viking?" Catherine started laughing so hard she snorted. She'd heard the stories about Libby's great romance with the mysterious Viking before she'd met Dale. "Well, Libby McGregor, hot damn. Now I really can't wait to meet him. Does he still look like a Viking fifteen years later? There is no way you're going without me now. Fix your makeup and comb your hair, we're going."

"I've died and gone to hell," Libby moaned. "If you breathe a word of this to anyone, I will fire you."

Catherine was still snorting but managed to catch her breath long enough to spit out, "You wish. My husband is your chief engineer, and my boys are already apprenticing. Although, a vacation sounds lovely. Maybe we'll take a page from your book and travel the world a bit. But don't worry, your secret's safe with me. I am your Senior

Lady-in-Waiting, after all. Protecting your secrets is part of my job. Scarlett is going to die when she realizes she missed this." Catherine picked up her laughing again.

"Oh, just shut it. Let's get this over with."

Fynnigan and Bastiaan were outside the stables, as part of his introductory tour when Libby and Catherine walked around the corner, coming up behind them. Fynnigan grinned at Libby, turned to his dad, and said, "Dad, I can't wait for you to meet King McGregor. Libby for short."

Bastiaan Van der Linden turned around and looked at Libby, stunned. He ran his hands through his red curls, his blue eyes going from confusion to understanding as he realized the responsibilities she'd left him for were ruling the Kingdom of the Talking Trees. His disbelief was countered by the crown she was wearing on her head.

He shook his head, and finally managed, "Elisabeth? You're King McGregor? This is the responsibility you left me for? You're not really an art buyer?"

They'd known each other so long, that he was one of the few people who still called her that. When she was younger, she thought Elisabeth made her sound more mature. It was after they'd broken it off, when Fynn was a boy, that she'd embraced the nickname Libby. He stood there, processing the fact that the woman who'd been in and out of his life for the last year was the King of the Kingdom his son had moved to. He flashed back fifteen years to the day of the wolf attack, the first time she'd left him, and the many times she'd left him behind to travel over the last year, including when she broke it off a few months ago to return home to her responsibilities.

She smiled awkwardly and shrugged her shoulders, as she felt her face flush. "Yeah. Um, welcome, Bas. Hi. I'm Queen, well King now, Aisling Elisabeth McGregor, ruler of the Kingdom of the Talking Trees. Although most people just call me Libby. I wasn't Queen when we first met, that came later, along with the nickname. And King is new. I'm not really an art buyer, just a collector who buys for herself.

I'm sorry I couldn't tell you before. I had no idea Fynn had recruited you, but I'm glad he did. I'll understand if you don't want to stay. If this is too weird. But I hope you do. And I formally welcome you to the Kingdom of the Talking Trees." By now her face was as red as her hair, but she extended a hand, per protocol. She knew she was talking too fast and screwing it up. She wished the ground would swallow her whole.

Bas took her hand, out of habit, but still stood thinking. Fynn was confused and looking back and forth at the two of them. *What the hell was going on? What was his dad saying about Libby leaving him?*

Then, still holding her hand, Bas finally spit out, "You lied to me! You lied to me about everything."

"No, Bas, not about everything. Just the magic and kingdom stuff. Everything else was real. Is real. This is the real me."

"And you always ran away! Why didn't you just tell me the truth? You never even gave me a chance to decide. You never gave me the chance to know the real you. I've been looking for you for months! You just disappeared." All of the anger and frustration at her leaving boiled to the surface.

"I did. I know I didn't handle it well. Good-byes aren't something I'm good at."

"No shit," he snapped. "Don't think I'm not still mad at you. I'm a little bit in shock or I'd be furious. And I'm going to be mad at you for a while. But"—he paused—"I've missed you. Is it allowed to hug the King?"

Libby grinned. "Not just allowed. Encouraged."

He pulled her in close and kissed her, wrapping his brawny arms around her and burying his face in her hair.

"Damn. I've missed you, Elisabeth."

She untangled herself enough to grab his face in her hands and look into his blue eyes. "I've missed you too, Bas." She grinned, before standing on her tiptoes and planting a kiss on his lips.

"I guess I need to get to know the real you and decide what I think about all this. Start over from the beginning. When I'm done being angry at you. This is all so fucked up."

"The real me is basically the me you already know, with a little extra. But, yeah, a start over would be great. Allow me to reintroduce myself. Bastiaan Van der Linden, I'm Aisling Elisabeth McGregor, Ruler of the Kingdom of the Talking Trees. My late father was King before me. I'm a widow; my late husband, King Dalen McGregor was killed in battle two years ago. I have no children of my own, so my eldest niece and nephew are my heirs to the throne. You'll meet them later. I recruited Fynn to the knighthood six years ago, when he became of legal age. Oh, and you should probably know that magic is real and I kind of have magical abilities and can talk to ghosts. Other than that, I'm the same person you knew. I'm sure you have a thousand questions. Feel free to ask me any of them as you think of them. Nothing is off limits."

Everyone but Fynn had discreetly disappeared from the awkwardness of the reunion, eager to dissect what they'd just witnessed.

Fynnigan was still sputtering in shock at seeing his dad and Libby together. "What the hell? Wait. You're the disappearing act? The mystery girlfriend? Dad, you and Libby? Libby, you and my dad? How long has this been going on? Since before you were Queen? What? Back when I was a boy? I think I need a drink. Oh my God! That's why you left after the wolf attack? I'd always wondered why you never came back to visit. Who else knew about this? Wait, that's why there were always lilacs at your house when I'd come to visit, because of Libby?" Fynnigan's brain was on overload, and the questions burst forth on rapid fire.

Libby looked at Fynnigan and laughed as she gave him a little smile. "Fynn, I told you it was complicated. No one knew it was your dad. C'mon. The three of us have some catching up to do." She looked up at Bas, who was still in shock trying to process this life altering revelation. "I'm pretty sure I have a bottle of that Jenever you like in the palace bar. We could all probably use a drink. Fynn, will you please show your dad to the bar? I'll meet you there shortly."

Fynnigan was still shaking his head in disbelief as he escorted Bas up to the palace, peppering his dad with questions.

She rolled her eyes when she saw Dale sitting on the horse arena fence, laughing, his arms outstretched as if to say, "Ta Da!"

"Really? Is this your idea of a joke? You've told me for the better part of a year that he wasn't the one and I had to let him go. More than once even, since I couldn't seem to ever stay away for long."

Dale hopped off the fence and sauntered towards her. "Ash, I told you to wait for the man who could love the real you. It wasn't right before. Now it's definitely a maybe. Now that you know who you are, he has the chance to learn too, and prove himself worthy. That's something."

"I'd punch you in the face right now if you could feel it."

"I know you would. That almost makes this funnier. I love you. The real you. I always have. Don't forget to give others, including this guy, the chance to know the real you. You deserve it, and so does he." Dale blew her a kiss and turned around and walked away from the palace.

Libby shook her head in disbelief, then started laughing.

"Yes. Definitely a maybe," she whispered as she turned and headed towards the palace.

And that's how the engineer and the King officially met. The rest is a story for another day.

Citations

p. 3 Endless Stream of Tears, written and performed by Dolly Parton

p. 6 The Mourning Bride, written by William Congreve

p. 9 Tales of a Wayside Inn, written by Henry Wadsworth Longfellow

p. 17 It's The End of the World As We Know It, written by John Michael Stipe, Michael E. Mills, Peter Lawrence Buc, and William Thomas Berry. Performed by REM

p. 63 Into the Mystic, written and performed by Van Morrison

p. 66 I will Follow You Into the Dark, written by Benjamin Gibbard, performed by Death Cab For Cutie

p. 111 Dancing Queen, written by Benny Goran Bror Andersson, Bjoern K. Ulvaeus and Stig Anderson. Performed by ABBA

p. 120 It's a Mother Fucker, written by Mark O. Everett, performed by Eels

p. 139 untitled poem written by Jon Storm

p. 189-190 No Stopping You, written by Brett Eldridge and Tom Douglas. Performed by Brett Eldridge

p. 195 Tender, written by Alex James, Dave Rowntree, and Graham Coxon. Performed by Blur

p. 199 Broken, written by Christian Medice, Mitchell Collins and Samantha DeRosa. Performed by lovelytheband

p. 203 When Ye Go Away, written by Charles O. Lennon and Michael Scott. Performed by The Waterboys

p. 211 In Memoriam, written by Alfred Tennyson

p. 214 Mama I'm Coming Home, written by John Osbourne and Zakk Wylde, performed by Ozzy Osbourne

CPSIA information can be obtained
at www.ICGtesting.com
Printed in the USA
BVHW040854190919
558888BV00014B/325/P